I0730972

Altered Horizon

Written by Richard Cutler

Edited by Lee Gjertsen Malone

Copyright © 2022 Richard Cutler. All rights reserved.

This is a work of fiction. Names, characters, places, and incidents are either a product of the author's imagination or are used fictitiously, and any resemblance to actual persons, living or dead, business establishments, events, or locales is entirely coincidental.

No part of this book may be reproduced or transmitted in any form or by any means, graphic, electronic, or mechanical, including photocopying recording, or taping without the written consent of the author or publisher.

Briley & Baxter Publications | Plymouth, Massachusetts

ISBN: 978-1-954819-36-8

Book Design: Stacy Padula
Cover Art: Maddy Moore

There is difference between wants and needs. This book is dedicated to everyone that provides needed help to others regardless of the species. While it is only the right thing to do, too many fail.

Contents

Introduction

My original plan for writing was not to create a book series, but as the title theme for this book explains, my horizons of long ago have been altered. And they will continue to be altered, but only time will be able to tell how as I reach for the apparent horizon before me.

In *Course Correction*, the first in this series of books, humanity has reached Epsilon Eridani's second planet from the sun, known as EEb, and established a colony called New Hope Island around a wormhole gate connected to Earth. This was not a simple task. Politicians had pushed this notion because there were more people on Earth than the planet's resources could support. As a distraction, these same politicians proposed that a Star Ship fleet should be built and sent off to build the Gate through which masses of people could move through, thus relieving the stresses placed on Earth. Unbeknownst to the astronauts during the voyage, Mother Nature had stepped in with the Death Flu and reduced the Earth-bound human population by 90%.

Survivors on Earth had to adapt to a world where high-tech systems couldn't be supported and governing bodies were mostly military. Clever people were still around, but the greatest intellect was isolated in the Star Ships. And these travelers had become almost forgotten leaving them ignorantly isolated while they continued their journey. Assistance from an alien benevolent order eventually led to a settlement established on EEb, but it was far from the original vision.

In the second book, *Carbon Neutral*, Earth's starships are sent on a mission of discovery. What was found was nothing like anything they had imagined as they helped the inhabitants of TCe rescue their ecosystem. What they discovered in the process expanded mankind's knowledge and in so doing, mankind's horizons were altered once again. What they didn't realize was that mankind was capable of taking on larger challenges, and others were watching.

Horizon is a word with meanings both physical and metaphysical. From a physical point one definition of horizon states

"The line of the apparent meeting of the sky with the earth and sea." In days of old, sailors would spend days, weeks, and sometime many months searching an unchanging horizon. The horizon was changed or altered when land or a storm appeared. The course of the ship might then be altered to either reach what appeared or to avoid it. This altered course brought on by the altered horizon pointed the ship in a direction that might be favorable, or not, depending upon the end result. In the case of a storm, the ship's captain might want to avoid it unless the ship's fresh water supply was low because a storm could provide the needed water. A choice needed to be made. This remains true today for anyone that moves towards any horizon. Choices need to be made based on what appears.

From a metaphysical point another definition of horizon states "The bounds or limits of one's observation, knowledge, or experience." When man travels through space, what are the limits? As more is observed, and more knowledge and experience are gained, aren't mankind's horizons perhaps altered with new realities? The answer has to be "yes." And with the perceived horizon altered might the course being followed also be altered? If it is, then the altered course may not be welcomed, but if it can't be changed, acceptance must be the response.

In each of the first two books, mankind's perspectives are changed. The perceived horizons observed were altered each time more knowledge and experience was gained. In *Altered Horizon* it is understood there is more to be learned, just over the horizon, but what the crews of the United Nations Stellar Commission starships discover is a dark secret that helps create a new and greatly altered metaphysical horizon for mankind; a future for mankind that is not at all predictable.

Disclaimer

I have used names of real places and stars in this story. There was no particular reason except to make the reader run to the atlas and star charts to see where these places might be. Any description by the author of these places is pure whimsy.

The people named and described in this story is pure fantasy. Any similarity to any person living, deceased, or yet to be born is purely coincidental.

Acknowledgements

There may be people that can take an idea, write a book, do their own editing, then publish the book, and finally get it distributed and advertised. Come to think of it, I think I have read some of these efforts or tried to. I'm not one of them. I get ideas that seem to generate words. The rest takes a team. Thank you Stacy Padula of Briley & Baxter Publications and her team: Lee Gjertsen Malone for editing and Sylvia Moore (Maddy) for the cover art.

Chuck Kantner, who likes my books, also went on the hunt for typos. He probably would have been good spotting enemy aircraft during WWII!

And as with most of my endeavors, I would be remiss if I didn't recognize my wife Gini who doesn't care very much for science fiction yet puts up with my nonsense.

Places & Names

Epsilon Eridani (EE): 10.5 light years from Earth
    EEb: Second planet from the star
    New Hope Island: Human colony and wormhole gate
Tau Ceti (TC): 11.8 light years from Earth; 4.8 light years from EE
    TCe: Fourth planet from the star
    High Point: Human colony and wormhole gate
    TCf: Fifth planet from the star
    New Polyarnaya settlement led by Captain Gigory Kazakov, later Elias Brown
    Downy: Leader of marooned aliens
YZ Ceti: 1.6 light years from Tau Ceti
    Two planets: planet c is uninhabitable and named Prosperity
Alpha Centauri (3 star system): 4.3 light years from Earth
    Star A: (Rigil Kentaurus)
    Star B: (Toliman)
    Star Proxima:
    Proxima Centauri b: a terrestrial planet, renamed Sanctum
    Gadan: the human commune on Sanctum
    Minda: Gadan Protector
Richard M. Nixon: U. S. President (1969 to 1974)
Melvin Laird: Secretary of Defense under Nixon
Tam-I-El: Rogue Order Leader
United Nations Stellar Commission (UNSC)
    Dr. Yvonne Blain: Operations Director
    Dr. Harlyn Jackson: Science Director
Union of African Nations (UAN)
    Princess Charm-E-Ine (Charmy): Benevolent Dictator & Order member
    Raman-I-El (Raman): Order member
Gabe-Re-El: Order Leader; UAN Commissioner to the UNSC
Star Ships:
<u>United States</u> (mission to YZ Ceti b)
    John Armstrong: Captain
    Suzanne Lehtola: Chief Academic and Science Officer (CASO)
    Alfred Lehtola: Ship's Chief Medical Doctor

Na-Ki-Ir (Naki): Order member
Ara-Ri-El (Ara): Order member
<u>Africa</u> (first mission to salvage Russia in orbit around TCf)
Katherine Hickey: Admiral
David Loring: Flight Lieutenant
Bill Yeakle: Chief Engineer
Schem-Hampha-Rae (Schem): Order member
Rag-U-El (Rag): Order member
<u>Africa</u> (second mission to salvage Russia)
Frederica Armanda: Captain
Kem-U-El: CASO and Order member

Earth Bound Fleet (TC to Earth):
<u>China</u>
Ying Wu: Admiral
Wang Fang: Vice Admiral of Academics & Science (VAAS)
Earl Null: Vice Admiral of Operations (VAO)
Lie Jie: Captain
Zhang Min: CASO
<u>British Commonwealth</u>
Noelle Null: Captain (married to Earl Null)
Kem-U-El (Kem): CASO and Order member
Brian Null: son of Noelle and Earl
<u>South America</u>
Juan Martinez: Captain
Ere-Mi-El: CASO and Order member

First Ships to Alpha Centauri:
<u>Orion</u>
Katherine Hickey: Admiral
Harlyn Jackson: VAAS
John Renaldo: Captain
Uri-I-El (Uri): CASO and Order member
Marine Sergeant Eric Green
<u>Perseus</u>
David Loring: Captain
Dr. Anna Giblin: CASO

Second Ships to Alpha Centauri:
<u>British Commonwealth</u>
Ying Wu: Admiral
Brian Null: Captain
Bridget Pardon: CASO

<u>South America</u>
    Juan Martinez: Captain
    Ere-Mi-El (Ere): CASO

Prologue

"Mr. President," said Secretary of Defense Melvin Laird to President Richard Nixon, "the situation with the Soviet Union is getting worse. It appears they are gearing up for a massive nuclear attack."

"Are they crazy? Well of course they are. What the hell is the matter with them? Even if we didn't retaliate, which I'd be forced to do, the nuclear fallout would eventually kill off everyone. They might as well just commit suicide and be done with it."

"Maybe not everyone would die," said Melvin, "but life as we know it here on Earth will certainly change."

"Yeah, that's for sure," said the President, "but it isn't as if there is anyplace else to go for safety."

"Actually, that may not be completely accurate, and that's why I'm here."

The President sat back in his chair and looked at Melvin with his hands folded and a look of curiosity and asked, "What are you talking about?"

"Mr. President, I need you to keep an open mind as I tell you of a proposal I received in confidence. I know this is going to sound bizarre, but I have come to believe it is possible for members of the human species to be removed from Earth and be safely established on another world. The goal would be to have this new settlement in a safe location until the day it would be safe to resettle Earth."

"Melvin," said the President, "you have been Secretary of Defense for two years. I know the pressures of the job, especially during this so-called Cold War must be getting to you, but really, 'bizarre' isn't a strong enough word. You have gone over the edge! But I have a few minutes for a fantasy tale to break up the day." And with a stupid grin on his face he added, "So tell me more."

Obviously quite uncomfortable, Melvin sucked in a huge breath and exhaled before saying, "Mr. President, you will need to shut off your tape recorder," and once satisfied that had been done he continued with, "I was approached by this very large, odd person dressed all in white with a proposal. How he managed to get to my office was a story all by itself. Apparently when he talked with people for a few minutes, he convinced them to let him pass and walk into my office with no announcement. This certainly got my attention, but not in a good way. Strangely, as he came closer I felt calm in spite of the intrusion and a willingness to listen came over me.

"He introduced himself as Tam-I-El from some kind of secretive order whose mission is to guide humans. I'm not sure what he meant by that. Anyway, this Tam is well aware of the potential for a nuclear holocaust and has a way to remove some people from Earth to another planet for safekeeping. The idea would be to have this colony grow and eventually people would return to Earth to start a new civilization."

President Nixon simply sat and stared at Melvin with the only movement being a slight shaking of his head.

Melvin continued, "Tam has plans for ships that could transport people in suspended animation to the Alpha Centauri solar system. This is a triple-star system and the smallest of the three stars has a terrestrial planet similar to Earth. In fact it would be far more environmentally agreeable to people there than here on Earth. Once there, the people would be revived and grow as a kind of colony until Earth is suitable for habitation again."

President Nixon held up his hand, "Melvin, stop already. This is crazy. So this Tam person doesn't actually have any ships? So where is this Tam going to get them? Or is he just going to conjure them up like this ridiculous story? I have better things to do than listen to this. And so do you, for that matter."

Melvin, feeling and looking more uncomfortable than before, took another deep breath and said, "Mr. President, please hear me out. I'm sure you'll be convinced when you hear from Tam directly. But to answer your question, we have the Air Force facility in Nevada that many refer to as Area 51. It is secluded and easily shielded from prying eyes. Four ships would be built, one at a time, loaded and sent off with staffing from Tam's people. This would take years to complete, but with enough Air Force and civilian staff, a ship could be built in nine months. I didn't understand the plans, but they appear to be very detailed. And before you ask, Tam would pay all expenses with gold and silver directly into the Treasury."

That got the President's attention and he said, "That would be a fortune! Our gold and silver reserves could certainly use it. I could even rescind the policy of no private ownership of gold. The voters would love that, but can this Tam character actually do this?"

"He says yes, and I believe him. Of course secrecy should be imperative."

"So we build these ships and even if they don't do anything, we add gold and silver to our treasury. That sounds good to me." Thinking for a minute, the President then asked Melvin, "So assuming this crazy scheme works, who goes on this adventure?"

"Ah! That gets a little tricky. Remember the goal is to preserve mankind so our personal feelings about this need to be put aside. Tam's people would take people and test them for suitability. Only the best of the best of our species would be selected from around the world so the broadest range of DNA would be represented. Meaning those with a family history of longevity and who are strong and healthy themselves would be selected. The plan, as outlined, would be to have each of the four ships carry 100 people for a total of 400 individuals. 'Go forth and multiply' would be the predicted scenario."

"So if I'm hearing you correctly, people would be snatched and potentially disappear." Shaking his head, the President added, "Wonderful, just wonderful. What about those that don't pass the tests?"

"Yeah, well, they will be released. I'm reasonably certain these released individuals will have stories to tell about being abducted by aliens. This could feed into all kinds of conspiracy theories since they will not be under any code of secrecy. Officially we should just ignore them. But maybe we get some stories of our own out there along the lines these people are crackpots, or maybe that these stories are an excuse to hide something else they were really doing."

President Nixon, now showing concern, said, "I'm not liking the idea of people being snatched like that."

"Actually I'm not thrilled about that part either, but it is for the greater good and isn't that really what we need to be looking at? We may not like it, but the possible alternative is the human race being completely eradicated. And by the way, Tam made it clear that he would prefer to work with the United States, but he does have other options. He didn't say that in the form of a threat, only to let us know where he stands.

"Also, the few Air Force mucky mucks that are aware of this are quite excited to have a chance to see some advanced technology. Tam's ships themselves resemble a shallow bowl and I am rather certain these things have been seen before when Tam's people were being careless. Apparently the propulsion for these ships is rather unique and we may not be able replicate it right away. However the ships don't really show up on radar and that technology appears to be something we could incorporate into new fighters and bombers rather soon."

"Okay, back to reality, Melvin. I don't believe any of this, but I'm willing to sanction the first steps. I want to eventually meet this so-called Tam-I-El, but in the meantime he should be paying as we go. That part seems pretty easy to agree to for now. We will play along. At least for now everyone involved must pledge secrecy. If even a hint of this gets out, there will be media frenzy and we'll look like idiots. Denying any of it at that point would be a political nightmare. Area 51 activities have to be top secret.

"By the way, where is this Tam-I-El staying? Is it here in Washington?"

"Yes. He said he would be staying at the Watergate Hotel until I got back to him." Melvin added with a smile, "I have been sitting on this for a few days trying to get up enough courage to talk to you."

"I can see why. This whole thing seems ridiculous, but who knows. If anyone is left alive, maybe we'll be remembered as the ones that saved mankind."

That conversation was between Richard Nixon and Melvin Laird on October 10, 1971. Three years later, after President Nixon resigned, Area 51 completed the fourth ship designed and paid for by Tam-I-El.

This should be the last one, at least for now, thought Tam-I-El. More than half of those tested failed and were sent back with a story that nearly no one believed. "These big people with wings flew down and took me to this strange place where they did weird things to me and then brought me back. I should have been scared, but for some reason I wasn't."

"Yeah, right. Aliens abducted you. Where were you really?"

But this abductee, a Mongolian, looked promising. She was in perfect health, strong, and had no genetic defects. She would be perfect for continuing the human species.

Tam-I-El and his teams had determined that 400 would be an adequate number. Three groups of 100 had already been selected and sent off to their new home in ships nine months apart. This last group just needed this one last person. This group, like the others, was made up of people from around the globe. The goal was to have the largest and healthiest gene pool possible so when children were born they would carry the best from each parent. A penchant for anger would immediately disqualify anyone for this program.

It wasn't exactly voluntary. People were snatched and if they proved worthy, they were "volunteered." That is to say, the ability of the abductors to calm people led them to accept their fate with little or no protest. Being told, "this is for the benefit of all mankind. You are among the chosen and will be going to a better place," yielded mixed responses. Those content with their life weren't happy about this at all. Some who were pulled from adverse poverty, abuse, persecution, and conflicts not of their making thought perhaps these large people, who dressed all in white and flew, were all part of the hoped-for rapture. None of this bothered Tam-I-El. He had absolutely no concern about the result of these disappearances on those left behind.

The new "home" had been carefully selected. It was a lush green valley with a clear river flowing through the middle. The soil was perfect for cultivation. There were caves here and there that could be used for protection until lodging could be built. There were four seasons, very much like Earth's temperate zones, though the storms proved to be unpredictable and much more severe.

Tam-I-El had been considering this enterprise for centuries. Each time he came out of stasis to help guide the people of Earth away from disaster and keep them on the proper course of development, he became more and more skeptical of their chances of survival. Self-destruction seemed to be inevitable. They were always trying to kill each other in stupid wars both large and small and ruining the same environment they depended upon. The mission of the Order needed to be amended and Tam-I-El decided he was the one to do it. The whole business of simply providing guidance was weak. Sure it had worked when mankind was less sophisticated, but now with the capability of nuclear weapons blowing up the whole place, subtle course corrections wasn't enough as far as Tam was concerned.

He had first convinced the other five members of his team and then three more teams that to save mankind, a new start was needed. A critical mass would be established on another world and be allowed to grow properly.

Almost as an afterthought, Tam and his people decided to include a few other Earth species, especially birds. This was more whimsical than anything, and was a bit of a challenge to place them in stasis. But somehow adding them to the indigenous population of the final destination seemed right.

The Order's Boss, made up of three beings that acted as one, had established this benevolent order to guide civilizations. Individuals and small groups might be shown a way to stay on a course that would advance their civilization. Natural disasters, disease, and even wars were allowed to run their course unless circumstances got completely out of hand. When that happened, a team, or teams, of the Order were activated to provide guidance. Direct interference and taking charge was not allowed. Tam-I-El and his teams knew this and knew that as a consequence of their actions, they would eventually be caught and banished. Tam-I-El was prepared for that, but assumed he could complete his plan before it happened.

Tam-I-El was convinced he was on a noble mission. In his mind it was a noble mission that no one outside of his group could comprehend. Convinced of that, his people shut off all communications with the rest of the Order and operated undercover. But while he managed to keep his clandestine activities secret, he also failed to realize that other Order members were hard at work deescalating the tensions between the major world powers and promoting greater cooperation. Tam-I-El, of course, would have assumed those efforts would fail.

Other assumptions would prove incorrect as well. The assumption that Tam-I-El could complete this mission might have been one too many, but as it turned out, other critical assumptions would prove to be wrong as well. The only real assumption to be realized was that he would get caught.

Chapter 1

Headquarters

Admiral Katherine Hickey sat at the conference table with the Science Director and Operations Director of the United Nations Stellar Commission. Both directors were new to their positions after the latest round of position changes. Katherine knew this and had quipped to her staff that the front doors of the UNSC had been changed to revolving to make it easier for the people that seemed to come and go on a rather frequent basis. Apparently it was difficult for the UNSC Commissioners to find qualified people willing to take the jobs, so they settled for incompetence resulting in quick dismissal or resignation. Katherine had a difficult time understanding this constant turnover as the Director positions didn't seem to require a lot of work as almost all of the heavy lifting was done by her and her staff. And there wasn't even very much of that lately.

The Operations Director this day was Dr. Yvonne Blain. Katherine had read Yvonne's curriculum vitae and it appeared the good doctor had spent most of her time—actually all of her time—accumulating degrees. She looked good on paper as long as you didn't look too hard. A perpetual student with zero real-world experience had been selected to manage the most technologically advanced worldwide endeavor ever imagined with thousands of people under her supposed supervision.

The Science Director was perhaps a little more prepared. Dr. Harlyn Jackson had at least spent some time on the Earth's orbiting space station overseeing some obscure biological experiment that no one, other than Dr. Jackson, seemed to understand.

The Admiral had left the fleet of starships orbiting Tau Ceti e and returned to Earth through the wormhole gates between TCe and Earth. She had been led to believe that this and subsequent meetings were to lay out the plans for the fleet's next mission. The six ships had been in orbit now for over two years in spite of promises of a "new, big, beautiful mission. When announced, the world will be amazed!" Katherine was pretty sure there had been no plan. If there had been, some idea of what it might be, or at least some word would have leaked out by now. These new directors had been in their respective positions for a few months now, meeting constantly with the commissioners. This gave Katherine the faint belief that maybe, just maybe, the secret plan would be revealed.

Things did not begin well, as Dr. Blain started with, "Well Kathy, we finally meet."

This told the Admiral all she needed to know. Apparently this jerk never read any notes prior to this meeting so once again the response used many times before was, "my name is Katherine Hickey. You may refer to me as Katherine, Admiral Hickey, or just Admiral, but my name is not Kathy."

Obviously not expecting that response Dr. Blain managed to sputter out, "Well you're a feisty one."

"Only when I need to be. So let's move on to the issues at hand. I have traveled twelve light years to be here and hope to bring good news back to TCe. What's the plan?"

Dr. Blain never rushed into anything so she was a bit taken aback by the Admiral's perceived aggression and said, "You have something against us?"

With a softer tone, Katherine said, "No, not at all. Perhaps I shouldn't let my frustration and the frustrations of my ships' crews be so domineering. Truth is, however, while you both are new to your positions, we are not, and have been waiting as patiently as possible for some mission to be presented to us instead of sitting around twiddling our thumbs. So has the UNSC finally come up with something?"

"Um, not exactly. As noted, we were hired not that long ago, so we're just looking at options."

"What about the 'big beautiful' plans your predecessors said they had?"

"Regrettably, I don't think any of them ever had a plan. Not a real one anyway, and that's likely why the turnover in these positions has been so frequent."

The Admiral stared at them for what seemed to be an eternity, looking from one to the other and then back again while she gathered her thoughts. Finally she said, very quietly, "At least you have the guts to be honest. Thank you for that. So why am I here?"

"We wanted to meet with you face to face."

The Admiral, at exactly five feet one inch, weighing in at 100 pounds even, and still wearing her hair in a ponytail certainly provided a less-than-intimidating appearance, but when she stood up and placed both hands on the table and looked down at the two directors she appeared to be a giant ready to strike. "Did it ever occur to either one of you that it might be a good idea for you to go to Tau Ceti and tour the fleet of starships under your command? I fully realize I'm not making any points here, but we have never had any directors or commissioners tour the ships. I take that back, the twin directors Richard Sylva and his sister Dawn Cohen who took over around 2096 were the obvious exception having been Vice Admirals. And they had vision. Are you going to be like them, or more like the directors with the baseless 'big beautiful plan'?"

"Now just a minute," said Director Jackson, "we are your superiors. You can't talk to us like that. Who do you think you are?"

"I am Admiral Katherine Hickey commissioned by the United Nations Stellar Commission. I know exactly who I am and until you prove otherwise, you may have the titles, but you are not my superiors."

With that, Katherine left the room leaving two somewhat stunned directors sitting at the conference table.

After a moment Yvonne said, "Wow, she's a hothead."

"Well," said Harlyn, "perhaps if we were in her shoes maybe we'd lose it too. I don't condone that behavior, but I'm just say'in, that she has a point. I think I'd like to visit the fleet and see how the Admiral operates."

"Harlyn, you go ahead and do that. I'll stay here and mind the store."

Harlyn smiled and said, "Of course you will."

Chapter 2

Wormhole Gates (2146)

Katherine had made a big show of frustration in front of the UNSC directors. She had chided them for not going to the fleet orbiting TCe. Instead they had ordered her to the UNSC headquarters on Earth. But while she was making a point, she actually wanted to come. It had been months since she had seen her husband Dakota Bickmeier and their daughter Celeste. While she had been busy being Admiral of the fleet, Dakota and a few technicians were building critical wormhole gate components for some yet to be identified mission. Celeste was sometimes with Katherine, but recently had wanted to be on Earth because of some "project" she was working on with her dad.

Katherine and Dakota had been on the Star Ship United States together when they were en route between solar systems Epsilon Eridani and Tau Ceti. She was the Admiral of the second fleet and he was the wormhole gate expert. Both were socially inept, but after years of avoiding the obvious attraction they had for each other, they married and nine months later had a daughter named Celeste. Because of their jobs, they weren't always together, but that didn't mean they weren't a close family. For now, however, Dakota was in Iowa building the highly technical components for at least one future Gate.

The cost of building the critical components was relatively small compared to the actual construction of the Gates, but there was no room for error. Both Katherine and Dakota speculated that the cost was so small relative to everything else that this effort was very much under the radar of the directors, and the entire UNSC Commission for that matter. The real cost of any Gate building was getting to its location and then doing the site work.

Critical to the functioning of any Gate was its location relative to a planet's magnetic poles. It had to be within five degrees of the 45-degree latitude corrected for magnetic declination. Once a site was deemed suitable, construction was no small task. That was why it took so many people and resources to build each Gate. Above ground with the actual Gate in the center was an array of towers, some reaching 1000 feet into the sky, stretching out from the center gatehouse over two miles. If that wasn't impressive enough, the entire above-ground array was mirrored underground. Some rather impressive engineering was needed to keep the placement of the ground surface mat of cables within a .02% tolerance from horizontal against the placement of the above- and below- ground systems.

All of this was powered with 1100 megawatts of AC electrical energy for transmission and 60 megawatts for receiving. Dedicated tunnels for the power conduits meant more excavation. Massive relays and transformers situated in a separate bunker required even more site work.

Each gatehouse had five levels, with the actual Gate through which people and things passed on one floor, oriented so that it was evenly split by the surrounding landscape grade. And while that one floor was safe, the energy needed to make everything work would cook anything that fell within the grid pattern on the surface. Support systems and controls were housed in the remaining four levels.

Dakota's shop in Iowa was built near the headquarters of the Star Struck Trading Company. Dakota had selected the location for two reasons. One reason was to be as much out of sight, and potentially out of mind, of the UNSC bureaucrats as was possible and second was to be close as he could to the people he liked to be near.

Star Struck Trading Company was established by Katherine's predecessor, Admiral Neil Dobson, his wife Kristie Marshal, and the now-CEO Sharon Hooding. All of who had been on the Star Ship British Commonwealth when Dakota and Katherine joined the fleet. These were good people allowing everyone that had been on the starships' crews to invest in trading opportunities; one of which was proving to be very profitable—the trade of carbon-based Earth pollutants, like carbon dioxide and carbon monoxide. The inhabitants of Tau Ceti e needed these "nutrients" and in exchange they allowed the mining of extremely rare and valuable minerals on their planet; minerals having amazing properties that were nowhere to be found on Earth.

The UNSC couldn't be bothered with the concept of trading, so the company simply filled a void. As it was rapidly becoming wealthy, it found it had a lot of influence over the UNSC and was gradually privatizing certain functions. In fact, it was the Trading Company that managed all the wormhole gate operations for the UNSC including the partial funding of Dakota's shop.

Katherine hadn't told Dakota or Celeste that she was on Earth. It was to be a surprise. She knew Dakota would be in the shop so she went directly there. It was snowing when she arrived and the temperatures were below zero, so when she opened the shop door, the swirling snow that entered with her got Dakota's attention.

"Wow, this is a surprise. I didn't know you were coming."

"Yeah, it's great to see you too, or are you disappointed?"

"Huh! No, no this is great," as he left his soldering iron and went over to give his wife a warm hug and kiss. "How long are you here?"

"Are you trying to get rid of me already?"

"What? Okay, let me start over. Honey, sweetie pie, what a fantastic surprise! I have missed you so much, this is like a dream come true…"

Katherine cut him off with, "Oh, you sweet talker, you. Where's Celeste, the real reason I'm here. It's nice to see you, but really."

"Okay, I deserve that. She's over there," pointing to a pile of some kind of wagon parts with wheels and a pile of metal. Sitting on an upside down bucket was a small figure wearing a face mask, face shield, rubber gloves, and a work apron much too large for her frame. It was a wonder the little figure could move. She was heavily involved with cleaning up some greasy mess and apparently didn't notice the newcomer.

"Hey, Celeste," yelled Dakota, "look who's here!"

The figure turned, threw off all the protective gear and ran over yelling "Mommy!" With a big grin Celeste hugged Katherine with all her might.

"I missed you kiddo," while Katherine hugged back. Looking past Celeste, she became curious and said, "What have you got her doing, if you don't mind my asking?"

"Um, well, we have a little project we're working on together. It helps me keep an eye on her while I'm working." And then after receiving a silent steely glare from his bride, Dakota added, "Do you remember me telling you that my family had an old car up in Alaska?"

"No."

"Oh, I thought I did. Anyway I took Celeste up there to see where my side of the family came from and there was the car sitting in a shed. No one wanted it, so I took it."

Slowly turning her head from Dakota and Celeste towards the pile, Katherine said, "And that's the car? How did you get it here? You obviously didn't drive it." Then, when there was no answer, and seeing Dakota was getting a little nervous, she added, "No, you didn't. You didn't take our daughter in that thing and drive here from Alaska. Tell me you didn't."

Crinkling up his face, Dakota said, "Well, yes and no."

"What does that mean?"

"We got it running and were halfway through Canada and the engine blew up. Star Struck Trading Company got it the rest of the way here with the understanding that Sharon's son Astron would be allowed to help with the restoration. Katherine, it was an adventure. A father/daughter bonding experience!"

"Good grief. I guess I can't leave you two alone for a minute without adult supervision. What is that thing anyway? It looks like a carriage."

"Kinda." Then with some excitement he added, "It's a 1914 Ford Model T. It's a horseless carriage."

Glaring at Dakota, Katherine said, "I'm not very happy about this."

During all this exchange, Larry Beal watched with amusement. Dakota yelled over to him, "Hey, Larry, watch Celeste for a while, I need to do some apologizing to the Admiral. It might take a while." Then with a little smile and taking her hand, he said, "Come with me dear, let me make it up to you."

Katherine said, "I'll be the judge of that." Both smiling, they left the shop and headed towards the house.

Larry said to Celeste, "They'll be back. In the meantime, let's clean up some more parts."

Chapter 3

Tam-I-El's Assumptions

Back in the 1970s, Tam-I-El really believed he had brought humans to a Garden of Eden to save mankind. Proxima Centauri b in the Alpha Centauri star system was a beautiful terrestrial planet. The gravity was slightly more than Earth's and the climate was very close to what he considered perfect, with four seasons. The valley he chose was large, with plenty of natural resources to sustain a colony of 400 for whatever time they needed to get settled. His plan included adding fruit-bearing vegetation and a few of Earth's other animal species that he believed should be protected.

The two larger stars in the system, Alpha Centauri A, called Rigil Kentaurus, and Alpha Centauri B, called Toliman, added to the wonder of the place. He envisioned the ring around the planet as something symbolic of safety. Safety from what Tam believed would be an eventual nuclear holocaust that would wipe out Earth's so-called humanity.

Tam had approached the United States government at a vulnerable time, when President Nixon had come to believe the world might suffer a nuclear holocaust. The offer from Tam to save humanity, even with what Nixon considered a bizarre plan, seemed worth the risk.

Four bowl-shaped ships were built under the umbrella of national security. When the first was completed, it was piloted by one of Tam's teams of six and loaded with 100 humans. When this ship, and when each of the subsequent three ships were launched nine months apart, it created a stir. The mission was supposed to be a secret, but flying saucers don't hide very well and so new rounds of UFO sightings surfaced followed with new rounds military denials.

Each "volunteer" selected for the mission was given a sedative, undressed, and placed in a stasis chamber with tubes inserted into each private body part. This is what members of the Order were required to do to themselves when they went into stasis, but the human subjects were in no position to do it on their own so it was done for them. Clothing and anything else the humans had with them were placed in a container next to each chamber. Those that had backpacks with anything that might look like a tool, such as a pocketknife, would later find themselves the richest members of the new society.

The people that Tam and his teams had selected were the best the humans had to offer; the best genes, the best health, and the most diverse DNA. This required picking people from all around the globe. While he knew this would create some issues initially because of the many languages involved, he assumed this would work out as some new mixed language would eventually emerge. Tam had made other assumptions as well, but as it turned out, this was one of the few assumptions that proved correct.

One assumption proved to be horribly false. When the human subjects were placed in stasis for the long journey, it had been assumed that their memory would be intact when they were removed. Tam's people retained all memories when they came out of stasis. Over the countless times he himself had come out, there were no issues of lost memory. Why he thought the humans would be no different was amazing and false.

It was a major disappointment to Tam's people when the first group reached their new home and it was discovered that the volunteers had only memory of the basics. They could talk using only simple words, and with each speaking a different language, communication was an issue. They could walk and were aware of their surroundings, but had no idea of how to make a fire, clothe themselves or even feed themselves. Their minds were essentially blank, ready to receive information. Team members that had accompanied them suddenly found themselves in a position where they had to show humans everything they needed to survive in their new home.

When this problem was discovered with the first group, it was too late. The remaining three ships, spaced nine months apart, were already on the way. Turning the ships around wasn't an option. Memory lose would have occurred no matter where they came out of stasis. Tam-I-El told his team "Maybe this is for the best. No memory means mankind has a completely fresh start." Privately he hoped the effects were temporary. They weren't.

Another assumption that proved false was that the new home would allow the humans to grow and prosper. Unfortunately, that also proved false, because Tam-I-El and his team never considered that the indigenous species of this new world might adapt to this intrusion in a most unfortunate manner.

All of Tam's plans were crashing down around him and he was now stuck in a recovery mode. He had understood that eventually he and his team would be stopped, but with the original assumption that this new colony, with memories intact, could manage on its own now proving to be false, he was in a panic. By the time the fourth ship reached his so-called Garden of Eden, Tam-I-El's people had only been able to teach the early arrivals the basics of making fire, weaving cloth, growing some crops, and gathering from the forests. With only these basic skills taught, Tam and his teams were captured and banished to a less-than-desirable place.

This left the Boss and its benevolent Order with a dilemma. What was to be done with this new colony of humans? They couldn't really be returned to their civilizations on Earth. They would be strangers out of time with no connections. It wasn't their doing that put them on this foreign world, but as they had no memory of where they had come from, this was now the only "home" they knew. A sanctioned team could possibly guide them, but the colony or commune was small and seemed to be coping. In the end, the Boss decided to provide a little more education on the basic of living and then leave this new colony of humans to develop on their own with no further interaction with the Order, at least for the time being. So it was, with a little more education provided for survival, the Order left.

This plan might have been completely workable, if not the most acceptable, if the Order had stuck around just a little longer to gain a better understanding of the planet's indigenous animal species. But they didn't, and some simple safeguards that would have made a big difference weren't provided. The resulting consequence was truly unfortunate.

Chapter 4

Garden of Eden

This new so-called Garden of Eden might have lived up to the name if the 400 humans brought there by Tam-I-El's people hadn't started with nothing. No memory of what had happened to get them to this place or anything prior meant that everything they might have learned on Earth was gone. Medical doctors, farmers, jungle warriors, and sheep ranchers were now equally ignorant, needing to learn but with no teachers. Each one did remember the basics of their own language, but that didn't help much with everyone essentially speaking a different language. Eventually this led to a new language that used many words from the languages they used to speak mixed in with other languages. One can only imagine how difficult these beginnings might have been; a true Tower of Babel, but without the tower. Tam had told them they were in the Garden of Eden, but that meant nothing. In time, as people started to exchange words, Garden of Eden simply became Gadan; just a name with no meaning.

The first 100 people had reached Gadan in the late 1970's. From then on generations had come and gone. It was a plus that the first people of Gadan all had above-average intelligence, they just had no memory of anything that happened before they arrived. They all had shared the same rebirth and would tell the story of arrival for the younger ones to learn and remember. Often this would be around a cooking fire before it became dark and before the huge raiding animals called tandoo might drag someone away.

"Tell me again Dalt how we came to be," said Zeen.

"I will tell you, but remember what I say, for one day you will be the storyteller."

"Yes Dalt. I will try to remember."

"No," said Dalt, "you must remember. Okay?"

"Yes, I will remember."

Dalt smiled. He was one of the older members of the commune and in excellent condition from a hard, but paced, work ethic instilled in him by his parents. Those of his age that weren't as healthy usually ended up as a food source for the tandoo. Dalt wanted to delay that fate as long as possible.

Dalt wore the usual warm-weather clothing consisting of a type of vest and what some might consider shorts. Men and women usually wore the same style clothing and all shared the same olive-colored skin, auburn hair and green eyes; the result of their ancestors coming from all over Earth, mingling their DNA, and the local environment.

It was unfortunate that the indigenous tandoo had readily adapted to the newcomers and found them easy prey. The tandoo never exerted any energy needlessly so culling the unhealthy and usually older, more feeble, members of the colony was their modus operandi. The effect on the Gadans was that the colony usually stayed between 400 and 600 individuals. Higher birth years would push this number a bit up at times. Because of the culling of the weak and the elderly plus some unseen factors, the commune as a whole was much healthier than what otherwise might be expected. This became integral to the Gadans story as a whole.

Dalt started, "We are the chosen ones. In the beginning, our people were born here coming out of a very deep sleep. Being born as adults, the birth was painful. Very large people that could fly with ease helped us as we were born. They showed us how to live here in Gadan and the first ones were told we should grow as a people and prosper. Our first people came in the warming season and were showed how to grow food. More people came in the cooling season and even later people came in the warm season and cold season. Our guardians said there would be no more and we were to make children.

"We were told that this place, Gadan, was special and we as a people were special. We were the chosen ones. Our fate was ours and we were to embrace that fate until one day when our people would go back from whence we came.

"But our guardians were taken from us by others of their kind. These new people told us that our guardians were not as they appeared. If fate allowed, Gadans would go back, but fate could not be predicted. Before they left in shiny flying bowls we were told to live for the moment and to embrace the end when it came.

"After the guardians and their abductors left, the tandoo showed us part of our fate as the old and the sick were taken. It was understood that the tandoo were taking individuals back and we needed to embrace this as part of our fate. Not everyone believes the tandoo are taking anyone back. Instead it seems that the tandoo actions are just painful and has nothing to do with going back. Still the tandoo are an accepted part of our life as a people, keeping us free of sickness and the ravages of age. We do believe that the guardians will return one season, free us from the tandoo and take us back."

Zeen asked, "Where is back?"

"Ah," said Dalt. Then looking up and pointing, "Back is up there past the clouds and the white dots in the sky."

"Is it wonderful up there?"

"There are no tandoo there, so it must be wonderful."

Zeen said, "I don't like the tandoo. I would like to go back some day, but I'd rather the tandoo not be involved," and Dalt smiled.

Chapter 5

The Missions (2147)

Dr. Harlyn Jackson, Science Director was rapidly becoming much more comfortable in his position and was taking it seriously. When he visited the fleet in orbit around TCe a thorough appreciation of what had been accomplished had made him feel quite inadequate. He was determined, however, to do whatever was required to be seen as worthy of his position. During his month-long stay with the fleet, Katherine gradually changed her thinking about Harlyn. True, he probably had not been the best choice for the job, but he asked a lot of questions and seemed eager to learn. Thoughts that he shared indicated he was perhaps more nimble in his thinking than Katherine had first thought. She had to concede, *Maybe this guy is the real thing.* And with that realization she started to share more of her thoughts with him.

When he returned to Earth and the UNSC headquarters, Yvonne Blain noticed a change. Harlyn spent a lot of time in his office doing calculations, drawing diagrams and communicating with Katherine. He also made several trips to meet with the principals of the Star Struck Trading Company. And since the wormhole gate factory was next door, he introduced himself to Dakota Bickmeier and spent a day with him tossing ideas around. Harlyn had to laugh when he discovered the personal project that Dakota and Celeste were working on. He thought, *Here was a man that is the world's only true expert of the most technologically advanced system of transportation between the stars. Yet here he is working on one of the earliest means of motorized transportation. Fascinating.*

What Harlyn wasn't doing was talking with was his boss, the Operations Director, or any of the commissioners. In fact he ignored several meetings of the Commission. While this did not go unnoticed, Harlyn had come to believe most of these meetings were a waste of his time. They were all talk resulting in nothing.

Still, no mission plan was put forth. Initially Katherine moved from frustration to anger, but as conversations with Harlyn became more frequent, she could see that at least he was developing a plan and she convinced herself, as well as the starships' crews, that "something was coming."

Finally ten months after his first meeting with Katherine, he announced that he wanted to present a plan to the Commission. The Commission members weren't expecting much, so they were in for a bit of a surprise.

"Ladies and Gentlemen of the United Nations Stellar Commission and Dr. Blain, I believe I have developed a long-range plan that will take us and the whole world to view new and exciting horizons. As you know, we have six Star Ships: United States, British Commonwealth, China, South America, and Africa are fully functional. Inactive and possibly remaining that way is the abandoned Russia.

"The UNSC's original mission was to find a new world to colonize with the purpose of taking pressure off an overcrowded Earth. That became moot when the Death Flu of 2071 killed off 90% of the people. As a result our mission shifted to exploration, but it seems to me that effort was not enthusiastically supported. The reasons aren't important, but it has been nearly three years since the TCe outpost was created. Both that outpost and the colony on Epsilon Eridani b have proved worthwhile for different reasons, but they certainly aren't what we Earthlings were seeking.

"Our starship fleet is in a holding pattern with crews only large enough to keep the engines functional. History has a habit of repeating itself if not studied, so indulge me for a moment. I happened upon a piece of history that I think fits our position. In the early 1900's, a Minnesota newspaper reported that the United States President Theodore Roosevelt wanted his naval warships on the move, and that they would rust and rot if left in the harbor. Around 1928, a professor by the name of John A. Shedd solidified Roosevelt's sentiment with a memorable quote, reminding us that great experiences are sometimes found over the horizon. He said, 'just as ships are meant to sail the seas, so too are we meant to explore new ideas and experiences. It can take courage to leave life's safe harbors, but the reward for such bravery is a life well-lived.' He finished by saying, 'A ship is safe in the harbor, but that's not what ships are for.' So I'm saying we need to do something with our ships."

The Chinese Commissioner interrupted with, "I don't know American history, but the rest I knew. So do you have something to say or are you just going to fill the air with words like the directors before you. Dr. Blain, do you two have a plan or not?"

"I have nothing to do with this. This is all Harlyn's noise."

"Okay," said Harlyn, "I'll cut to the chase. There are multiple parts to the plan that I developed in conjunction with the Star Struck Trading Company and Admiral Hickey.

"First, one ship and crew will try to restore Russia to service. We know that whatever contaminated the ship killed all that couldn't be rescued. We need to decontaminate the ship and get it back into service. For now my thinking is that Russia and the rescue ship will remain in a holding pattern in the TC solar system and we will make plans for these ships later based on the level of success we have with the decontamination.

"Second, one ship will go to YZ Ceti. The two planets there don't appear suitable for a settlement so I'm not proposing that we build a wormhole gate. Instead, the mission would be to find and potentially bring back information and rare minerals we could use. YZ Ceti is only 1.6 light years away. Since this mission is mostly enterprise driven, I propose this ship be turned over, or leased, to the Star Struck Trading Company. The Company is more than willing and is well positioned to staff the ship. They could possibly complete this mission in five to six years. They would then rejoin the two ships at TC for a mission yet to be worked out."

When Harlyn stopped to judge the reaction in the room, someone blurted out, "What about the remaining three ships?"

"So I have your attention now. Good. Third, the remaining three ships will return to Earth."

"Return to Earth. Why?"

"The trip will take about twenty-five Earth-based years. Maybe less. In any case it will be less than the twenty-eight years it took the fleet to go from Earth to EE. While those ships are on route, the UNSC will build two more ships to be completed prior to the arrival of our returning ships.

"Fourth, this new fleet of five ships will then leave Earth for Alpha Centauri. In this case, the purpose will be to build a wormhole gate and hopefully create a true colony on one or more of the planets."

"Why do we need the ships to come here first? Why not go directly to Alpha Centauri?"

"For one thing, Alpha Centauri is almost completely opposite Tau Ceti from our sun for a total distance of over twenty-four lightyears. Even if we found a crew willing to take that trip, a stop over at Earth should be welcome. Also it occurred to me as I toured the fleet, there aren't that many people here on Earth that have seen the ships. I think it would be good for morale to have the ships in orbit around Earth so people can see them. Finally and most important of all, they need to pick up the Gate components."

"So how far away is Alpha Centauri?"

Harlyn now knew he really had their attention and answered with, "it is only 4.3 light years away."

"Well, what the heck! It's practically in our back yard; just down the road. Okay, answer me this. If Alpha Centauri is that much closer than Epsilon Eridani, how come the ships weren't sent there first?"

"That's an excellent question. I believe the data available at the time indicated that an Earthlike planet was more likely to be found around EE. There is also some indication that there was some outside influence that steered us away from Alpha Centauri. Something I don't quite understand. Anyway, as we know EEb in fact is very much like Earth. It just happens to be occupied. Newer research indicates Alpha Centauri is also likely to a have a planet we could use, and maybe this time it won't be occupied."

"That's a lot to take in. Have you and Yvonne worked out the details? I suspect there are more than a few."

With that, Yvonne said with panic in her voice, "I have nothing to do with this!"

"Well maybe you should," said the British Commissioner. "This seems pretty bold to me having ships going in different directions, but I kind of like this bold initiative. I'll make a motion that the UNSC directors flush out the details of the plan as presented, after which a decision to proceed or not will be made."

The motion was seconded and passed unanimously. After all, the commissioners didn't need to do any work, so why not?

Harlyn was rather pleased with himself. Yvonne was not pleased at all and made sure Harlyn knew it when the commissioners adjourned. "How dare you do this without my permission!"

"I dared," said Harlyn, "because something needed to happen and you weren't about to do anything. I'm sure you conveniently forgot I tried to get you to listen to my ideas more than once, but you couldn't be bothered. So now, either work with me like the commissioners expect, or resign."

Doctor Yvonne Blain seriously thought about the resigning part, but decided that since Harlyn was doing all the work, she'd stick around and get some credit. She could resign later and blame Harlyn if things didn't go well.

Chapter 6

Interesting Times (2148)

Gabe-Re-El was shocked back to the present, a kind of defibrillation that forced his heart to reset and start pumping. While he had no way of knowing for certain until he saw the actual year, he felt like he hadn't been in stasis for very long. If true, this was not good at all. For now, however, it was the old routine of coming out of stasis.

It would take a day or so for all the body parts to recognize that they were connected and for the stasis fluid in the lungs, stomach and digestive track to purge. Gabe certainly knew what was coming. This was far from the first time he had been subjected to this misery.

Within an hour, the vomiting and the convulsive discharges started. This would last at least five hours and there was nothing he could do but use a form of mental yoga to get past the pain and stench. A mask of sorts would take the vomit away while pumping nearly pure oxygen into his lungs. Tubes stuck into the most private body parts would take much of the stasis fluid away from the body, but the smell from the process and the general body odor from laying in stasis for any period of time was less than pleasant. It simply felt so unclean and degrading. *At least no one could see what was going on,* was his fuzzy thought.

At hour six the convulsions stopped. Now with enough brain function to study the monitors above the bed he could get some idea of what was going on with the purging functions and how long he had been inactive. He had been under for only a couple of years. *I might as well have stayed active,* he thought.

At hour twelve, Gabe started to feel his body responding and part of that response was a developing hunger for food: real, chewable food. This gave Gabe something pleasant to think about and a plan for the immediate future. Protocol was to get the body functioning first and fortunately that meant food and drink. Though his movement was still limited, he could at least plan a meal and later, through verbal commands, get the robotics to start gathering food and preparing a feast. Comfort food, that's what he wanted. But that would have to wait until hour fourteen when his mouth could form some words.

Finally past hour twenty-three, the tingling in Gabe's arms and legs subsided enough to allow him to slowly remove the mask and those miserable tubes.

"Ah, much better!" he said out loud to the monitors. "Man, am I hungry!"

He shifted his seven feet two inch frame so his feet could touch the floor. Using his hands and currently limited body strength, he steadied himself and looked around. There were no surprises. The soft glow showed the same dull gray walls he looked at when he was going under. Though they and the somewhat darker floor looked cold, they were in fact pleasantly warm, a good sign that the environmental systems were working.

Gabe made it to the galley and though extremely hungry, he grabbed only a quick bite of a biscuit and some water before heading for the shower. He really needed to get clean and dressed. Once that was completed he felt better and was ready to truly settle into eating. The robotic kitchen staff had conjured up steak, a half dozen eggs, scones, grapefruit juice, and coffee. *That should hold me for few hours*, he thought. There would, in fact, be a lot of food consumption for a few days, even more than usual, before his body recovered to its normal weight of 300 pounds.

For now it was time for business. What Earthly dilemma had triggered the need for him to be brought out of stasis? As one of the most senior members of his Order on Earth, the need for him to address situations was usually reserved for the most serious issues. Knowing there would not actually be a response, he said to the robotics, "What is it this time? Ever since humanity started reaching for the stars, everything has become more complicated." There was, of course, no response.

In the control room, Gabe settled into a chair and fired up the monitors. "Ah, let's see now."

He wasn't too impressed initially with what he saw. Talking to the monitors, which also didn't talk back, he said, "Hmmmm, the United Nations Stellar Commission has a new mission for the fleet.

That's nice. Wait a minute! The eventual goal is to go to Alpha Centauri! Damn!"

Gabe wasn't one to panic, but a mission to that star system really had the potential to be extremely embarrassing for the Order, possibly exposing the Order to the entire world. Up until now, very few people knew about the Order with every effort designed to keep it that way. Only guidance was allowed and that was to be restricted to those that needed it in order to keep mankind on a positive course of development. Direct action was forbidden. Occasionally in the past an Order member would go rogue and action, including discipline, would be administered depending upon the severity of the offense. In the recent past, Charm-E-Ine allowed herself to be placed as the leader of the Union of African Nations with the title of Princess Charm-E-Ine. While certainly against protocol, the end result was extremely positive. The Boss determined that simple removal from the scene was appropriate, allowing her to be brought back into the fold.

There were far more serious incidents in the past, however, resulting in complete banishment of multiple perpetrators to an "undisclosed" location. One particular incident was what concerned Gabe now. While the incident had been dealt with in perhaps questionable ways, it appeared as though it might be exposed. If that happened, or wasn't handled properly, it would jeopardize all future interactions with the people of Earth.

In this embarrassing case, there was a leader named Tam-I-El who had led his team in a completely wrong direction. In addition, he managed to recruit three additional teams for a total of twenty-four Order members going rogue. Tam's intentions were noble, but the end result was a disaster. A disaster that had been covered up, or more correctly, had been conveniently explained away by conspiracy theory groups and seemingly ignored by the authorities. And then there was the little clandestine effort to use false data to make the planet look less attractive. This effort led the UNSC to send the ships on a much longer voyage to Epsilon Eridani. A fresh look at Proxima Centauri, without Order interference, now made it appear much better. If, however, the Earth's Star Ship fleet discovered the result of Tam's actions on the second planet of Proxima Centauri and exposed it, the consequences couldn't be imagined. *Fortunately,* thought Gabe, *we have some time to develop a plan.*

Of a more immediate concern was what was happening on the African continent. When Princess Charm-E-Ine—or Princess Charmy as she had come to be known—was head of the government, Africa found itself as the world leader economically. It even funded its own Star Ship. But while Charmy left behind a solid government, the lack of her "charm" allowed previously vanquished issues to return. This included a few individuals looking to carve out their own fiefdoms. The good news was that it could be brought under control with some swift action, even if it meant bending a rule or two. Gabe would put this on his "get it out of the way" list so he could focus on problem number one: Tam's mess.

Another variant from protocol was not really his fault, but Raman-I-El had created a problem. Being in stasis for long periods of time could create changes in an individual. The nature of the changes could vary, but in Raman's case it developed into something serious. Raman had been in stasis for over 3,000 Earth years, or ten times longer than was acceptable. He might have been in stasis even longer or, more likely have perished, if the Earth's star ship fleet that happened upon Raman's crashed ship hadn't rescued him. The other five members of his team did, in fact, perish. Most considered this event serendipitous, but there were some that calculated the chances of this happening as being so astronomically unlikely that some other influence must have been involved.

In any case, Raman became a valued member of the fleet's crews because he was able to translate all forms of language, just as all in the Order were capable of doing. As time with the fleet went on, he also developed the ability to communicate instantaneously with Princess Charmy. And then an additional side effect developed, providing premonitions of future events. However as these abilities grew, Raman also gradually lost self-awareness and became more and more unresponsive to the world around him. One result of all this trauma was an extremely close relationship with one of the crewmembers, Sharon Hooding. So close in fact, that Sharon had a child. This was something that had never happened previously between any Order member and a human and was certainly far outside of acceptable protocol. To make matters worse, Raman was so far out of it mentally by the time the child was born, he couldn't seem to understand or accept that he had anything to do with creating a child.

Sharon Hooding took her child, and with no involvement from Raman named him Astron Hooding. From a personal standpoint, Gabe wanted to know how Sharon and Astron were getting on, but he also needed to know from a professional standpoint if Astron was more like Sharon or more like Raman. Hopefully his scrambled DNA had provided the child with the best of each parent.

Gabe considered all of this and laid out the makings of a plan in his head. To implement it, he decided he needed the rest of his team and the team that had ended up with both Charm-E-Ine and Raman-I-El. In the meantime, he needed to have more food, and perhaps a nice bottle of Chianti to wash it down. Maybe that might settle the extremely uneasy feeling in the pit of his stomach. *What was that ancient Chinese curse? Ah, yes, "may you live in interesting times."* This was all going to be interesting.

Chapter 7

The Other Team

After Gabe started the reactivation of his own team, he sent a signal to activate the South American team members of the Order. This team had some unique collective experience, but it also had two members who had created some of the issues that now needed attention.

Evan-Ge-Line was the first of the second team to be brought out of stasis. As was typical, Evan would be brought out with no apparent reason evident. She would focus on getting back into a functioning mode and then she would find what was going on. First her mind would click in with the fuzzy realization that she was coming out of stasis. Then as the agonizing process was activated to shed stasis fluids and tubing, she would gradually become more alert; first to the process itself, then to her surroundings and finally to fully functioning.

She was between fuzzy and some clarity when she looked around the stasis room to see if she was the first one. Apparently she was, as the other five chambers were occupied. She looked again. *Wait a minute,* she thought, *there were only four of us before and now there are six? Do I remember this wrong? Did the other two not get killed?*

It would be many hours before she had her answer.

When her chamber opened and she was able to get up, she looked carefully at her sleeping companions. Three she recognized immediately; they were her teammates and friends. *But who are these other two and how did they even get here?*

Confused, she put that thought aside as the number one priority was to get cleaned up, eat, and get dressed. *At least one thing is normal,* she thought as she settled in at the dining table. The drones had gone off looking for food as she was coming out of stasis and the robotic help had prepared a huge comfort meal to her liking. And that included a huge pitcher of champagne and orange juice.

Satisfied for the moment, she went up to the control room to determine what was going on. The first thing she saw was a very unusual handwritten note. Thinking, *Who writes notes on paper anymore?* she read, "You have probably noticed two new people added to your team. One is Charm-E-Ine and the other is Raman-I-El. I am designating Charmy as team leader, at least for the short term. Both were left alone when their teams were killed, something of which, unfortunately, you know about all too well. You will need to activate the rest of your companions and when ready, come to Alaska to join up with my team and me. All will be made clear then. We have a number of issues that need to be resolved. We have some time for resolution, but you shouldn't delay. That said, it will not be necessary for you to make any extra efforts to avoid being observed on your trip here. Gabe-Re-El."

Speaking to the robotic staff getting the expected nonresponse, she said, "Well that was helpful—not! That Gabe can be a royal pain." And the word "royal" triggered a memory.

Charm-E-Ine. I know who that is. She was the one that went rogue, created the Union of African Nations as Princess Charmy and funded the Star Ship Africa. Wow! But who's that other dude? He's new to me.

It actually would have been a surprise if Evan didn't know who Charmy was. Among her people Charm-E-Ine had become something of a celebrity. Few ever went rogue, and no one had ever gone to the extent she did. *Hmmm,* she thought, *There was a bunch that did something quite unacceptable years ago, but they were banished, while this Charmy was promoted to team leader. I'm confused.*

Remaining confused, she activated the controls that would take the others out of stasis. A couple of days later the six of them prepared to head for the volcano of Augustine Island, off the coast of Alaska, to meet with Gabe and his team. Just like Evan, her original team members were somewhat baffled by the presence of Charmy and Raman. Some information came to light as they all prepared but there were no real details.

When ready, the six of them put on their antigravity packs and took off. They packed very little food, relying on diners and food stores for most of their meals using the standard gold and silver coins they all carried for payment. If they entered a reasonably sized town or village, they would split up. It was not necessarily to be discrete, as there was nothing discrete about these large people with long hair and dressed all in white. It was more to avoid too much strain on the small diners when they ordered their meals. The amount of food they consumed was almost shocking to anyone that witnessed the dining experience.

They didn't go out of their way to display their unfurled antigravity pack panels when arriving and leaving these towns, but they took Gabe's suggestion literally and didn't hide them either. Many who saw this display started believing that something more significant was on the horizon. Church attendance increased.

It took about a week for Charmy's team to meet up with Gabe's team.

But they were not prepared to hear what Gabe had to say.

Chapter 8

Assignments

When the South American team showed up, the first thing on the agenda was a feast, as any excuse for a feast was a good one. There was plenty of food, wine and conversation. Much of the food gathering by the drones was done secretly to avoid awkward stories. In addition to food, barrels of wine might disappear from a winery; usually the best. But left in its place would be the usual gold and silver coins worth much more than the wine. The vineyard owners would scratch their heads, but couldn't really complain to the Police. "Why yes officer, I found some gold coins where my wine used to be."

During the feast, Gabe laid out his plan to address what he saw as problems. It was actually multiple plans and that was why he needed the two teams. There were plenty of other teams he could activate, but that would happen only as necessary. However, as those assembled were shocked to learn, eventually all the teams would be activated for something quite unprecedented. But that would be some time in the future.

Gabe's plan was to break the teams up into smaller groups with each group addressing a specific issue. The biggest issue, as he saw it, was the need to mitigate past transgressions by members of the Order. Usually Order members dealt with issues created by mankind, not issues generated by the Order members themselves. This particular issue created by an Order member was unprecedented and complicated. Minimizing the effects of what would be the eventual discovery was going to be a major headache.

While some knew about this, others did not, or had only heard bits and pieces of the story. Gabe explained the actions of rogue Order members who believed they were the ones going to save mankind. They had gone far outside of what could be considered acceptable and created a mess. This had been a few generations ago and while it couldn't be corrected, discovery would have serious consequences. So far discovery had been delayed by misdirection, but unfortunately, things were in motion that would certainly bring it to light.

This first issue needed the most thought. As Gabe explained, "Over a period of centuries, people would mysteriously disappear. There were numerous reasons for this that had nothing to do with the Order, but disappearances in the 1970s were directly tied to the Order. Some people claimed they had been abducted by aliens and after some kind of testing by the aliens they were returned to Earth. Few believed these stories, and in fact most were fiction. Interestingly these fictitious stories were the ones with the most graphic detail of invasive testing by little green men. However, some stories were true as the result of Order member Tam-I-El and his people trying to determine the best candidates for their clandestine activity. If the selected candidates failed the testing, they were returned. If they passed the testing, they disappeared from Earth forever.

"The Order caught up to Tam-I-El and sent him and his followers into exile. What they had done, however, couldn't be corrected. A painful decision by the Boss was to leave these people alone to fend for themselves and essentially let things develop as naturally as possible. My opinion is that was an unconscionable error on our part. It was our people that made the problem; we should not have just walked away. Things are now in motion that will eventually expose this error so now something more than just guidance is going to be required. I don't think we can solve the problem, but I think we just might be able to make the Order look, well, less bad. Awkward is not a strong enough word. This mess might likely lead to destroying everything the Order hoped to achieve in the future if we were to stick around.

"On another front and in the very recent past, another member of the Order had also gone rogue. While the efforts weren't sanctioned, the result was much more acceptable, though as it turned out, too fragile."

With this statement, Gabe looked directly at Charmy who said, "What?"

Smiling, Gabe said, "You know what. It was you. Do you want to tell the story?"

"No," she said. "Be my guest."

And then to the others he told the story. "In the not so distant past our not so innocent friend over here decided that our Order wasn't doing enough to help Africa. It began when Charm-E-Ine's African team were killed, leaving her alone. The Order assumed that she had been killed as well when Erta Ale volcano erupted, destroying her habitat with her fellow team members inside. Charmy, as she was referred to with affection, did some soul searching and finally decided that the mission of the Order was worthy but the protocols in place were too restrictive. She decided to do what she could for Africa as a whole before dying a natural death. Then with the help of an African village, she was raised to power, forming the Union of African Nations. She was portrayed as Princess Charm-E-Ine or Princess Charmy, the last of a noble Nubian family, and assumed the role of Benevolent Dictator over most of Africa.

"During her reign, Africa prospered. Seeking to be seen as a global power, the UAN funded and staffed the newest Star Ship in the fleet, Africa, a ship that helped rescue the mission to Tau Ceti. When the Boss finally realized what was happening, I was sent to bring Charm-E-Ine back in line. But it wasn't quite that simple, was it Princess Charmy?"

Charmy said, "Okay rub it in, you jerk," while the other ten Order members who already knew at least some of the story looked admirably at her.

Gabe chuckled and went on saying directly to Charmy, "But what you built is falling apart. The person you chose to take over can't do the job. It has been decided to give it one more shot to have the UAN function without Order interference. What that means is that you are to return to Africa and hopefully fix things so they stay fixed."

Charmy didn't know this last part and was more than little distressed to hear that what she thought was a lasting legacy was falling apart. Now somewhat chastised, Charmy said, "I'm sorry, I'll get this fixed."

Turning his attention away from Charmy, Gabe went on, "Another problem was actually started three thousand years ago give or take a few centuries. Another team had been sent to Earth back then, but while the team was in stasis during the trip, their ship collided with an asteroid eventually killing all on board except our friend Raman-I-El. By chance, or perhaps by the design of some unknown force, Earth's starship fleet discovered the wreck and rescued Raman who was still in stasis. The amount of time Raman had been in stasis had damaged him but also gave him some amazing abilities; both of which were enhanced over the length of time he was with the fleet. The positive attributes helped save the fleet. But during this period his cognitive abilities declined. In the process he strayed from acceptable practices and ended up having a son with the ship's Head Bartender. Something he didn't seem to comprehend as anything he had done."

Raman winced at this and said, "You're not painting a very pretty picture of me. I'm better now…I think."

"That was the bad part," Gabe said, turning to the rest of the group, "but there is more. There is an extremely rare gene that can occur among our people. Charmy was born with this gene, but it was so rare, she had been told, 'don't even think about it. It is so rare you're probably the only one alive with it.' The gene allows thoughts to be transmitted over any distance, including light years, instantaneously. Charmy did in fact forget about this rare ability until she was connected to Raman. Apparently, the long stasis period for Raman that damaged part of his brain also mutated the same gene possessed by Charmy. Their ability to communicate was one factor that rescued the fleet. But it also drew Raman closer and closer to Charmy until she was his only focus." Then looking at Raman asked, "Is that about right?"

"Yes, I suppose that's fair."

Gabe continued, "These two finally met when the TCe Wormhole Gate became operational. That's when I convinced the two of them to rejoin the Order. That's how they ended up filling the two available spots in your South American team. One hoped-for result for Raman was that a more standard period of time in stasis would repair his mind. While Raman certainly seems more cognitive, I think it is still too early to know if he has retained the communication ability. I'm going to have Raman assist Charmy with Africa, but not until he has paid a visit to Sharon Hooding and their son Astron."

Most of the Order had never heard the story of Raman and those present were quite shocked to hear it. It had always been assumed that those that left their home world made it to their final destination. It was unsettling that not only was that assumption false, but that the accident seemed to be a secret.

Gabe could see that the others were distressed over Raman's story. He needed to get their minds off the subject so he said, "Now on a less serious side, I admit I thought it would be fun to add two people to the South America team to see the reaction when everyone came around."

"Yeah, very funny," said a very insincere Evan. "Charmy is right. You can be a jerk."

Ignoring Evan's comment, Gabe went on with, "I did think that naming Charmy as the team leader was a good idea, but I honestly never expected circumstances to be what they are right now. Since I'm breaking the bigger teams up into smaller units, we'll forget about leader designations." Then, smiling, he added, "Except for me of course".

"Of course," said Ara-Ri-El. "Heap big cheese Gabe-Re-El not gonna play second fiddle to us lowly second-rate cheeses." Only Ara laughed as the others stared at him for this poor attempt at humor.

Gabe ignored Ara, saying, "As you have likely noticed, the idea of working behind the scenes and advising per Order protocol is being put aside for the African continent. We are also putting a lot of standard protocol aside in everything else we'll be doing in the near future. It all relates to our long-range plans. Suffice it to say the quiet ways of the Order working behind the scenes is starting to shatter. More and more people with influence are becoming aware that we aren't just an oddity, but are in fact from another world. And while our intentions, and most actions, have been to benefit mankind, the people of Earth are starting to take exception to this interference. We'll have to put that concern aside for now and focus on the issues we might be able to control.

"There are some activities in the works that require direct action from us if the outcomes are to be successful. This is not a passing thought. It has been decided that for now the ends justify the means. It is hoped that this a correct assumption."

"So that takes care of two of us," said Na-Ki-Ir. "I assume there is more. Yes?"

"Oh, for sure," said Gabe. "You're not off the hook. It seems the UNSC has come up with plans for the starships. They are going to split up the fleet for multiple missions. One of these missions will eventually lead to the discovery of the commune on Proxima Centauri b. This is where Tam-I-El had set up his so-called Garden of Eden for his abducted humans. Everyone that was brought there originally was placed in stasis, but humans are not of our kind and they didn't fare very well. Physically they were fine, but their memories were wiped. They were taught a few basics to survive and they have survived quite well for the most part, but the current generation is not prepared for what is about to come. While we can't fix everything, we can at least prepare them a little for what will happen. What degree of preparation they will need is unclear until we have someone there to evaluate the situation. Evan-Ge-Line, I am assigning this task to you."

Evan said, "Ummm okay, I guess. Can you perhaps provide a few details, like how do I get there?"

Ara piped in with, "Gee you want everything. I thought you were smart."

With a steely glare from both Gabe and Evan towards Ara, Gabe said, "Don't you have something to do? If not, find something." Then to Evan he said, "One of our ships will be arriving here in a couple of days. You'll have the team from Australia to help you. You'll need to fill them in as best you can. You'll be in charge. This ship is a standard design for six, so one of you will take turns being out of stasis at a time. The trip should take about four years. I suggest a nine-month watch per individual. It is completely up to you on how far you want to go with the preparations once you reach this so-called Garden of Eden. That decision-making includes when you think you need to leave, if at all. Since the fleet from TC will take about twenty-five years to get here before it can leave for Alpha Centauri, I think you'll have plenty of time.

"When Earth's starship fleet finally leaves Earth for Alpha Centauri, Ur-I-El will be on board and will help with whatever needs to be completed."

Ara-Ri-El said, "I'd like to go on that mission."

With the look of suspicion on his face, Gabe said, "Why?"

"It would be a whole new audience for my jokes!"

Ere-Mi-El said, "They wouldn't get your so-called jokes. We don't think they're funny, why would they?"

"I'm crushed," said Ara.

Gabe said, "You don't look very crushed, but you might be when you hear what I have for you."

"Oh goody," said Ara.

"One ship, the United States, is going off in a different direction to explore the 'c' planet around YZ Ceti. The Star Struck Trading Company, with its goal of finding valuable minerals, is funding this mission. What they don't know is that there are mineral deposits on that planet with the potential of solving many of Earth's environmental issues. Now, I know leading the humans to these deposits is far outside our normally acceptable practice for the Order, but the results could be nothing short of spectacular. Naki, I hate to do this to you, but you can probably control our friend Ara as well as anyone, so you'll go with Ara on this mission. I'm making arrangements for you to have an official rank."

"I have to be on the same ship with Ara?" Naki asked, then with the faintest of smiles added, "You don't like me very much I guess."

"We'll have great time!" said Ara. Naki groaned.

"I don't suppose you're done, right?" asked Kem-U-El.

"You supposed correctly. Star Ship Russia was abandoned in orbit around TCf when the crew brought something on board that killed just about everyone. Since the engines can't be shut down, they are in idle mode with no one attending to them. If something isn't done soon, there will likely be an explosion that will finally destroy the ship. The UNSC wants to save the ship and has assigned the Africa crew to try and do exactly that. This is likely the shortest and most dangerous mission. Schem, I'm assigning you this mission with Rag. Even though you don't know anyone in the crew, you have the most experience on the star ships than anyone here because of your trip from Earth to EEb. I think they will need your help."

"So," said Kem, "what about the rest of us?"

"I didn't forget you. You and Ere are going to be on British Commonwealth and South America as the Chief Academic and Science Officers. I made these arrangements as well. China will be the other ship in this small fleet as they head back to Earth. Once the fleet reaches Earth, it is planned that two new ships will join them and then they will be heading to Proxima Centauri b. And that is when mankind will discover the so-called Garden of Eden and legacy of Tam-I-El."

"That's a long trip back to Earth. Are you expecting trouble?"

"I am, but don't know what."

"So Gabe where does that leave you?" asked Naki.

"I am going to stay here on Earth and try to keep the UNSC and Star Struck Trading Company under control. Cast-I-El will help me."

Charm-E-Ine had listened quietly through this briefing. When Gabe seemed to be done she said, "So Gabe-Re-El, you had told me I had been a naughty girl when I went rogue and established the Union of African Nations. You convinced me to abandon my dream and rejoin the Order and follow its protocols. I broke the rules alone! And now, if I'm hearing you correctly, you are asking the bunch of us to do what you had originally said was wrong. Is that correct? Are you being a hypocrite?"

Ara said, "Who cares, this is all fantastic! The chains are off. We can do anything we want now! I feel like a politician or maybe a parent, 'do as I say, not as I do.' I vote for forgetting mankind right now and we party. All in favor?"

"Not so fast" said Gabe. "There is one more thing…" And when he finished making known what he had been told directly from the Boss everyone was silent as his words sunk in. Finally Gabe said, "There is no vote on any of this. You are either in or you're not."

In the end, no one dropped out. Smiling Gabe said, "Thank you. I think our Order is doing the right thing, but only time will be able to tell. I think we will all be making big decisions as we go along. Now then, since we are going out to save the world, actually multiple worlds, I guess we should prepare ourselves and continue with our feast. Our drones and robotic kitchen help have gathered and prepared some exciting dishes. Schem, as the former Head Bartender of the Star Ship United States, I give you the honor of pouring the wine. "

Schem-Hampha-Rae thought this wasn't much of an "honor" but said, "It will be my pleasure."

Chapter 9

Preparations (2148)

The decision to divide up the fleet had been an interesting one, and one that Admiral Hickey hadn't fully contemplated. But there was logic in the divide-and-conquer scenario. Now it was up to the Admiral to decide how best to do it. It wasn't just the ships that would be divided up; it was the crews as well.

One ship would stay in the Tau Ceti solar system and try to salvage the Star Ship Russia. That required the least amount of travel but potentially would be the most dangerous assignment.

One ship would go to YZ Ceti on a mining exploration mission. This would be a relatively short trip of maybe six years, depending upon what might be found.

Three ships were to eventually end up at Alpha Centauri after a stop off at Earth, where supposedly two new ships would be joining them on the next leg of the journey. That would be another 4.4 light years away or about a nine-year trip. This eventual mission was to build the next wormhole gate.

But, of course, these ships had to get to Earth first, the longest assignment.

The Admiral called a general staff meeting of the Vice Admirals, Captains and CASOs to lay out the overall plan and to get their reaction. There was general enthusiasm, but then the decisions of who would do what had to be made, and the enthusiasm quickly faded. It was understood that the current skeletal crews on the ships would either be added to or there would be a completely new crew assigned. It would be up to the officers as to what they wanted to do.

The Admiral went first saying, "there will be two Admirals. Since I have seniority, I have decided I will stay in the Tau Ceti solar system for the Star Ship Russia salvage mission. This is considered the most dangerous because we have no idea what is in store. But it is somewhat selfish as well. Star Ship Africa is the ship that will remain here as my flag ship. It is the smallest, having the smallest carrying capacity. I will not have anyone designated as a Vice

Admiral or CASO. I will act as Captain and have two assistants named by the UNSC and the Trading Company. My goal is to minimize the crew size as much as possible.

"Remaining here means I will be able to occasionally reunite with my family, assuming nothing goes wrong, of course. Dakota needs to stay on Earth at least for the foreseeable future as he is building more wormhole gate components. One of these will be going to Alpha Centauri with the plan to finally create more than just an outpost on a planet. While the outposts and Gates here at TCe and on EEb are important, it isn't close to the colonization of another planet. The UNSC thinks Alpha Centauri might be the one.

"Whoever takes the Admiral position for the trip back to Earth will have Star Ships China, British Commonwealth, and South America. Obviously the crews can be changed once the ships reach Earth. These three ships will likely remain in orbit around Earth for refurbishment before leaving for Alpha Centauri with the additional two new ships. I'm thinking this will be the most fulfilling mission in even though in total it will very long."

As soon as Katherine stopped, Vice Admiral Yin Yue jumped up and said. "I want that job. I'm the most senior next to you, so I get to choose."

Katherine smiled, thinking, *Of course you want this. You have been Vice Admiral for a couple of years and always wanted my job.* But then she thought, *I don't think this is going to work.* Instead Katherine said, "that is what I was expecting you'd say, but think it over carefully. Because the trip is so long, you have first choice of the crewmembers, but they must be willing. Understood?"

Smiling Yin Yue said, "Aye Aye, Admiral."

"That Leaves the United States for the mission to YZ Ceti. Other than the ship's operating staff, most of those going on that trip will be geologists, chemists and other earth science experts, plus mining engineers and equipment operators. The entire crew has been hand picked by the Star Struck Trading Company but with approval from the UNSC and me."

These last statements got everyone's attention. "Why is that?"

"The Trading Company is funding this particular mission. It hopes to discover something of commercial value. They are thinking long term. Admittedly, they are taking a financial gamble but with the hopes for huge profits as the incentive. Admiral Yin Yue has made her choice. Everyone else, take a couple of days to determine what you'd like to do, and let me know. If you want to talk to me, please do. This is not a trifling decision. Oh, do I really need to tell everyone to pass the word along to your crews? They need to make decisions as well. I will be talking to the people on the ground and then heading to Earth to help in crew recruitment. Dismissed."

Yin Yue left with a huge self-satisfying smile thinking, *Admiral Yin Yue. That has a very appealing ring to it!*

Chapter 10

Shore Leave

Admiral Katherine Hickey had selected the salvage mission of Star Ship Russia for herself knowing it had the potential of being the most lethal, but she also felt strongly that it was necessary and wanted to make certain due diligence was observed for all-around safety. While it was true that the ship was in orbit around TCf, doing no one any good at the moment, it also posed a real threat to the planet or perhaps something else still unknown.

The ship had four engine pods still functioning in idle mode plus one other spare engine pod. But there was no one on board to take care of these temperamental hybrid fission/fusion engines. *Well,* as she corrected herself, *no one on board alive that is.*

When Russia became contaminated, everyone on board died a painful death. Only a few were rescued when they were able to isolate themselves from the rest of the ship. One other, Captain Gigory Kazakov, managed to survive by taking a shuttle to the planet's surface where he expected to die, but didn't. Whatever it was that had come from the planet and killed the crew was not harmful if you stayed on the planet. It was like some kind of addictive drug. In time, crew members who had mutinied convinced the Admiral to let them join the Captain and together a colony of sorts was established named New Polyarnaya after Gigory's Russian village. They weren't entirely alone, however. The colony shared the entire planet with sheep-sized animals covered with a feather-like coat that seemed to be telepathic. Just like the humans, these creatures may have been trapped there as well.

Getting Russia back into the operational fleet with all the Gate and construction resources that were still on board would be fantastic. But the dilemma was how to do it without jeopardizing another ship and crew.

Katherine sent a message off to Gigory asking him if he had any ideas. She would give him one month to think about it. In the meantime, she asked for volunteers for the mission and gave everyone who said yes a one-month shore leave. Those electing to go back to Earth permanently would stay on board and run the ship while replacements were located.

Africa was the smallest ship in the fleet with the smallest crew. Because of the risk factor, Katherine was making the crew even smaller; the smallest possible. Africa would have just enough to operate and to staff Russia with a skeleton crew if the mission was successful. Still, that meant a crew size of about 1700. Katherine also decided that with the travel distance between TCe and TCf being minimal, no special amenities were required. But that meant this was a truly bare bones, potentially dangerous mission, so recruitment might be difficult.

Katherine gave herself shore leave and returned to Earth to help recruit replacement crewmembers and to see her husband and daughter. While there was a thought of reestablishing some of the Gates on Earth's closet neighbors in the solar system, no one in the UNSC indicated any urgency. Even the long-term goal of establishing a wormhole gate on Proxima Centauri b was so far away, it almost didn't matter. So with no pressure from the UNSC and being somewhat out of sight and out of mind, the Gate components production facility was anything but a beehive of activity.

Celeste, on the other hand, was up to her elbows restoring the family 1914 Ford. This provided a significant distraction for her dad who found this ancient piece of technology fascinating. And that is where Katherine found the two of them. Huddled in the corner with the Ford.

Katherine stood at the entrance door to the shop, looked at the two of them, put her hands on her hips, and said, "I see you two are hard at work saving mankind. Seriously Dakota, are you getting any of the real work done?"

"Well yeah! I have people!"

Looking over at Larry, Katherine said, "It appears to me your 'people' are more interested in the Ford. Good thing I came back to check on you," and she laughed.

Celeste and Dakota moved as one to give Katherine a proper greeting with lots of hugging and kissing. Dakota asked, "How long are you going to be around this time?"

"On Earth, about a month. I'm splitting my time between recruiting and quality family time. This new mission has me a little spooked."

"You know, honey," said Dakota, "you don't have to do this mission. You could assign someone else."

"Perhaps, but I feel like it's my duty. We'll figure it out. For right now, though, it is time to go out to dinner." Looking at Celeste, Katherine said, "I can just imagine what your father has been feeding you."

Looking wounded, Dakota said, "I'm offended. I can cook!"

"Ah huh. Go get cleaned up, we're going out."

"Aye Aye, Admiral dear."

Then looking at Celeste she said, "And you, young lady, we have a lot of scrubbing to do before you are fit for public exposure."

During dinner Katherine learned that Astron Hooding had been regularly coming over to the shop. He was four years older than Celeste, but instead of bossing her around like big kids often do, he did whatever she wanted, much to the embarrassment of Dakota. Astron was a big kid for his age, actually nearly any age, and extremely smart. Dakota was one of the few people that knew the story behind Astron's father, and he concluded that explained a lot about Astron.

One aspect of Astron that didn't seem to fit his physical ability was his penchant towards organizing thoughts and design. Everything he did seemed oriented towards creativity. He amazed everyone with his ability to take a plain piece of paper, and while seemingly just doodling during a conversation, draw people's faces with such detail it might be considered a photo. Sometimes he would sketch a person's hand, the hardest part of the anatomy to get correct, but would do it with such exactness and speed it took the subject's breath away.

Astron's creative ability went well beyond the arts, however. His creative mind could see solutions to issues few others could, including both humans and Order members. In his mind he could organize anything from seemingly unmanageable chaos. While he was as interested in the old Ford design, Celeste was much more interested in the mechanics. How did things fit together to make something functional. While Astron didn't care to get his hands dirty, he would if Celeste asked him. Celeste, on the other hand, could be found up to her elbows in grease. Dirty fingernails and grease smudges on her face was not her concern. Astron and Celeste made quite the pair.

The town was as close to a company town as any. The biggest employer was the Star Struck Trading Company and with the Gate assembly facility next door, most of the town was space oriented. Any visitors to the area wouldn't have been surprised, though likely amused, that the one real restaurant was named Over the Moon. Its food was proclaimed "out of this world," and if you wanted a drink you had to mix your own with "space shots."

Katherine ate well on the ships, but there was something special about eating in a quiet restaurant on Earth with no constant background noise and vibrations from machinery that never shut down. She couldn't help but notice that Celeste was looking so grown up. That is, once you got past the grease-stained hands. Celeste was already much taller than Katherine, though at Katherine's height, it really didn't take that much.

During dessert, and feeling rather mellow, Katherine said, "The Commission makes me nervous. They have laid out plans for the ships, but I don't think they have the will to follow through to the end. I suspect my next visit with the Commission is going to be interesting, but first things first. We'll get the ships on their way. When Russia is dealt with, we'll see where we are and if the Commission is still committed. That being said, are their Gates ready if they should ask for them? Or just old cars?"

"Hey, everybody needs a hobby! And yes, all the high-tech stuff has been engineered, tested, and packed away here for two Gates. The non-high-tech materials have all been set aside in warehouses owned by the Trading Company. The construction equipment and supplies needed to build a construction camp have all been identified and can be assembled in short order. We, of the great and glorious Gate manufacturing facility, are all set. 'We are all dressed up, but have no place to go.'"

Katherine smiled, shook her head and finished her after-dinner Madeira wine before the three of them left and were "Over the Moon" as they held hands.

Chapter 11

Mission to Earth (2149)

Ying Yue was initially thrilled to be named Admiral for the voyage back to Earth. She would have three starships under her command. This was the recognition she always craved. But then reality set in. She was now a very trim and fit seventy-seven-year-old woman still ready to take on the role. Her CASO, whom she had planned to be her Vice Admiral, said, "No, I've had enough. I'm going back the Earth through the Gate. I'm not up for what looks like a boring trip of twenty-five years."

That's when Ying Yue realized that she would be over 100 years old before even reaching Earth, let alone taking on the trip to the Alpha Centauri system. For the first time in memory she cried. She thought, *Why is life so short?* Reluctantly Yue went to see Admiral Hickey to give up what she always wanted, the title of Admiral. When Katherine named Yue as Admiral she half expected Yue would take the job, but would groom someone to take over during the trip. Whether Yue considered this or not, it didn't matter now. Katherine understood completely what Yue had decided and wasn't surprised. Katherine did say, however, "Are you willing to hold the title of Admiral until we have new crews? I think it would be important for someone with your knowledge to help select the crews and your successor."

That somewhat boosted Yue's morale. She would be Admiral, just not the way she wanted, so she said, "Thank you, that means more to me than you could know." And with that, Admiral Ying Yue started recruiting to fill the rosters of three starships.

A fellow countryman from China ended up as Admiral for the mission. He was Ying Wu. Wu had distinguished himself as a test pilot after graduating first in his class at the Chinese Air Force Academy. Some thought that at age twenty-eight he might not get the respect required for the job, but Wu projected an authoritative figure that went a long way in the decision. Wu stood at five feet seven inches and weighed in at 155 pounds. Just like Yue, his uniform fit perfectly and was always pressed. Katherine wondered about this "kid" being able to take on the role, but changed her mind as soon as she met him. She actually had to laugh to herself. *He reminds me of me when I applied for the job.*

Both Yue and Katherine were a little surprised how easy it was to recruit Wu. Very few qualified people were even interested in talking about the job whereas Wu seemed to be almost begging for it. Not that it would have made a big difference in the actual recruitment, but the UNSC directors could have shared with the Admirals a little background. It seems that while Wu came from a financially well-off family, he had a gambling problem and got himself into trouble with the wrong people when he couldn't pay off his huge gambling debt. He might have found himself with broken legs except for his social status, but that reprieve was soon coming close to an end. Wu needed a place to hide and the space fleet seemed like a good place. He made a deal with the UNSC directors to pay off his debt in exchange for no pay. Financially, that was a good deal for the UNSC. After all, it wasn't as if Wu would be jumping ship! Wu also promised not to gamble, though he found it amusing that the biggest gamble of his life was taking on this less-than-certain mission.

Wang Fang was selected as Vice Admiral of Academics and Science. Fang generated a lot of curiosity about to why she wanted the job. At fifty years of age, this would likely be her final professional position. She wasn't the first choice, but she was the only one with any qualifications willing to take the job with the one condition that she would be allowed to continue her research of microbes and how they might survive in space. It was agreed and her lab was transported through the TCe High Point Wormhole Gate and up to the Star Ship China. This new VAAS wore her uniform only until the fleet left orbit. After that she and her staff were always seen in lab coats. The primary duty of the VAAS was supposed to be calculating course direction and timing when the ships went from acceleration to deceleration and back again. It soon became evident after leaving orbit, however, she didn't care about anything related to her position and left it to the three CASOs to figure out.

It was becoming more and more evident to Yue as she recruited that this task was far from easy. Without some extenuating circumstances, individuals weren't all that thrilled about a long voyage whose only mission was to get the ships back to Earth. There were no expectations of discovery, no possible establishment of a new Gate or colony, and certainly no grand cause to save humanity. Incentives had to be invented.

The incentive for the new Vice Admiral of Operations was simply money. For both Earl Null and his wife Noelle it was a good pay, nothing to spend it on for about twenty-five years, and full retirement when they got back to Earth. The money was the incentive to go, but doing the best job possible was Earl's goal. Trained as a nuclear engineer, he specialized in the design of the fission/fusion concepts used to power the starships. He stood straight at an even six feet, weighing in at a muscular 195 pounds. The expression on his rugged bearded face was one that seemed to penetrate. He wanted only the best from his operations people, even when it was a struggle to get it; because even though he was more than competent, many of his staff weren't nearly as good at their jobs as they should be. And he was determined to make them better.

Once a young engineer brought Earl a report and left it for him to read. It sat on Earl's desk for a couple of days before asking the young engineer to come see him. Waving the report in the air Earl asked, "Is the best you can do?"

"Umm, let me work on it."

When the report was once again submitted, it sat on Earl's desk until he told the young engineer to report in. Earl said the same thing as before only more forcefully, "Are you sure this is best you can do?!"

Frustrated the young engineer took the report back and a few days later resubmitted it. When asked this time if this was the best he could do, the young engineer said with some irritation, "Yes!"

"Good," said Earl. "Now I'll read it. I want only the best from my staff. Don't waste my time with anything less. Got it?"

"Yes sir." A lesson was learned.

Noelle Null was much like her husband and though it wasn't desirable to have a spouse in the line of authority, the UNSC and the Admiral made an exception and named Noelle Captain of the British Commonwealth as part of the deal the Nulls negotiated. Their son, Brian, was five years old.

Headquarters assigned the British Commonwealth CASO with no input from Katherine or Yue. He was six feet eleven inches tall, and weighed in at 280 pounds with not an ounce of fat showing. He had blond shoulder length hair. If that wasn't enough to set him apart, his name of Kem-U-El certainly did. Katherine and Yue shared knowing looks when he showed up. They confirmed their suspicions when they took him aside and asked if there was any relationship to the fellow they had rescued many years ago. Kem smiled and said, "You know if you go back far enough, we are all related." That was enough confirmation for them, but they wondered out loud to each other, "Is there something going on we don't know about?"

They really started to wonder when the CASO for South America showed up and was named Ere-Mi-El. He was a little guy compared to Kem at six feet eight inches tall and 250 pounds, but he had the same hair and body build. When asked if they were related, they said, "Oh, we're cousins." There was no enlightenment from the UNSC headquarters.

Juan Martinez was selected as Captain of the South America. His incentive for the trip was protection very much like the new Admiral; protection from creditors of the most unscrupulous kind. Also to get away from a woman he had left standing at the altar. Juan also came from a wealthy family, but was disowned when he couldn't control his playboy lifestyle. He drank, womanized, and bet on almost anything with money he didn't have. Contrary to these uncontrollable impulses he was able to focus when needed and was an admired Captain of a Chilean ocean research vessel that made numerous trips to the Antarctic. Juan was five foot eight inches tall and 160 pounds with a pencil-thin mustache and slicked-back black hair. He had promised to change his ways. No one believed him, but a Captain was needed.

One of the operating engineers was selected as the China Captain. Lie Jie had the unique history of being the baby born at New Hope on EEb just before China left for TCe. Li Jie learned from experience and had gained specialized training that only someone raised on a Star Ship could get. He took his job seriously, no matter what it was. So seriously that he never even visited Earth when he had the chance. He saw no need. His seriousness, however, also translated into very little compassion for anyone that might need it.

His CASO, Zhang Min, more than made up for it in the compassion department. Her petite size of an even five feet and ninety-five pounds and inability to stand firm on any subject made her a pushover. Zhang had great academic credentials and interviewed well, but could almost be described as a recluse. When it came time for technical skills to be applied, however, she was in her element and brilliant.

As far as the rest of the crew was concerned, the UNSC found itself in an even worse position than when it was trying to outfit the ships for the trip from EEb to TCe. Even with the financial incentives, pickings were meager. The most eager to go were the least qualified, many of whom had stories like Juan's. In the end, however, Star Ship China had a crew of 7800, British Commonwealth had 6,500, and South America had 6,100. With each ship designed for a crew of 18,000 and plenty of room for equipment to build a wormhole gate, there was certainly no crowding.

As far as most knew, the usual non-human crew included fish farms, honeybees, canaries, and a few service dogs. There were no Second People from EEb in the crew. There were, however, two bug ship crews from TCe with their bug shaped airships. It wasn't clear why, but their leaders had persuaded them to volunteer.

On March 4th, 2149, China, South America, and British Commonwealth uncoupled from United States and Africa and headed for Earth with the hope of breaking a record and making the trip in twenty-one years.

Chapter 12

Salvage Mission (2150)

When Katherine returned to the fleet from shore leave, she contacted Captain Gigory Kazakov to see if he had any thoughts on salvaging Russia. He did, saying, "Admiral, as I told Admiral Dodson before he turned the reins over to you, I would try to do whatever I could to make up for my transgressions. I meant it then, and I make the same pledge to you. With that off my chest, I do have some observations that might help. We don't have very sophisticated equipment down here, but with what we have, a couple of us seem to think that whatever kills people is in the air. We think it is some kind of pollen given off by the grass that grows everywhere. When it is inhaled, the person is contaminated. Does that make any sense?"

Katherine, Schem-Hampha-Rae, and Rag-U-El listened and when Gigory finished, Katherine said, "I guess that's possible, but why is it not deadly on the planet? Instead only deadly when you leave?" When she said this, she looked directly at Schem and Rag for a response. None came, as for once they also had little knowledge beyond what Gigory had to offer.

Because of the distance the response wasn't immediate, but when the response did come back, Gigory was saying, "We're not sure. I think it is one of three things; the planet itself provides an antidote, the pollen stuff is addictive, or maybe the pollen has to be fresh to avoid ill effects. That is, once inhaled, it has to be refreshed continuously by breathing. We're just guessing, of course."

Katherine asked, "So you think it acts like an addictive drug?"

"Actually, not like an addictive drug, but that it is an addictive drug. Once you use it, you're hooked or die."

"Hmmm," said Katherine, "So how did it kill the crew that hadn't been exposed?"

Gigory thought he had an answer with, "This pollen stuff was carried back to Russia in the shuttle and in the ignorant shuttle crew.

The ventilation system carried it around the ship, but without it being refreshed with new pollen, it was deadly. Thinking back, remember I went back to the ship a couple of times to get supplies. Each time I went, I removed my spacesuit so I didn't have the fresh pollen. I don't know if it is pollen, but I'll keep calling it that. Anyway, I would start to get sick, but when I returned to the planet's surface, I recovered."

"So," said Schem, "the ship is still contaminated. Contaminated with old pollen?"

"That would be our guess," said Gigory. "Maybe old pollen can infect you, but only new pollen can neutralize the effect. But we really don't know."

Rag said, "So if it is old dead pollen, wouldn't that make it neutral?"

And Schem added, "What if we were to bring the grass up to the ship and let it grow. Would that provide a continuous antidote pollen so a crew could work?"

Katherine thought for a nano-moment before saying, "Maybe, but that won't get us anywhere. We need to interact with the ship. We can't do that if it's always going to be a one-way trip to the ship. Besides we're only guessing at this pollen scenario."

"Yeah," said Schem trying to lighten up the conversation, "and if it was a one-way trip, it would get pretty crowded over there."

Katherine looked at Schem and couldn't help but smile while saying, "Yes, that too. But seriously, that's not an option. We need a plan."

When the United States uncoupled from Africa and headed for YZ Ceti, Africa headed towards TCf. As the ship got closer, communications became easier with Gigory and a plan was finally laid out.

Knowing this wasn't going to be a certainty, they went ahead with a plan mostly formulated by Gigory. It was a combined effort among Gigory, his people, and the crew of the Africa with Gigory taking the first steps.

Gigory dug up and brought as many living plants as possible onto his shuttle. The goal was to use the shuttle as a place where he and a small crew could refresh. The shuttle docked in the shuttle bay and they left the shuttle wearing their spacesuits. From there they went to the ship's bridge where they could control the ventilation system on the entire ship, with the exception of the autonomous engine room pods. Gigory vented the entire ship bringing the vacuum of space inside. Given some time, it was theorized that any sealed pockets of contaminated air would eventually escape.

For the next phase, Gigory had asked for volunteers, warning them it might be hazardous, but the worst part was going to be the disposal of thousands of bodies; bodies that had been unattended for far too long. With zero gravity, bodies might be found just about anywhere. Extrication could prove difficult and it certainly would be gut wrenching.

Part of this phase also included volunteers from Africa. Surprisingly, Katherine had little trouble finding the burial crew, but there was some reluctance among the shuttle pilots for fear of bringing contamination into the shuttle and then from there into Africa. Eventually, Lieutenant David Loring stepped forward to take command of shuttle #1.

The third phase to be performed simultaneously was to check the engines' operating status and the engine pods for radiation contamination. The leader of this advance group was Bill Yeakle, the Chief Operating Engineer of Africa. He made it clear to Katherine that he would be the perfect choice for this mission. He knew what to look for as far as the engines were concerned, he was seventy-four years old and had received a lifetime dose of radiation that had resulted in terminal cancer, and finally he had lost his wife and partner of fifty years one year ago and simply found little to keep himself going. "Still," he said, "I'm not on my death bed quite yet and feel pretty good. But if something goes wrong, I wouldn't be much of a sacrifice."

Looking at Bill, no one would guess he had issues. He was tall, upright, wore his uniform with dignity, and with his slicked-back white hair looked like he could have been a character actor in an old British war movie.

Katherine stared at Bill for a minute and with more emotion welling up than she expected simply said, "Thank you, Bill."

Bill and Katherine selected four volunteers to work with Bill. For some reason they decided they needed to call themselves something and came up with "Africa Core." When Katherine heard this she just smiled.

When Russia was abandoned, Engine Pod #5 had been inactive and uncontaminated. It was transferred over to the United States to replace one of its failed and ejected pods. It was understood that Russia's Pod #2 was not contaminated and operating, but Pods #1, #3, #4, and #6 were contaminated.

The focus for Bill's team would be Pod # 4 initially. Safety precautions and contingencies were laid out. The contingency plan was that if any of the Africa Core volunteers started to get sick they would not be allowed back in the shuttle, but would be brought down the planet's surface where they should recover. It would be a one-way trip to the planet's surface, but at least they would be alive. That was the theory anyway. For obvious reasons, the Africa Core members were considered heroes.

When everyone felt as comfortable with the plan as possible, they got started with a mini spacewalk from the shuttle to the contaminated engine room pod #4. The spacewalk provided just enough distance between the shuttle and Russia, protecting the shuttle and the reluctant pilot. Next, they entered the pod's airlock. Still wearing their spacesuits, they vented the pod with the vacuum having no effect on the actual fission/fusion engine. With the pod vented to space, the airlock was left open making it easier for body disposal. Just like on the main part of the ship, each body was brought to the airlock, a few words of prayer were said and the body was launched into space. The team was grateful that, at least in the engine room pods, there weren't any children to deal with.

Once the engine pod was cleared, every surface was wiped down with a sanitizing agent. No one knew if this would be effective at all, but it couldn't hurt. Next the pod airlock was closed and an aerosol disinfectant was released in the pod's ventilation system. With zero gravity, the droplets were scattered and was slowly attracted to all surfaces. The concentration was high so it was theorized that the most inaccessible areas would receive treatment.

Next, the airlock was opened again, venting any remaining aerosol and hopefully any residue contamination.

All of this was following a theory that any "pollen" that came on board initially might be harmless after all this time. If not, the vacuum might render it ineffective, and if not that, then sanitizing with two methods and a final dose of vacuum might do it. This took days to complete and it was only one engine room pod.

The big test came next. Compressed air rich in oxygen from TCe was released into the pod and the ventilation system was turned on once again. When the atmospheric pressure in the pod registered normal, Bill Yeakle removed his spacesuit. There was some tempered jealousy as Bill was able to eat a full, unencumbered, meal and wash it down with a beer. Based on the time for the first of the Russian crew to become ill, if Bill didn't have any symptoms over that same time frame, the rest of the volunteers could remove their suits.

Thirty-six hours later the hoped-for celebration did not come to fruition; Bill was in severe pain. He found his way through the connecting tube to the bridge and from there to the shuttle bay and Captain Kazakov's shuttle. Once inside breathing the pollen filled air he felt a little better, but until he was brought down to the planet's surface he wouldn't fully recover.

This was a huge disappointment for everyone. For the Africa Core, there was a lot of anxiety over what to do next. They were in their spacesuits so they were safe, but now what? How could they get back to the Africa shuttle and safely enter if there might be contamination on the outside of their suits? The answer was: they couldn't.

Lieutenant Loring announced to Katherine, "I'm not letting them in." And while it was obvious he was thinking of his own well-being, he added, "We shouldn't risk bringing whatever this is back to Africa."

Katherine was sick to her stomach. Even though the Africa Core team had volunteered, there had been a relatively high level of confidence that the cleansing scheme would work and this crew would return to Africa. Contingencies be damned, this was not good. Katherine knew there were very few options, and none of them very appealing. She looked at Schem and Rag and said, "There must be a reason you two showed up for this mission. So far you haven't said very much. Was this expected?"

Schem said, "Katherine, I, that is we, had as much knowledge of this as you. I'm being honest. The thought was that if needed, we might be able to provide some suggestions along the way. I think the plan, especially the contingency plan, was well considered under the circumstances. Perhaps the degree of optimism on everyone's part was simply too much. I don't see where you have much of a choice here for the volunteers."

Scowling, Katherine said, "Well that's not much help."

"Sorry," was the only thing Schem could offer.

Katherine knew the volunteers wanted to get back onto Africa. But she had specifically selected these people because they had no family ties so if something went wrong, it would result in the least worst-case scenario.

The four volunteers collectively conferred with Katherine and all agreed the only apparent choice was to join Captain Gigory and the people on TCf. Maybe someday a miracle would allow them back out of isolation. Gigory offered, "It isn't bad on the planet's surface. The environment is good and people are mostly content. We will make you welcome."

And so it was. Bill Yeakle and his Africa Core would join the community on TCf.

The remaining issue was what got them here in the first place. What was to become of the once proud Star Ship Russia. If nothing else, the dead needed to be tended to and the ship should be made as secure as possible.

Gigory broke his people into two groups; one group to deal with the engine pods and the other to deal with everything else. Gigory was actually in pretty good shape to handle the engine room pods as far as personnel was concerned. When the ship had been abandoned, the engine Pod #2 staff had isolated themselves from the rest of the ship so that the pod and staff remained uncontaminated. This staff was rescued but eventually ended up on TCf. Now he had Chief Engineer Yeakle in the mix which meant he had the right people to operate and maintain the engines. Even if the ship wasn't going anywhere, everyone agreed the engines should be maintained.

So the strategy now had Gigory's people working to clean out the engine room pods. The original failed protocol for the decontamination was still followed. It was agreed that it wouldn't hurt, and besides the decomposing bodies had certainly made the on-board environment something that needed sanitizing.

The engineering group first focused on Engine Room Pod #3. Once they went through the airlock from the connecting tunnel tube into the engine room itself, it became abundantly clear from the displays on the control panel that the plan was now about to change. Everything indicated the engine was about to go critical and blow. Everyone was ordered back into the airlock and the ejection sequence was initiated.

When Gigory saw the pod disengage he demanded, "What's going on? I didn't authorize this!"

"Sorry Captain, there wasn't enough time. This thing is about to blow." Which it did. No engine had ever been ejected before from a ship that was in orbit, meaning that in this case it didn't go nearly far enough from the main part of the ship before it went off. With no movement of the ship, the pod was still nearby when it erupted into a massive explosion. The explosion blew off the stern antennae array and slowed the orbital speed of Russia. It also rocked Africa, but no serious damage was observed.

Other than actually loosing a precious engine pod, this didn't seem to create additional issues, but on further analysis, the number crunchers determined that Russia was gradually loosing altitude. If not stabilized it would eventually crash. It was clear that Russia wasn't going to join the fleet anytime soon, if ever, but that didn't mean it should be allowed to crash. If it did, the resulting explosions and radiation contamination on the planet's surface were unthinkable.

Rag suggested, "If you use Captain Kazakov's shuttle and the three shuttles from Africa, you should be able to nudge the ship back into a stable orbit. All the contamination issues are inside the ship so there is no danger of bringing anything back to Africa."

Katherine was in no mood so her response was less than subtle. "Thank you, Rag for pointing out the obvious." And over the next couple of days, the shuttles kept nudging Russia until it returned to a stable orbit. Katherine ordered that the four remaining engine room pods be rotated into the proper symmetrical operating configuration. It was a small consolation, but at least Russia looked good.

Over time, the operating engineers would periodically return to Russia, making sure the engines were operating correctly in idle mode and use the ship's thrusters to keep it in a stable orbit. Unfortunately, this also meant that the one previously uncontaminated engine room pod would now be contaminated as engineers would be entering and leaving its control room.

Bill Yeakle unfortunately showed that the formula for decontaminating the ship hadn't been discovered as yet. Still, there was a lot of work to do, but it was now all left to Gigory and his people. So once the operating systems and orbit was stabilized, Gigory's people went back to the original mission of cleaning the ship. The main reason for the cleaning mission—to get the ship back into service—had vaporized, but still everyone felt a need to properly tend to the dead and to clean the ship as best as possible.

Body disposal was now the priority, and without question the most disturbing. With no gravity force, there seemed to be bodies everywhere. There was no other way around this task, but as much dignity as possible was given to each of the dead Russia crew members as they were brought to the airlocks. A nondenominational pastor recorded each name before "burial" and said the same words of prayer over each one as the attendants launched each body into space. Often this was accompanied with tears, especially for the children and interestingly, the service dogs.

Beside body disposal, it was decided that everything that wasn't an actual part of the ship was to go; plants, beds, clothes, wine, everything. Much of this was brought back down to TCf, where any contamination would make zero difference. If it couldn't be used off into space it went.

Finally after one week shy of a year, the efforts on Russia were deemed satisfactory. Gigory topped off his shuttle fuel tanks and brought the onboard volunteers back to TCf for the last time, where they were congratulated for their efforts. At least these people had somewhat redeemed themselves in the eyes of the Admiral and the UNSC.

Back on Earth, no one had wanted to jump the gun, so there had been very little, if any, thought about what Africa and Russia would do next if the salvage operation had been successful. Now that success had eluded them, the UNSC, as a group, felt some relief. They didn't need to devise a plan for Russia. Only the Science Director, Harlyn Jackson, seemed disappointed. He had a plan and now reluctantly filed it away. But he wasn't going to sit still. He started devising a new plan. One that he hoped Katherine would approve.

As for Katherine, who was without any orders, she would give the future some serious thought. She had learned the "lead, follow, or get out of the way" rule and was formulating her own plan as Africa headed back to TCe.

Chapter 13

Mission to YZ Ceti (2150)

It seemed fitting that the Star Ship United States would be the one to head to YZ Ceti as it was the United States-based company, Star Struck Trading Company, that was footing the bill. The Trading Company was doing quite well, but it still wasn't in the extremely wealthy category. If the company could find and retrieve rich deposits of minerals needed on Earth or even on the two colonies humans had on other planets, its category could change. For this mission it wasn't hard to find investors, and the United Nations Stellar Commission was more than willing to send the ship off with someone else paying the tab. "At least one ship will appear productive," quipped one commissioner.

YZ Ceti is only 1.6 light years from Tau Ceti. And while 1.6 LY isn't a trip to the local grocery store, the distance compared to other celestial bodies was small. Still the calculated round trip, including time to explore the orbiting planet, would be at least six years. Paying a lot of people for that period of time would be prohibitive for the Trading Company so the crew was kept small, and in lieu of a full salary each crewmember would receive a share of the profits on anything of value they might find. Each share would be determined by the rank of the individual. Essentially, everyone was taking a chance.

To provide cargo space for anything of value that might be found the crew was limited to 3500. With the ship designed for 18,000 people plus Gate components and construction equipment, there was now plenty of storage space. The only drawback was the need for each crewmember to put in extra effort to make the mission work.

The people selected for this mission were chosen following a different thought process than used for other starship crews, and as a result many crewmembers were cut from a rather coarse piece of cloth. That didn't mean they weren't smart and capable of running a starship, but it did mean they had a very rough-and-tumble streak in them. The engineering team and the bridge crew weren't quite as rough and tumble, but they also weren't very polished either.

The captain for this mission was selected by the Trading Company and then cleared by the UNSC and Admiral Hickey. John Armstrong had been a United States Air Force Colonel, which was quite an accomplishment for someone who had simply enlisted and was now relatively young at forty-one years old. He'd flown experimental aircraft and was a certified shuttle pilot. Not only were his arms strong, like his name, he was as solid as a brick. He was five feet eleven inches tall and weighed in at an all-muscle 210 pounds. His chiseled face said, "I mean business," but he could party with the best. For this mission uniforms weren't required, but Captain Armstrong insisted that all officers wear crisp clean uniforms whenever they were on duty in an attempt to maintain some level of decorum.

The Chief Academic and Science Officer (CASO) qualifications for the mission were altered. In this case she was a mining engineer with an advanced degree in geology. She knew every detail of the periodical table and her hope was to add to it and become famous…and wealthy. Suzanne Lehtola was five feet five inches tall and a strikingly beautiful blonde, making it difficult for some to understand how she could be so brilliant. Her husband Alfred, however, did know how smart she was and it was that intelligence that won him over. Of course, her stunning looks helped.

Alfred Lehtola was the ship's Medical Doctor. He would normally take a back seat to his wife, but when it came to his job, he was remarkable. One of the things that enticed him to go on the mission was the opportunity to study the effects of what was sure to be a hostile working environment for the miners. His appearance was very much on the nerdy side, making some wonder how he managed to secure such a beautiful wife. He would say, "being persistent and begging worked!" Suzanne, on the other hand, only saw his beautiful mind.

The Captain wasn't quite sure what to make of the two crewmembers that had been assigned just before they were leave TCe orbit. They were strange fellows with equally strange names of Na-ki-Ir, who apparently went by Naki, and his equally strange partner Ara-Ri-El, who went by Ara. They were supposedly specialists, in, well, "something." Naki was supposed to be an expert on DC electrical power generation. Ara was supposed to know something about planet geology. Neither of these skills appeared to be anything useful to John. Both were also language experts, which also made little sense as everyone spoke the same language on the ship, English, and the chances of finding anything or anyone with any other language known to mankind was as close to zero as one could get. And since no one had ever been to this planet, how the hell could anyone be any more of an expert on geology than his CASO? It made no sense, but neither of these guys could be ignored. Naki was six feet ten inches and looked to weigh about 275 pounds. Ara was six feet seven inches and looked about 240 pounds. Both had shoulder length hair and as John learned early on, these two guys were eating and drinking machines. *Oh well,* thought John, *The office must have a reason.*

In fact, the office did have a reason. Gabe had convinced the Trading Company that Naki and Ara would be essential in the success of the mission. This was done, of course, with no facts; just his power to make people agree. He would eventually prove correct but it did require knowledge that no one outside of the Order could know. Gabe had given Naki and Ara specific instructions that went beyond, far beyond, established Order protocol. On February 11, 2150, Star Ship United States separated from Africa and headed for YZ Ceti, with the crew settling in for a long voyage.

By late 2152 the ship was in orbit around YZ Ceti c, one of the two planets circling the star. With no other ship to connect with, the United States crew found itself with zero gravity. Gravity on the planet's surface appeared to be slightly more than Earth's, so that part seemed appealing. But that was the only thing that looked appealing. Meanwhile, the other planet in this solar system was extremely close to the star, leaving the surface of the planet nothing more than a caldron of molten material.

YZ Ceti c was a little better. The surface was solid in most places, but the temperatures averaged over 200 degrees Fahrenheit, which likely burned off any potentially useful atmosphere. The reason for coming to this planet at all was strictly a financial gamble. As unappealing as it might be for settlement, scientists suspected that it held easily obtainable riches. Of course, "easy," in this case, overlooked the surface conditions. Those who would do the actual work did know about the surface conditions and planned accordingly. The ship was loaded with special suits for the mining crews and it was hoped that the shielded mining equipment would last long enough to be useful.

Spectral analysis of the surface had Suzanne nearly jumping with excitement. Not only did she find rich deposits of gold, and known rare-earth minerals, she detected some elements she couldn't readily identify. "I'm going to be famous," she said to Naki and Ara as they looked over her shoulder. "Oh, I mean *we* will be famous."

Ara laughed and said, "Where shall you start. Oh, I mean where shall *we* start," and laughed again.

"Very cute," said Suzanne. "I think we should tell the Captain to start over here," she said as she pointed to a particular sector on the screen. "This looks like it might have a good concentration of some rare earths; very valuable stuff, and maybe over here. Does that look like a pool of gold?"

Naki and Ara looked at each other, and remembering what Gabe had told them before their departure, shrugged. When Suzanne was studying her instruments, Naki mouthed silently to Ara, "Why not?"

Turning his attention back to Suzanne, Ara said, "I agree, but do you see this area over here where you found something new? That needs to be explored."

"Well yeah, but I think we need to mine the material that will pay for this mission first, then go exploring if we have time."

"We need to do both. Trust me on this."

Suzanne looked at Ara suspiciously. Ara had never expressed any strong feeling about anything before and now he was being very insistent. She thought about that for a few minutes and finally said, "Okay. It'll be a bit of a challenge for the shuttle pilots having three sites changing out crews frequently, but I'll talk to John. If we don't find anything interesting at your site, the three shuttles can go back to supporting the actual mine sites. It would be great to load up and head back early and enjoy the riches we harvest."

Naki and Ara were looking down at her with huge smiles as Ara said, "Oh, you're going to be rich all right, and have more fame than you can imagine."

"You seem awfully sure of yourself."

Ara just smiled as he viewed the sensor equipment and said, "Trust me. I'm from the government and I'm here to help."

"What?" said Suzanne.

Naki said, "Ignore him. He's making another tired joke."

"You are a very strange individual, Ara," said Suzanne.

Before sending anyone down to the surface, the Captain followed the usual protocol over the next couple of weeks just to make certain there wasn't some kind of weird life form with a civilization on the planet. Once he determined with a comfortable degree of certainty that there weren't any "smart" rocks or something else weird, shuttle #1 was sent down with a geologist, mining engineer, and a few miners. The shuttle left them on the surface for a six-hour shift while it returned to the United States for a relief crew. The first order of business was to build a shelter under which the crews could eventually work twelve-hour shifts. If everything worked as planned, there would be some processing of any valuable ore before it was brought up to the United States in order to use the ship's cargo hold efficiently.

All did go as planned and Ara commented, "Well, that's once in a row!"

Efforts then started on the second site. This also went as planned and within days the first ores were being loaded onto the shuttles and brought up to the mothership. The excitement over how easy this was had everyone thinking of the fortune they'd be sharing.

The third site identified by Ara, but appearing to have no commercial value, was next—but only after convincing the Captain. "I don't know Suzanne, this looks like a waste of time and resources," he said.

"I thought so, and maybe it is, but Ara and Naki are convinced we should go take a look. They seem to know something and they are supposed to be experts aren't they?"

John was sitting in his chair looking across the conference room table at Suzanne. He said nothing for a full minute. Finally, he said, "Those two haven't done much of anything—except eat and drink—since we left on this mission and now they are gung-hoe to get down to this worthless looking site? Did they ever say anything about the areas we're looking at now? You know, where we actually found something useful? What could they possibly know about something no one has ever seen? They are the strangest guys I have ever met and I've met some real winners!"

"John, I can't disagree, but I'm thinking these guys were sent for a reason. What that might be, I don't know, but I'm concerned that if we don't listen to them, they're going to give a very unflattering report that might make us look bad. I'm not suggesting a full-fledged operation. Let's just go down, grab some samples and come back. I mean, we're already here and everything seems to going better than expected, so it really wouldn't be a big deal."

"All right, you convinced me. Go do it before I come to my senses."

And so it was. Ara, Suzanne and a small party left for the planet's surface with the goal of trying to identify the minerals that weren't identifiable from the ship.

Once the shuttle was on the ground and everyone was in protective gear, Ara said to no one in particular, "Ah! What a glorious place. I see lots of potential. Steam baths over there, sauna over there, maybe some hot tubs over there," as he pointed out some very ugly-looking steam vents. That might have received a polite chuckle, except the surface they were now walking on was anything but serene.

One of the instruments they had was a gauss meter to measure any potential electromagnetic activity. Ara didn't seem to be surprised, but Suzanne was shocked, both physically and mentally when she stepped out of the shuttle. With each step, sparks rose around her feet giving a disconcerting tingling feeling. She was even more than a little concerned when she saw the same sparking around the shuttle. The pilot was not happy about this at all!

Suzanne couldn't believe it when Ara said, "Jumpy are we? Not to worry, it will be just fine. Let's just figure out what this is," and with a smile said, "and name it. How about Lehtolarite?"

"This is scary stuff and you only want to pick a name? We don't even know if this a mineral! You're nuts!"

"Well, you're not going to just call it 'scary stuff' are you? Do you know what it is?"

"No. And you don't either." Then, looking straight at Ara, Suzanne added, "You don't know, do you? How could you?"

Ara said with a stupid smile, "I do know what it is; it's Lehtolarite. Remember? I mean we could call it Ararelrite, but that doesn't trip off the tongue, does it?" Then, more seriously, he said, "Handle it carefully, but you have nothing to worry about. Probably. Let's grab a healthy sample and get it back to your lab for analysis."

"'Probably?' You are not making me feel very warm and fuzzy."

"Take off your suit and you'll at least feel warm, but not fuzzy."

"You're not just nuts, you're a jerk." To which Ara just laughed.

Very carefully, several hundred pounds of Lehtolarite were easily chipped from the surface and placed in plastic totes. It was easy digging, but extremely nerve-racking because each strike with a pick and each shovel full gave off little electrical sparks. Curiously Ara cautioned the party not to close up the totes. Once on board the shuttle, the pilot couldn't wait to lift off, and in his haste nearly forget to close the hatch.

In the relatively cool shuttle and with no contact of any kind the sparking stopped. This was very curious and Suzanne wondered if they had wasted their time getting this stuff. Sitting there in the totes it looked gray and useless. It remained useless looking during the return to the ship and then on down to the laboratory. John was waiting for them and asked, "Was it worth it?"

Reluctantly Suzanne said, "I don't know. It was pretty scary getting these samples, but now it just sits there. Maybe it has to be part of a larger critical mass or something. I'm not sure what to do with the stuff."

"Well, what's done is done. At least we don't need to think about it any more. Have fun with it."

Ara said, "I didn't think we should keep calling it scary stuff so I named it Lehtolarite."

John looked disgusted, shook his head, and left the lab just as Naki strolled in. Both he and Ara already knew what the stuff was, but Naki didn't want to make it too easy for Suzanne so he asked, "What've you got?"

Ara said, "Lehtolarite."

"Lehtolarite?" asked Naki. "You call it Lehtolarite? Cute. Have you figured out what it is?"

Ignoring the Lehtolarite banter Suzanne said, "We were just about to get started with some experiments. I'm not sure where to begin exactly. I did take a look at a sample under the electron microscope and as far as I can tell its makeup doesn't appear to match anything on the periodic table. In fact, I don't see where it might even fit into a grouping. It is lightweight like aluminum, but that's the only thing it has in common. I thought we really had something when we first saw it, but here in the lab it just sits there. I don't see any properties that make any sense."

Ara knowingly looked at Naki and said, "It was pretty warm down there and this stuff was sparking around everything touching it. No harm was done, but it was a little spooky."

"Yeah," said Suzanne, "But now that we have it back here, it doesn't do anything. Maybe there needs to be a whole lot of it to interact somehow."

Naki said, "Heat it up a little."

"Yeah," said Ara, "Heat it up a little."

Suzanne looked at Naki and Ara, then hesitatingly took a fist-sized sample and placed it on steel lab bench. She grabbed a heat gun and blasted a little heat at the sample. It sparked. Startled, but curious, she gave it a little bigger blast and it sparked more.

Ara said, "So what's the electric potential when you give a little heat?"

Suzanne had one of her assistants bring a multimeter over and with the positive probe on the sample and the negative probe on the grounded steel bench leg, Suzanne gave the sample a short blast of heat. "Did we get anything?" asked Suzanne.

"I'll say we did," said the assistant, "DC voltage was off the scale!"

"Wow," said a somewhat-confused Suzanne. "I have no idea what's going on."

Ara said, "I think you should consider what could be made with this," with a huge emphasis on the word "made."

"Don't you think we should know what it is first? Making it do something before we even know what it isn't very good science."

Naki said, "You can learn a lot when you manipulate it into a useful product."

Ara added, "And it shouldn't blow up or anything like that. Just take it slow."

Suzanne looked at Naki and Ara standing next to each other smiling and she said, "You two know a lot more than you're telling me. Am I right?"

Not exactly lying, Ara said, "I'm truly hurt. What would make you say something like that?"

"Because you're both being jerks, that's why."

Chapter 14

Lehtolarite

The United States returned to TCe loaded with mineral-rich ore. As planned, some refining had been completed on YZ Ceti c to concentrate the "good stuff," though gold, silver, industrial diamonds, copper, and rare earths were so plentiful that the actual mining and refinement was exceptionally easy. The gamble for all involved appeared to be paying off much better than anyone could have anticipated.

The planet that looked so unforgiving from a distance, and actually still did, had turned into a treasure chest. With the expected wealth each crewmember would gain, they decided all names for the planet that might have been given by astronomers was meaningless. They named the planet Prosperity.

But while the ship was loaded with the customary minerals that meant wealth, it also carried the newly discovered mineral named Lehtolarite. Suzanne, Naki, Ara, and the lab assistants did some crude experiments on the ore as they had headed back to TCe. The first thing they discovered was that they hadn't mined enough. The mineral rich ore that they did have was showing some exciting properties. Exciting because what they were witnessing was unlike anything anyone could have imagined.

When they landed on the site where Lehtolarite was discovered, every step, every little disturbance produced what appeared to be intense static electricity. Admittedly, they were all wearing protective spacesuits, but still there seemed to be no detrimental effects. Even when collecting samples, the mineral didn't hinder their efforts, as scary as it was in doing so.

Closer analysis on the ship indicated that it was, in fact, a mineral and wasn't anything organic. The lab resources on the ship were somewhat limited, but under an electron microscope, it appeared as though Lehtolarite had at least two basic elements that defied association with anything on the periodic table. If this were to prove true, Suzanne would see these elements added to the periodic table and she would have exceeded her dreams of being famous.

For now, however, the limited time they had returning to TCe would be spent conducting simple experiments to try and gain some understanding of what the stuff could do. At room temperature, the blue/gray mineral displayed nothing. There was no apparent radiation, nothing! It just sat on the lab bench like a lump of, well, just a lump! When Captain Armstrong witnessed this first hand, he looked at Suzanne and commented, "We wasted time getting this stuff? I gotta say, I'm rather underwhelmed."

However, subsequent tests showed something quite different. Any positive heat differential excited whatever produced the static-like spectacles. Any light source that wasn't LED also produced the phenomena. Suzanne was convinced she had something special in her possession, but didn't know yet what that potential might be. That wasn't her focus. Not yet anyway.

Suzanne had speculated that Naki and Ara already knew what this stuff could do based on the comments they made, but had no idea how they might know. And as what seemed to be part of their MO, they were being strangely more secretive than usual. "What are you two not telling me? Is this stuff dangerous?"

Naki said, "Well anything not used properly could be dangerous, but not by itself." And then he added, a bit too quickly, "But not that I'm aware of, anyway."

With an extremely solemn face, Ara said, "Yes, this stuff is dangerous, but only for you. You are going to be so rich and famous you might get trampled by people just trying to get near you for an autograph." Then he laughed.

Suzanne stared at Ara while Naki said, "Really? That's not funny you idiot." And Ara laughed again.

Eventually the Lehtolarite was transported through the TCe High Point Wormhole Gate back to Earth where it went to the Star Struck Trading Company labs. There seemed to be a lot of this stuff on Prosperity and it certainly seemed like it could be useful, but being of the scientific ilk, Suzanne and her assistants felt compelled to try and identify what was in its makeup that allowed it to do what it did. After all, it might just be a combination of things that were already on Earth rather than something completely new.

Gabe stopped by to see Sharon and Astron. He said he just happened to be in the area. Both knew, however, Gabe never just happened to be anywhere. He casually mentioned that he'd heard about this Lehtolarite substance and wanted to see it.

Sharon said, "So you just happened to be in the area coincidentally when this Lehtolarite mineral shows up. And you just happen to know it is here when no one told you."

"Naki told me."

Sharon laughed saying "Okay, I'll give you that, so what's the interest?"

"Oh, just curious." There was a little more small talk, but it was obvious Gabe wanted to go to the lab as soon as possible, so off went Gabe and Sharon as Astron followed along. When they got to the lab, it seemed the technicians were testing the Lehtolarite with everything they could find. Gabe watched a little while then asked, "Does it melt?"

Suzanne, who was in the lab with her Lehtolarite, "Yes, and at a relatively low temperature. It is easily extracted from the ore and its strange characteristics seem to be enhanced once refined."

Gabe said, "I suggest making a thin sheet and see what it does in the sunlight."

Suzanne looked at Gabe shaking her head and said, "You are just like your buddies Naki and Ara. You guys all know something but you're making me find out the hard way. You're collectively becoming a needless pain in my derriere."

Gabe smiled and invited Suzanne to join him as he left with Sharon and Astron to have a light lunch of four one-pound hamburgers, fries, and three pints of stout. Sharon commented, "You know, Astron can really pack away the food. But you, Gabe, make him look like he's on a starvation diet."

During lunch Gabe seemed to be steering the conversation towards the present day accepted conversion of sunlight through photovoltaic panels to make electricity. The technology had reached a plateau of about forty percent efficiency. By itself that wasn't bad, but everything that went into making the panels, their relatively short useful life, and then the decommissioning of them had been a problem from the beginning. In addition, forestlands had been cleared to make room for the solar farms; the same forests that convert carbon dioxide into oxygen. To many that seemed counterproductive.

The death flu pandemic in 2071 had left ten percent of mankind alive, but the remnants of the constructed infrastructure was still in place in many areas. Much had been done to clean things up, but at the same time energy was needed to continue on. Electric everything meant electricity had to come from someplace. Someplace that didn't add to climate changes and in the best of all worlds, would reverse the trends.

The discovery of the carbon-deprived, oxygen-producing, indigenous species on TCe was first thought to be the answer, but the logistics to make that mutually beneficial exchange was still proving difficult. This new, supposedly serendipitous, discovery of Lehtolarite might be the answer. "Supposedly discovered" because as Suzanne, Sharon, Astron and a few others had determined, members of the Order had led them right to it.

Sharon said, "So Suzanne, what do you think about this namesake mineral you found?"

"I'm not sure what to think. I'm the one working with it and I still can't believe what we're seeing. So far we have treated it with acids, bases, heat, cold, light and dark. Everything we've tried so far seems to lead in one direction. The stuff converts light into DC electricity and stores it in direct proportion to the size and shape of the refined material—and at remarkable levels. It has reacted to sunlight and even the slightest increase in temperature. It's still early, but we've tried to see if there is anything that might make its qualities deteriorate and so far, nothing. Of course we are currently only looking at the characteristics exhibited right in front of us. Maybe there are even bigger and better potentials for the stuff.

"Experiments indicate a simple process could shape it into just about anything. We had enough to make some small solar panels and there are no harmful byproducts detected. The capacity to store electricity is just as remarkable. I'm thinking a thin panel placed on the roof of a motor vehicle could power the vehicle even in a nighttime rainstorm. Even heavy construction equipment might have plenty of power. We are, however, having some difficulty regulating the discharge of power when we try to tap into the electric potential."

"Gabe asked, "What are your two experts telling you?"

"Oh, they're a fine pair, especially that Ara. What a jerk. His words of wisdom after we made a panel were 'snow might be a problem, but people eventually should learn to stay home when it snows.' Brilliant."

Astron, who had been quietly listening, just laughed.

Sharon had to smile as well, saying, "This Lehtolarite might be the magic pill everyone on Earth had hoped to find. I'm pretty psyched. Climate change has created so many problems over the past 200 years. This stuff could really make a difference. You are going to be very famous. Oh, and very rich!"

"Yes," said Astron, "And Star Struck Trading Company has the only access to it. We just need more—a lot more."

Later on, Astron casually mentioned to Dakota what was going on with the Lehtolarite. Dakota was fascinated and made a point of visiting Suzanne in her lab where he made a proposal that at first Suzanne rejected. But after more coaxing from Dakota, on the verge of begging, she relented. Dakota had an idea that was whimsical but also might provide an interesting demonstration for a Lehtolarite use.

Even later, when the discovery of Lehtolarite was made known to the world, Dr. Suzanne Lehtola learned that Ara was at least half right in the short term. People really did want to meet her and they intruded into her life to such a degree that she volunteered for another mission to Prosperity just to get away. The predicted "rich" part would come later, once the mining of Lehtolarite became serious.

Chapter 15

Raman's Reunion

Gabe-Re-El had another reason for being at the Trading Company headquarters besides the Lehtolarite. He needed to have a private conversation with Sharon. He had known about Sharon's history even before he met her years ago on her return to Earth through the wormhole gate. He knew she had apparently moved on emotionally from her relationship with Raman. Her son, Astron, remained the only tangible evidence of that relationship. A very real, tangible evidence to be sure.

Gabe hadn't planned to ever bring up the subject of Raman again, but recent events and the long-range plans of the Order had caused him to change his mind. He had come to believe that Raman needed some closure with respect to Astron before he could move on. Of all the encounters Gabe had over the centuries, this one made him the most uncomfortable. And uncomfortable was not something he was used to feeling.

After dinner he found a private moment to talk to Sharon. She knew something was on Gabe's mind so she said, "Something is bothering you. What can I do for you?"

Gabe thought, *She wants to know how she can help me. That's a switch,* but said, "How is Astron? I mean really. He seems fine to me. We haven't talked about him, but I do think about him a lot because, well, I guess I don't need to explain."

"No Gabe, you don't need to explain. But to answer your question, we're both doing fine. Really. Astron is growing up rather quickly and is obviously going to be a very big man. He eats like a horse, just like his father. As you've seen, he is a very serious kid, which has me a little concerned, but not much. He does make friends quite easily, and I find it amusing that Celeste Bickmeier has him wrapped around her little finger in spite of the age and size difference. I'm guessing it is because they have a common bond of being born in space, but who knows. Why are you asking now?"

"I have something to ask that has the potential of being awkward. I will tell you what it is, but take a little time to think about it before you respond. As you certainly remember, Raman was, well let's say, out of it by the time he reached Earth. You knew he had been in stasis for thousands of years when your starships found him, causing all the odd things you witnessed. It was believed, or perhaps more correctly hoped, that a more normalized period of time in stasis might have restorative effects on his damaged brain. I found a place for him and making a long story short, he has been brought out of stasis. He clearly remembers his earlier life and the rescue and how he was integrated into the starships' crews. He remembers with great affection the early years with you, but it appears the memories are increasingly fuzzy leading up to coming through the Earth Wormhole Gate."

"Oh I remember all that for sure, and how I lost him to this Princess Charmy person he'd never met, and how it broke my heart. Why are you bringing all that up now?"

"Because Raman would like to see you and Astron. Actually, I'd like him to see you and Astron to help bring a little closure for him. Not to renew an old relationship, but to try to address his now recognized transgressions."

Somewhat stunned, Sharon said, "You were correct. I need to think about this."

"Ummm," started Gabe, "There is something more for you consider. The restorative effects of stasis include age."

"What does that mean?" said Sharon as her stomach started to feel like it was doing flip-flops.

"It means he has returned to age thirty-three and that might be hard to deal with. Take a couple days to think this over and how you might explain any of this to Astron, if at all. In the meantime if you have any questions, you can likely find me in the evening at Over the Moon."

With that, a somewhat flummoxed Sharon watched Gabe leave. She had told Astron about the relationship she had with Raman and how Astron had come to be. But that was more of a history lesson, with no thought of how Raman might reenter her life at any level. She had, in fact, moved on from Raman. Sharon caught up to Astron and Suzanne without saying a word. When she got home and Astron went off to his room, she went to the liquor cabinet and pulled out a glass and a bottle of twelve-year-old single malt scotch. She wished she had some ice, but shrugged that thought off as she poured herself a double shot.

Three days later, Sharon found Gabe in the diner having breakfast. He had just finished a three-egg omelet loaded with everything and was about to start on a huge stack of pancakes. Every head in the diner was watching Gabe, though he didn't seem to notice. As Sharon sat down the waitress asked her if she wanted coffee, and then with a smile asked, "You want the same thing?"

"Huh? Oh, no thanks, coffee would be just fine."

"That's probably good, I think we're running out of food for this guy. Is he training for a hot dog eating contest or something?"

Sharon and Gabe just looked at the waitress who threw up her hands and walked off.

Sharon said sarcastically, "Looks like you have a fan club. Have you been living here?"

Sharon almost hurt herself laughing when he said, "Nope; just breakfast. There's a great pub a few blocks from here that I go to for lunch and the restaurant for dinner."

Sharon shook her head, but from the years she spent with Raman she knew how much these people could eat. With regained composure she said, "I would like to see Raman, and Astron should meet his father, but only as a relative, not his father. I think this age business is something I don't want to try and explain. I think it will be tough enough for me to deal with. But let's do it."

Another three days later, Raman was at Sharon's front door. He knocked and she opened it. Sharon's heart raced. When Sharon and Raman first met after his rescue, they were about the same age, if you ignored the 3000 or so years he had been in stasis. What Sharon saw today was the very same person she had seen then. Feelings poured in, but she had girted herself for this moment and showed no emotion.

Raman, on the other hand, saw a sixty-eight-year-old woman for which he was not prepared. She was still pretty, but not as he remembered her. With only the vague memories of the later years with Sharon, he only had clear memories of when she was younger.

He gasped, leaving Sharon to say something. "Raman, come in. Can I get you something to eat or drink?"

She couldn't believe it when he said, "No thanks." And trying to compose himself. added, "You have a nice place here. It's a lot more comfortable than any starship."

Sharon ignored that and called out, "Astron, please come here. I'd like to meet one of your cousins. He has the same name as your father, Raman-I-El, but I'm sure you can address him as Raman."

Astron said, "Very nice to meet you. Are you a space traveler like my dad?"

Sharon had told Astron his father had died in space. In a sense that was true. The Raman she had met back then essentially faded away and became dead to her.

"Yes. I was away for a time and thought I should meet you before I go on another trip."

"I'd like to go into space someday. You look like my dad."

"Yes, I suppose I do. It's a family thing."

"Nice to meet you, I have schoolwork I need to do," and Astron left, leaving his mother and "cousin" awkwardly trying to think of something to say.

Finally Raman said, "I am so sorry for the way I treated you. I hope you understand it wasn't my fault, but that doesn't mean I don't have many regrets now that I better understand what was happening. I am sorry about Astron and please know that I would now do anything for you both."

"Do not apologize for Astron. He is my joy and reminds me constantly of the best times we had together. It is good you wanted to come. I have wondered about you and now am pleased you are healed. I doubt I will ever want anything from you but you need to understand that it is probably best we never meet again." Sharon showed Raman to the door, closed it, and bent over crying uncontrollably.

Astron came to her, hugged her, and asked, "That was my dad, wasn't he?"

"Yes," was the only thing she could say.

Chapter 16

Pokola, Union of African Nations

It seemed like only yesterday that Princess Charmy had abdicated her throne and rejoined the Order when she went into stasis. While she was ninety-five years old at the time, she still looked stunning.

In fact, for Charmy, returning now really could have been yesterday because she had been in stasis, where her time had stood still. Actually, for her, time had reversed. The stasis/rejuvenation process had returned her to her base age of thirty-three. But that wasn't true for the Union of African Nations. Charmy thought she had selected the perfect people to lead the UAN when she abdicated, but it didn't work out as planned. The designated Benevolent Dictator crowned as Prince Adudada had a good heart and the best of intentions. But he was weak and as simply a member of the human race, he certainly did not have that special ability Charmy had over people that provided a calming effect and gave them a willingness to cooperate.

Under Princess Charmy, the problem of small-time petty dictators went away. Some by choice and some at the hands of the people who only wanted to live in peace and prosper. In some cases, suicide for those people was the way out when they couldn't bring themselves to find peace and calm.

With the fighting stopped, people discovered they could concentrate on making a better world rather than simply trying to survive. The end result made the UAN a world leader. Prosperity, technological advancement, and environmental repair occurred so rapidly people were almost giddy with pride. So much so, the UAN had funded the starship appropriately named "Africa."

Unfortunately, this new union was more fragile than had been anticipated and it started falling apart soon after Princess Charmy abdicated, taking her charismatic ways with her. The UAN had needed a longer time to become so firmly established that it wouldn't slide back to the old way of doing things.

New petty dictators reemerged with the vision of ruling Africa. Except their typical, very shortsighted rule of Africa would be for their personal benefit. Of course, there was more than one, which meant fighting started all over again. With ridiculous promises and forced recruitment, armies were raised. The central government found itself constantly trying to suppress rebellious activities to the detriment of everything else. One tyrant was brazen enough to organize an armed attack of the capital. Fortunately that was suppressed, but not before showing the vulnerability of the government.

The journey from Alaska took over a week. They flew mostly at night and slept during the day in secluded locations with their glowing shields to protect them. Charmy had learned early on to shed the formal uniform of the Order and Raman never really ever had one, so they both wore what they thought would blend in, which it mostly didn't. Flannel shirts and jeans were out of place once they crossed into the southern United States and then further south. Their need to eat was also something that certainly kept them from blending in.

They didn't carry a lot of food with them, so buying food at grocery stores and stopping at diners was the norm. Raman had developed a huge love for beer while in the starship fleet so whenever he could, that was the first thing ordered; usually four or five pints to wash down enough food for a family of five. Charmy tried to be a little more discrete, but she also needed to eat. Of course, just their size, let alone Charmy's stunning looks, always caught the attention of everyone when they entered a dining establishment. Stares simply intensified when they ordered. "When was the last time you two ate?" was a familiar question.

When done, they asked if payment with gold and silver coins would be a problem. It never was except for the gasping of the people around them. "Who pays with gold and silver?"

When Charmy and Raman were approaching Pokola, the UAN capital, Charmy said, "We need to do this right. I want to make a grand return to the capital so it becomes the only news to be broadcast. I need you to make this work."

"Okay. Whatever you want, just tell my what to do."

"You may have to wing it a little after we get started, but here's how we start…"

Without the usual thoughts of secrecy, Raman now wore what was close to the standard Order apparel of a loose-fitting white shirt and matching trousers. He used his antigravity backpack to fly into Pokola purposely at dawn, to be symbolic, but also to allow the all-encompassing glow that emitted from his backpack and surrounded him to make an impression. Flying in with the rising sun behind added to the effect. Raman descended slowly into the capital square with hands raised and one leg slightly lifted. Once on the ground, he stood with his antigravity panels unfurled for few moments with the accompanying glow.

Word traveled fast of this aberration and soon the square was filled with people, including many government officials. There were perhaps a thousand people in the square when Raman rose and floated twenty feet upward and stayed motionless for a few moments with his hands once again raised before speaking. "Citizens of the Union of African Nations. I bring you greetings from Princess Charm-E-Ine."

The assembled crowd looked to one another murmured, "How can this be? She abdicated years ago and must no longer be among the living."

After another full minute, Raman went on, "The Princess is not pleased with much that has happened in this union of nations that she built. She has the ability to do many things and has used this ability to return as her former self, resurrected towards the goal of restoring the greatness of this land, returning peace and tranquility. Consistent with her goals of a peaceful transfer of power, she will not force Prince Adudada to return the power of Benevolent Dictator to the Princess. If the Prince wishes to stay in power, that will be respected. If he wishes to step down, the Princess will retain his services as a trusted advisor if he so chooses.

"All that I have said will come to pass in three days, but only with the blessings of the people. Those in positions of authority are to vote on this transition of power before it can occur. Your legislative bodies are to render a decision and present that to the Princess when she arrives. She will abide by the decision."

What Raman had not said was that Charmy had secretly visited the Prince and he was relieved to have this opportunity. He in turn had already talked to the government leaders and all wanted a change back to the way it had been. And that was done without any of Charmy's abilities influencing the Prince or anyone else. They all realized he was in over his head.

Three days later, as promised, Princess Charmy flew in and landed well outside the capital in a forested area. She gave Raman her antigravity pack and walked out onto the main thoroughfare. As she walked, word traveled fast of her arrival. At first a few people joined in the walk, but as the procession moved towards the capital, more and more joined in. She walked as though she was alone, seemingly ignoring those that only wanted to be near and hopefully have an opportunity to touch her robes.

Few remembered Charmy when she was first in power. Many remembered when she had abdicated. None expected the young and beautiful rejuvenated Princess that was walking into Pokola now. No one knew how she would enter the capital, but expected some sort of grand entrance after the impressive announcement from Raman. Instead she wished to portray herself as more humble. Some were disappointed in this approach, but most gave it a nod of approval. For those that had memories of her from before, she wore the colorful clothing she had adopted when she had been in charge to help solidify her identity.

The rapidly growing, disorganized parade of thousands moved along silently. Every vehicle on the road had to stop as the flood of people flowed around them. Some drivers abandoned their vehicles and joined the procession. As Charmy moved towards the square in front of the capitol building, thousands more were waiting to see her. As she moved to the capitol steps, the flood of people stepped back, clearing a path, only to have it fill in behind her.

On the steps stood the Prince and the legislative leaders. The Princess stopped at the foot of the steps and waited, saying only, "Prince Adudada, what is the government's desire?"

The Prince removed the diamond-incrusted ruby medallion from around his neck, the symbol of authority, and walked down the steps and placed it around Princess Charmy's neck. The cheer that arose from the crowd was thunderous. The Princess was escorted to the top of the steps and bowed to the crowd, and smiling, blew kisses before entering the building.

Inside, all but a very few came to praise the return of Princess Charm-E-Ine and to pledge allegiance. The few that did not attend were some of those that needed her attention. Many in attendance wondered, but no one asked, how she had become younger by some sixty years. It was chalked up to being a miracle; a double miracle that not only returned the Princess, but had returned her as her former youthful self.

Inside, addressing the government leadership, the Princess said, "Gentlemen and Ladies, thank you for this honor of welcoming me back. We have much to do and I plan to start first thing in the morning. It is now early in the day. By 4:00 PM this afternoon, I would like to see the list of the most serious issues facing the UAN. I shall assume that list will include those individuals that have disrupted the peace and tranquility of our unified nations. That will be my primary focus.

"Prince Adudada has agreed to be an advisor at my side, for which I am most grateful. In addition to others that I shall choose, I have returned with Raman-I-El who will help bring the lasting peace we all want."

"Forgive my asking," said Prince Adudada, "but will you be leaving when peace has been restored?"

"My longevity here has not been decided. For now, assume I shall never leave." And with that statement there were many smiles and nodding heads of approval.

Chapter 17

UAN Restitution

Ajani Bankole watched the news and saw the reception Princess Charmy received upon her return. He noted that this woman was much younger than the one he saw abdicate and doubted this was actually the same person. "Who does this impostor think she is just walking in and taking over? That will not happen. I am the next great leader, not this person. My army will crush her if she tries anything."

Ajani had started quietly when Charmy abdicated. He knew exactly what he wanted and how he was going to get it. He had promised other dictator want-to-bes great power and wealth if they followed him. He gave the most ruthless the highest ranks and sent them off to create an army. He didn't care how that was done or how it would be paid for. He had already been intimidating enough to get sufficient cash to buy weapons. With these weapons, he was able to plunder even more.

The central government initially paid little attention. By the time they realized what was going on, they found it was too difficult to rein things in. Fighting took the place of peace and with the fighting, prosperity starting losing pace. Seeing what Ajani had done only stimulated others to try and grab a piece of Africa for themselves. The UAN was coming apart.

Princess Charmy understood that things would be different this time. The first time she led Africa forward, she had done so quietly and gradually built up the momentum needed to create the union. It was different this time because she was very much in the spotlight. She hoped it wouldn't be the case, but thought a more militant approach might be needed. To that end, she asked for and received funds for a larger security force.

Also, unlike the first time, now she had another Order member to help and Raman would do anything Charmy asked. She named Raman Internal Ambassador and gave him the mission to meet with each of the rising warmongers, strongmen (and women), poachers, and gangsters. Raman decided he would start with the most widely recognized individuals and got word to Ajani Bankole they should meet.

Ajani agreed but thought, *I shall send a message back to that so-called Princess that I am not some fool to be trifled with. I will send this idiot back in a box.*

Ajani thought Raman would arrive in a more traditional way. That would be either military escort, or perhaps by helicopter. In either case, his well-armed followers were to gun him down. Raman was still naïve, but wasn't stupid. Charmy's advisors had told him to be on his guard for treachery. With that warning he decided to use what he had to make a difference.

To the surprise of Ajani's guards, Raman flew to Ajani's headquarters using his antigravity pack with his panels outstretched and his glowing protective shield activated. This was a vision the guards had not expected. To some it was simply too frightening as they saw a "celestial" being coming down in front of them. More gang-like rather then a well-disciplined armed force, many dropped their weapons and fled. Some did stand their ground as Raman came closer; they took aim, and fired.

Raman might have flinched, but if he did, it wasn't noticeable as the bullets were either deflected or ricocheted off the protective golden shield. One or two of the guards looked at their weapons thinking they had misfired, but by this time even more had dropped their weapons and ran. Their pathetic commander was upset at the desertion and fired at them, and some dropped to the ground. Raman simply kept on coming, though more slowly now.

Raman, with his hands and arm raised and one leg slightly lifted as the means to control the antigravity pack, landed ten feet in front of the closest guard, though the term guard hardly fit the man's description at this point as he was completely petrified. The panels furled, but the glow remained as Raman walked forward. "This is not the way to greet Princes Charm-E-Ine's Internal Ambassador," he announced as he moved even closer. "Put your guns down and step to one side or face the wrath of one that has been insulted." As he said this he thought, *I hope they don't call me on that. I have nothing very "wrathy" to really offer!*

The commander in charge, perhaps more afraid of Ajani than Raman, stepped forward and wasn't about to let Raman pass. But

Raman, at seven feet tall and nearly 300 pounds of sculptured muscle, reached over with one hand, grabbed the man, lifted him off the ground, and placed him to one side as if he were nothing. "Out of my way little man and go home." And that is what he did.

As if nothing had happened, Raman entered Ajani Bankole's headquarters, turned off the protective shield, and walked over to the clerk saying, "I have an appointment with Mr. Banklole. Please tell him Princess Charm-E-Ine's ambassador is here."

Wide-eyed after seeing the scene that had just transpired outside, the clerk lied, saying, "Please enter, he is expecting you."

In the office Raman said, "Mr. Banklole, I believe you were expecting me. Thank you for the most gracious reception you prepared for me."

"You insult me," said Ajani. "You may address me as 'Eminence Leader.'"

"That's fine with me. Eminence Leader, you are coming with me. It is obvious you have no respect for the true leadership of Africa and therefore you are under arrest. You will stand trial for sedition, though that will only be a formality. The Princess has no more patience for the likes of you." And with that declaration, military vehicles pulled up in front and the UAN's solders burst into the building, dragged Eminence Leader out into the street, and escorted him rather roughly into an armored vehicle.

The UAN Colonel in charge turned to Raman and said, "Sir, where to next?"

"You have solders to take charge here?"

"Yes sir."

"Excellent. According to my list, it appears the next one is about seventy-five miles south of here. I'll meet you there late this afternoon."

"Yes sir," said the smiling Colonel. "It shall be our pleasure," he added, as he signaled his troops to move out.

Over the next five months, the campaign to clean up the strong man infestation went on. Some were easy and some were not. Some tried to blend back into society, but this time that wasn't going to be allowed. Every one that had taken a militant position against the government was tracked down and arrested; often with the assistance of the citizens who were tired of these petty thugs.

In one case, if it hadn't been so pathetic it might have been comical. Well, actually, it was comical. Firearms were once considered by many to be a symbol of power and the more guns a person had, the more power that person had, or so many people foolishly thought. To entice these people into buying even more guns, the manufacturers kept making more effective guns; guns that were increasingly more effective at killing. By the time the Death Flu pandemic of 2071 had faded away there were far more guns than people, so manufacturing all but stopped. Petty dictators had no trouble getting weapons, but most were old, poorly maintained, and only a few thug leaders were smart enough to trade weapons so an armed force had some consistency. Added to this was the lack of new reliable cartridges. Entrepreneurs soon learned refilling spent cartridges and making new ones with no quality control was an easy way to make money. Naturally old weapons, made by different manufactures, and loaded with bullets of poor quality was a combination that didn't favor the end users.

Kandake Amanirenas, an adopted alias because it invoked power, was a dreamer with delusions of grandeur but little grasp of reality. She managed to recruit followers only because the recruits had even less of a grasp of reality. It seemed anyone with a measureable IQ was disqualified from her "army." Yet with no training and no discipline Kandake somehow still expected the best from her recruits. In this case, however, no matter how good they might have been, it wasn't going to matter as they faced Raman. When Raman entered their compound the fun started. As usual, some fled as he approached, and some fired—or tried to fire—their weapons, but with no success. These people threw down their useless weapons and fled. Only the dumbest of the bunch stood their ground for a little longer as the guns failed to fire, blew up, or in some cases managed to send the bullet backwards into the one shooting the gun. Raman smiled, shook his head, and tried not to laugh at the comical scene laid out in front of him. Raman guessed that this fool, Kandake, must have looked in the mirror and saw herself as the new Princess Charmy and had somehow convinced others she was the one to take Princess Charmy's place. Delusions of grandeur have no boundaries.

The petty thugs that wanted power were one group, but perhaps the ones that really angered Raman were the poachers. There was no need to kill innocent animals, especially those that had been brought back from the brink of extinction, or in some cases had become extinct and were then brought back through applied science. There was plenty of good food available for anyone willing to put in any effort at all. So poaching was to feed other unrealistic wants, rather than needs, and if not stopped it would eventually destroy much of the ecological restitution that had been so successful. Raman took great pleasure in the capture of these truly selfish people.

In the end, each of the people that had plotted to overturn the great works of the UAN were placed on trial and, depending upon the severity of the crimes, appropriate punishment was applied. The citizens of Africa were so fed up with the worst kind of behavior that it was proposed that the very worst ones be placed in a Restitution Prison, as they called it. It was proposed that those that had been responsible for the most heinous of crimes be placed in this very special hospital prison where they would be "allowed" to make restitution to society by donating organs as needed. Princess Charmy was rather appalled at the notion and it never happened. However, the very thought that something like that might occur gave gang leaders something to consider and the violence nearly disappeared.

Chapter 18

Home Front

With the mission to salvage Russia abandoned, Katherine decided to take time to go back to Earth to see Dakota and Celeste. There really wasn't much for her to do at TCe and though it was unlikely much would come from it, there was still the need to discuss what might be a regrouping with the UNSC.

When Katherine arrived, she wasn't at all surprised no one was home. Dakota and Celeste spent so much time in the wormhole gate construction facility she wondered why they hadn't simply moved in. Sure enough, they were in the shop. And sure enough, the technicians were boxing up Gate parts for yet another Gate while Dakota and Celeste were polishing the brass on the 1914 Model T Ford. It wasn't much of a surprise that Astron was helping as well. He was now seventeen and towered over just about everyone. He didn't seem to mind that Celeste, four years younger and much smaller, was still telling him what to do.

As what was becoming a common practice, Katherine hadn't told them she was coming home, so when Celeste saw her, she dropped her polishing cloths and ran over yelling, "Mommy!" After the obligatory hugging, Celeste asked, "Are you here for a while this time?"

"Maybe. Do you want me to hang around?"

"You're being silly mommy. Come see the car. It's all done. Daddy taught me how to drive."

Scowling at Dakota, Katherine said, "You taught her how to drive this thing?"

Faking shock, Dakota said, "This isn't just a thing. This is fine piece of historic art. Just look at how shiny it is!" Then after Katherine and Dakota hugged, he said, "Wanna go for a ride?"

"Umm, not right now. I see you recruited some help. How are you doing Astron?" How's your mom?"

"We're just fine. ma'am."

"'Ma'am?' That makes me feel old. I'm hungry, what's for lunch?"

Dakota said, "We had some chili. There's some there on the stove, if Astron didn't eat it all."

Katherine shook her head. "You know we do have a house with a kitchen."

"So?"

"So when was the last time you used it?" While Dakota was taking too long to come up with an answer, she said, "Really? You have to think about that? You don't have that issue, do you Astron?"

"No ma'am."

After Katherine had a bite to eat, she let Celeste give her a ride next door to the Star Struck Trading Company offices. Smiling, both Astron and Dakota were in the back seat. Katherine held on for dear life in the front seat while her daughter was motoring along. Katherine couldn't help but think, *I travel almost at the speed of light, but this is far more frightening!*

Sharon saw the old car pull up and came out to greet everyone. "Hi Mom," said Astron. "We got the car running."

"So I see." Then looking at Dakota she said, "I didn't know twelve-year-olds were allowed to drive."

Celeste said, "I'm thirteen."

"Oh yeah, that makes a big difference. Katherine you look rather pale. Come on in."

Once settled in, the kids went to show off the car to some workers leaving Dakota, Katherine and Sharon alone. Katherine asked, "So the company is doing good?"

"We have been bringing back a lot of valuable material through the High Point Wormhole Gate. I wouldn't say we are flush with cash at the moment, but the outlook is phenomenal, especially with this new substance Lehtolarite found on Prosperity. If we can bring back enough of this stuff and make the products we think we can make from it, there is no telling the amount of wealth it could bring. What is particularly exciting is that the wealth would come while providing a major benefit to every aspect of the Earth's environment."

"That seems a bit over the top to me," said Katherine.

"Yeah, perhaps, but it looks so good potential investors are lining up, with one investor that might not be a surprise."

"You mean the UAN?"

"Yup. Gabe-I-El came to see me wearing his UAN representative hat, and without UNSC knowledge apparently. It seems to be becoming clear that the UNSC is considering reneging on the plan to build two new ships."

Katherine went nuts, saying, "Are you kidding me? Those jerks. They made a commitment. What's their problem?"

Sharon, trying to calm Katherine, said, "Wow, calm down there lady! It seems money is the issue. At least that's the excuse. Truthfully, I don't think they are visionaries, with maybe a couple of exceptions, and those people get ignored. Anyway, Gabe convinced me, I mean the company, that it could be worthwhile if we took over. We haven't, of course, but we are positioning ourselves to be able to do it. We can easily raise the money. In the meantime our engineers have been developing a new ship design. And I'm proud to say, Astron was the one that came up with the concept. The design should mean a much smoother ride during the turning cycles. The engines remain the same UNSC design."

"Smoother than that old car?" asked Katherine. Sharon just laughed, while Katherine continued, "So Sharon, you've done pretty well for yourself. This is a long way from your Head Bartender days."

"Yes, I feel pretty lucky. I have plenty of money and Astron is a wonderful kid, though for obvious reasons to those of us that know who his father is, I do watch for anything unusual. He has latched onto Celeste, who does most of the talking while his mind seems to going a mile a minute. He is very smart.

"I was hoping I'd see you soon. Raman is back and now off to Africa with Charm-E-Ine. It's best I don't see him again. Gabe, on the other hand, comes by regularly to talk about the mission for the new ships. We don't see any good reason why new ships shouldn't leave for the Alpha Centauri star system before the fleet makes it back from Tau Ceti. Scouting for a suitable construction site and some initial work could be completed before the rest of the Gate is brought along. For some reason, Gabe wants to zero in on a planet that circles the smallest of the three stars, Proxima Centauri, specifically one planet. Of course the ships would have to be built first."

"That's interesting," said Katherine. "Seems like there is a lot of visibility from his Order lately, with a lot more push than I thought they were allowed. I mean it used to be we didn't know they were around. Now they seem to be everywhere influencing policy, especially Gabe."

"Now that you mention it," said Dakota, "He has suggested I go on this mission. For me it wouldn't be a problem. We have all the high-tech critical components completed for more Gates. That's what the guys were boxing up. The stuff for the overall site is big, but nothing fancy. That can be assembled in a couple of weeks if necessary. So sweetie-pie, if you're looking for a family outing, Celeste and I could go."

"Sweetie-pie? What do you want?" Katherine said as she looked over at a winking Dakota.

Sharon said, "You two need a room?" Then added, "This may be asking a lot, but Astron is always asking about the starships. I think he'd like to go. Would you be willing to take him as well?"

Dakota said, "He's always hanging around us anyway when he's not in school, so why not? He'd still have school."

"Hey, wait a minute," said Katherine, "The Admiral hasn't even said you can go. In fact, I'm not sure this Admiral wants to go. And let's not forget that the UNSC hasn't agreed to anything yet. And by the way, did you forget we still need ships?"

"Oh."

In the end, however, they did all decide to go. Of course there were still a few minor details to be worked out. Little things like UNSC's agreement and the construction of the ships. That meant the next stop would be the UNSC headquarters. Details, details!

After a few days at home, actually in the house and not the shop, Katherine headed out. The UNSC directors seemed anxious enough to see her that a military jet was sent to pick her up. This was not normal for the UNSC so it made Katherine wonder, *what's going on?* The flight might have been uneventful, except that the Science Director, Harlyn Jackson was on board to greet her. The suspicion meter in Katherine's head went right off the scale.

For the first half hour of the flight, Harlyn was the most gracious of hosts. He asked if she wanted a drink and Katherine, thinking that she wanted to brace herself to eventually find out what was what, accepted a Mai Tai Harlyn made that was absolutely perfect. She took a few swallows, swished the ice around in the glass and said, "Okay, Harlyn, what's going on? You're buttering me up for something."

"Well maybe," he said, and then when Katherine just sat looking at her drink and taking a sip or two he sighed and said, "I need some information and a favor."

"You're asking me for a favor? Aren't you my boss?"

"First some information, or insight I guess. This guy Gabe-Re-El comes by a little too often as far as I'm concerned. I mean, he is the UAN Commissioner to the UNSC so I could live with that, but when he is talking with Yvonne and me, it's as if we're being brainwashed or something. I feel as though anything he says must be correct. Then when he leaves I start to question myself. I decided to come on this little trip because Gabe will be nowhere around. He will be at headquarters as a Commission member when we arrive, so he does have an official right to be there."

"What does he want?" asked Katherine.

"He wants the two new starships launched as soon as they're ready. He is very insistent on exactly where they are to go, and he wants you in charge."

"Okay, I guess, but didn't the UNSC already decide this?"

Harlyn continued, "We were going to wait until Admiral Wu brought the fleet back and then all five ships would go together. But Gabe-Re-El said, and I'm quoting, 'The UNSC shouldn't wait. The others to can catch up.' When Yvonne said the UNSC was going to delay ship construction, he said, 'That is unacceptable. The Trading

Company has a newer design for the ships and they will fund the enterprise.' When he said it, Yvonne and I thought, *Sure, why not?* So this is what I'm asking. What can you tell me about this Gabe-Re-El and his band of so-called benevolent Order members?"

Wow, thought Katherine, *How much can I say? Things seem to be moving a lot faster than I realized.* She drained her drink and asked for another, and Harlyn readily obliged. With the fresh drink in her hand, she said, "I will tell you what I can, but there is more to this, I'm sure." For the next hour plus, Katherine told Harlyn about the beginnings of the Order on Earth, as she understood it. How they had saved the very first fleet from disaster, how Raman was rescued, and about his ability. "There are many more of his kind than we know. Many centuries in the past they were more confrontational towards individuals they thought could lead large segments of the population to live better lives. Then, until very recently, they have been operating quietly; trying to guide the course of humanity in a positive direction in a more advisory capacity. But I have observed that lately they are being a lot more direct in their actions. They act as though time is running out. Princess Charm-E-Ine of Africa is a prime example."

"Really?" said Harlyn. After thinking for a minute said, "Of course she's one of them. How could I not see that? So what's the big push for Alpha Centauri?"

"Honestly, I don't know. I mean it seems logical that we send ships there based on what we know today. I'm sure the fleet would have gone there first instead of Epsilon Eridani if we knew then what we know now. But the sense of urgency from Gabe is puzzling." After a pause, Katherine added, "Hmmm. I wonder if the Order had steered us away from Alpha Centauri previously." After another pause and almost as an afterthought, Katherine quietly said, almost to herself, "I suppose if the two ships get there and it turns out we can't build a Gate, we would have wasted resources on only two ships instead of five."

Harlyn cleared his throat, "Okay, that was a bit disturbing to hear how we've been manipulated. But I suppose we might have killed ourselves off if a course correction wasn't made once in a while. I have to think about that."

"So what's the favor?" asked Katherine.

"I want to go with you to Alpha Centauri. You can assign me to whatever position you like. Well, maybe not dishwasher."

Katherine held up her empty glass and said, "Maybe bartender, but you know you could make yourself Admiral. Besides who said I was going on this trip?"

Harlyn laughed, "Gabe said you were going, so it must be so!" Then more seriously, "Listen, I know my limitations. I'd make a crappy Admiral," and they both laughed.

Chapter 19

New Ships (2152)

When Harlyn and Katherine arrived at the UNSC headquarters, Yvonne was trying without success to get the commissioners to focus. Yvonne was not doing well on her own so when Harlyn and Katherine entered the chamber, her first panicky words were, "Harlyn, where have you been. You were supposed to be here."

"Sorry. I didn't want to waste any time," he lied. "I went to get Katherine so we could debrief on the plane."

Yvonne scowled at him and said, "Whatever. I'm glad you are both here now. This is important. There is no money or commitment for money to build new ships."

Katherine having been briefed knew this, but playing her part, said, "But Director Blain, the UNSC made a commitment. Are you reneging? Are we bringing back starships and crews to Earth on a wasted, decades-long mission?"

This seemed to put most of the commissioners into a form of panic mode while trying to slink down into their seats out of sight. The UNSC Commissioners were keenly aware they had made a commitment to build two new starships to complete a fleet of five. Now, apparently, it looked like they had made this commitment without any clue as to how they would pay for the construction of two new ones. This was a sick joke.

Looking at Yvonne and Harlyn, one commissioner said, "Well now, you're the ones that said we'd build two more ships!"

"Yes, and you agreed," said Yvonne.

"How did the last one get built?"

"You mean Africa? The UAN paid for it and staffed it. Remember?"

"Oh, yeah. Well what do we do this time?"

What followed was a lot of noise with no realistic suggestions. It appeared to be another case of "lead, follow, or get out of the way," except in this case everyone was trying to get out of the way.

Finally Gabe, with his commissioner hat on and playing somewhat coy, smiled at Katherine and said, "I have an idea. But once again the UNSC will be giving up some authority if we pursue this." Katherine was a little surprised this hadn't been brought up before. It seemed obvious Gabe was trying to get his idea to be moved forward by someone else.

Willing to shed any responsibility Yvonne quickly said, "Great. What is it this time? Somebody else might build the ships?"

"As a matter of fact," said Gabe without hinting in the least that he had a deal in hand, "it is. The Trading Company could build the ships with the help of investors. I think if we make a proposal to the Trading Company giving them control over anything they discover, they might go for it."

"Yeah, but," started the South American Commissioner, "what about the three ships under UNSC control?"

Trying to be funny and break the tension in the room, Harlyn said, "First off 'Yeahbutts' are big hairy critters in the Arctic Circle. We have no Yeahbutts here."

"Very funny," was the not so sincere response.

"Secondly," said Harlyn, "we can propose anything we want. We don't have to give up everything. Maybe they'd 'rent' our ships, or maybe we'd share everything. After all, we have the wormhole gates. Besides, it isn't as if we've not done something like this before. Did you forget we allowed the Trading Company to lease the United States?"

Yvonne trying her best to get control said, "Are we agreed to at least ask the Trading Company?"

All heads nodded in the affirmative. Gabe remained stonefaced.

Katherine took control. "Director Blain, excuse my bluntness, but the Star Struck Trading Company has already anticipated this possibility and have investors lined up pending the decision of this

Commission. They have also designed a modification to the ships that would make them a new class, called the Constellation Class. The Company CEO, Sharon Hooding, is simply waiting to hear if it is a go or no go."

There was stunned silence in the room. As a group, the UNSC suddenly realized they were about to play second fiddle to a private enterprise.

Katherine went on, saying, "There are conditions. I am to be in charge. Once the ships have been completed, they are to leave for the Alpha Centauri system with whatever they can carry to start building a Gate. The rest of the fleet will carry everything else needed when they catch up. I will have the final say on the crew of the new ships. The Trading Company will have control of the Gate operations once completed. The Trading Company will take any profits from any discoveries. The UNSC Science Director will be assigned as my Vice Admiral of Academics and Science."

Harlyn acted surprised with this condition and looked at Katherine appreciatively.

Gabe sat trying hard not to smile.

Finally after a few minutes that seemed like hours, the British Commissioner said, "What do we get out of this? Sounds like the Trading Company gets everything."

Katherine was on a roll and never skipped a beat, She surprised even Gabe when she said, with no hesitation as she thought, *I hope Sharon won't mind my doing this,,* "The UNSC will receive seventeen percent of any net profits. That, of course, means after the crews are paid. Plus the UNSC will have a say in any kind of settlement or colony that might be established. Scientific discovery will be shared independent of who makes the discovery."

Yvonne was dumb founded. She would have been happy to leave the fleet parked at TCe, but Harlyn had made the sweeping proposals, and now with details emerging it was getting complicated. Apparently some negotiating might be in order. *I want out of this*, she thought. But that wasn't going to happen.

The Japanese Commissioner said, "I'm not saying I'm agreeing to this, but I'm curious. What's the new ship design?"

"I can only give you the overall design concept, but from what I have come to understand, it will make for a smoother ride. The original design for the ships was based on a constant acceleration and deceleration providing an artificial gravity. When the maximum determined speed was reached, acceleration stopped and the ships turned around and started decelerating. With a 1.5g and .5g provided through this maneuver, there was some semblance of normalcy as it pertained to this artificial gravity. But this period of transformation leaves the ships with a zero gravity pull and everything floats around, causing a major disruption with every turn. Later a version of what we call a skid steer was proposed and implemented. When initiated, the ships make a gentle turn while under power and when the ships have turned 180 degrees they start the opposite acceleration/deceleration cycle. This requires a lot of space, but as has been pointed out more than once, there is a lot of room to maneuver out there in space. The gentle turn, if done exactly vertical to the artificial horizon, either up or down, creates a centrifugal force that is tolerable. But a turn that is any degree off of vertical, even with the gentle turn however, people and things have to adjust to the side centrifugal force created by the turning."

The Japanese Commissioner said, "I didn't know this was an issue."

Katherine said, "That's because you haven't been there to experience it. I have. And while it was something we all learned to live with, it was, and still is, unpleasant."

"So why not always make this skid steer turn vertical to the artificial horizon?"

Katherine said, "That isn't always the best approach when you're trying to stay on course. And if the ride can be made better, why not? The mathematics involved is tricky. The option to make the skid steer turn in any direction makes life so much easier."

Katherine went on, "Now then, the new ships would still be powered with the same UNSC engines, but our shipboard operating engineers have a few safety upgrades that need to be implemented. The engines would remain risky, but this should make them a little less temperamental. The main body of the ships, however, will be different. It will be an approximately 880-foot sphere that will house most of the activities; living quarters, bridge, recreation, and some food production. The ships will still make the skid steer turns, but we think they can do it more quickly if necessary because the sphere will rotate so the g forces will always be straight down. That means no side centrifugal force to contend with. The bow and stern sections of the ships will be conical shaped with pointed ends armored against any possible collision and holding the communications arrays, just like the current fleet. This area will hold the shuttlecraft, additional food production areas, and storage of the equipment for the Gate construction. The design is complete."

Yvonne asked, "And this all came about when?"

Gabe and Harlyn were both impressed by the way Katherine was apparently making this presentation on the fly with no preparation. They didn't know she was doing a lot of guessing when she said, "Oh this has been in the works for some time. The Trading Company is very progressive in its thinking. Not seeing much in the way of action from the UNSC prompted some initiatives."

"Well that's rather insulting!"

Katherine only looked expressionless, ignoring the comment, before saying, "And these next new ships will be called Orion and Perseus."

She just listened with the faintest of smiles when Yvonne said, "So you have thought of everything."

"Not me, and honestly, I don't think the Trading Company has considered everything either. After all, it is the UNSC that has the mandate from the participating countries to do space exploration. Keep in mind that the Trading Company has a more-than-willing major financial partner in this so it is conceivable that in the near future the Trading Company could afford to just go ahead without the UNSC if it didn't need the UNSC engines. Given enough time, that might not be an issue either." As Katherine got up to leave she said, "Think it over. The Trading Company has made it clear it is there to help if you want it." And she left the room.

Harlyn also excused himself for a few minutes and went into the hall. He found Katherine sitting on the floor with her back against the wall. "Are you all right?" he asked.

"Yes, just exhausted. I didn't plan any of that."

"Maybe not, but I was very impressed. I will be honored to be your VAAS."

Katherine said, "We talked about it. You do realize that's a demotion. Instead of me working for you, you'll be working for me?"

"Oh, somehow I think you'll cope," said a broad-smiling Harlyn as he went back into the chamber.

Chapter 20

The Mobile Ones

The three indigenous species that occupied the fourth planet from Tau Ceti, referred to most commonly as TCe, were nothing the humans could have imagined. These creatures converted carbon, preferably in the form of carbon dioxide, into oxygen with such efficiency that they had created an environment so out of balance it forced a war of survival among the different species. At first the humans thought the environmental problem created on TCe could balance the excess carbon dioxide issues on Earth, thus helping both planets. It didn't work out that way, but the humans were able to make a significant contribution to helping TCe with the carbon neutrality issue.

When the fleet was preparing to leave TCe for Earth, the indigenous species of the planet decided that those referred to as the Mobile Ones should be included in the voyage. The Tall Ones were the thinkers of TCe, resembling extremely tall trees. They never left the soil where they were "born." Their counterparts were the Mobile Ones and, as the name more than implied, they could move about freely. To the humans they looked like a short piece of wood with a green top and roots that moved like legs. Without their airships their movements were slow, but their airships, designed by the Tall Ones, were incredibly fast and maneuverable and easily proved they were able to shoot down a shuttle when the humans first arrived at TCe. These days things were a lot different, with the indigenous species of TCe and the humans cooperating for everyone's benefit.

For the trip to Earth two airships, which looked like large bees, and their crews of three each were volunteered to go, even though the concept of volunteering was something the Mobile Ones and the Tall Ones didn't really understand. If something needed to be done the most readily available Mobile Ones simply did it. So it was that six Mobile Ones and two airships were pressed into service for the trip to Earth on board China.

For the human crew, this wasn't much of a hardship since each Mobile One stood only about one inch in height and the airships were no more than eight inches in length. Plus Mobile Ones only needed some rich soil to feed on and the carbon dioxide that the humans didn't want anyway.

Each crew was made up of a pilot, a flight engineer, and a fire control officer. As they all looked exactly alike, at least to the humans, and having no designations that could be understood, they were referred to with the not-so-clever names of, Pilot 1, Engineer 1, Fire Control 1, Pilot 2, Engineer 2, and Fire Control 2.

Being as small as they were, each crew was assigned a human crewmember to provide what was needed. Often this was simply transportation. After all, Admiral Wu didn't want the little fellows getting crushed by accident. That sort of thing wouldn't be considered in a favorable light back home! Occasionally the crews would fly their bug airships, but after a couple of collisions with people in the corridors the flights were limited to large recreational areas, and even then it was more for entertainment.

Kem-U-El and Ere-Mi-El could both communicate directly with the Mobile Ones using their strange wood-creaking language, but they were assigned to the other ships. So the written English language was the communications of choice with the Mobile Ones with humans using magnifying glasses initially to read the small written words. In time there would be an electronic means of communication so messages from the Mobile Ones could be seen on a large screen. For the humans, this made the exchange of ideas painfully slow.

The purpose for the Mobile Ones to join the mission was to gain knowledge. The Mobile Ones were charged with learning as much as possible about the strange creatures called humans and their very interesting machinery. At the same time the humans really wanted to learn as much as they could about these strange creatures that looked like little trees, but weren't.

The plan was for the Mobile Ones to reach Earth themselves and/or by any offspring that might be born on the ship. With information stored in their collective memory, this would be shared with the Tall Ones and the other Mobile Ones. The Tall Ones back on TCe and their colony on Earth's Coat Island in the Hudson Bay had learned to work with and trust the humans—well, mostly trust—but they remained quite confused about how they functioned. Unlike the Tall Ones and the Mobile Ones that shared all information and acted with a collective consciousness, the humans mostly operated as individuals with their own memories and individual sets of skills. Yet somehow the humans were able to work together for a common cause when it suited them. When it didn't suit them, individual humans could create all manner of chaos for the rest. Somehow this social interaction must have worked, however, as evidenced by the technology they had developed. The Tall Ones felt if they could understand human behavior, perhaps some of that behavior could be incorporated into their collective memory for their benefit. In the meantime, the bug ship crews were enjoying the rich CO_2 atmosphere on board China.

It was customary for members of the bug ship crews to be at different stages of life. The reason was the need to pass knowledge from one generation to another. When a younger member was added to a crew, their "root" system allowed downloading of knowledge. The Mobile Ones were not the youngest of their species when volunteered for the mission and now it was time to prepare for the future. Pilot 2 informed Vice Admiral Null that it was time for his engineer and Fire Control 1 to perform the ceremonial reproductive activity.

Earl was naturally curious what this was all about, but the translation through the written word was not making much sense so both Pilot 2 and Earl had Kem video-in so the dialogue could be better understood. Once connected, Earl asked through Kem, "What does that mean? Or maybe the question is, what's involved?"

Kem spoke with Pilot 2 for some time, using the creaking language, and finally turned to the Vice Admiral and said with a somewhat furrowed brow, "Apparently the Mobile Ones have developed some understanding of the human reproductive process and while they think it is bizarre, they can see how it works. Their means of reproduction seems more aligned with the fruit trees on the horticulture decks, though I'm guessing it is even more aligned with the Tall Ones reproduction. It seems the actual activity is simple enough, but there is some ceremony involved. Back on TCe, there would be far more Mobile Ones going through this at one time and it would be a time of reflection and celebration, though I think their idea of celebration is lot different then what you and I might consider. In this case, Pilot 2 would be honored if you, the Admiral, Captain Lie Jie, and their human handlers attend the ceremony. Pilot 2 also asked if Ere and I could attend. That's up to you, though I can tell you this is an important occasion for the Mobile Ones and it might be a good way to establish stronger relations with them."

"So can you enlighten me a bit more?"

"I'll try. On TCe, the Mobile Ones tend to the Tall Ones, which includes, what I guess we'd call, pollination similar to what honeybees do. The Mobile Ones do things a little differently. There are certain periods each year when older Mobile Ones gather in an area. They call it something I don't fully comprehend, but for lack of any other term I'll call it a nursery.

"The Mobile Ones that are preparing to reproduce gather in a cluster. Around this cluster is a circle of as many companions as are available. It appears there is a lot of fast movement by the clustered group, but as we have seen, their idea of fast movement might be hard for us to recognize. Anyway, one member in the cluster, with some unseen stimulus, will shake and what we might call pollen goes into the air. Once one does it, it triggers all those in the cluster to do it and the pollen, or whatever it is, mixes. It then falls to the ground where it creates the nucleus of many tiny Mobile Ones."

Earl asked, "So this is like cross-pollination, or some kind of egg fertilization?"

Kem said, "I guess, though it might be more like a seed, or for these guys it might be something all together different. And before anyone asks, I already asked if we could get a sample and they were horrified at the question."

"So 'no' then?" said Earl.

"A bit stronger than 'no,'" said Kem.

"Then what?"

"Well," said Kem, "the tiny little things start to grow in the soil and when they get to a certain age, they are able to move and leave the nursery taking their place in their society."

"Okay," said Earl, "So how many new Mobile Ones will come out of this and how do they learn anything?"

"There might be just one, but more likely a dozen new little guys. I find the learning part interesting. While the mini Mobile Ones are in the nursery, their roots, or feet, or whatever those lower appendages might be, are sucking up nutrients from the soil. But they are also sucking up the knowledge that the older ones are sharing when they are feeding in the same area and their lower appendages touch. So when the new guys are able to become mobile themselves they are already educated. They all seem to have the same basic knowledge. It is their eventual assignments that dictate what they actually do, not what they learned."

"So what happens to the older ones?"

"It appears they do this reproductive thing only once while in their prime. Maybe a few do it more than once. Anyway, they continue on for a few more years at least, and then eventually die and through a rather interesting process, return to the soil in some sort of complicated composting ritual that is usually private."

Earl asked, "So when does this take place?"

"Tomorrow, 10:30."

"Hmm. This better be worth it. I'm sending a shuttle over to pick you up and then Ere to attend the ceremony."

The next day at 10:30 on the lower horticulture deck, Engineer 2 and Fire Control 1 were in the middle of a large tray of soil set aside for the ritual. Around them was a loose circle of their shipmates and around them were the invited guests. It seemed like forever, but it was actually about forty-five minutes before there was any discernable movement. Suddenly Engineer 2 started shaking as if in a stiff breeze and immediately Fire Control 1 started doing the same thing. What looked like dust came from the their tops for a few seconds and then the dust settled to the soil. Their crewmembers made considerable creaking noise for perhaps a minute while the two stars of the day stayed in the middle. Then it was over. The humans were informed that Engineer 2 and Fire Control 1 would take turns monitoring the growth of their offspring for about eighteen months, until the newest Mobile Ones could leave the nursery. In time they would replace their parents in the bug ships, and any additional Mobile Ones would likely build additional bug ships.

With the conclusion of the ceremony, Earl said to the Mobile Ones, "We have our own traditions when a baby is born. You are invited to the lounge where we shall drink a toast to your offspring. I will have the richest soil we have brought to the lounge for you. Would that be acceptable?"

And it was. It was a rather strange gathering, with the five Mobile Ones on the bar with their platter of soil, much to the chagrin of the Head Bar Tender. Around them were the humans that had been at the ceremony. In spite of the size of the Mobile Ones, there was no "small" talk. There was very little talk at all from the Mobile Ones which seemed a little awkward at first, but eventually the humans, Kem, and Ere decided this was as good as any excuse for a party and did exactly that.

When they were back at their airships, the Mobile Ones concluded that the humans were a very strange species. The humans, once alone in the Lounge, concluded that the Mobile Ones were a strange species. Ere and Kem agreed that both humans and Mobile Ones were strange species. But they all agreed, to themselves anyway, that the little ceremony had an impact on all as it opened their minds further to understanding.

Chapter 21

Intervention (2153)

Evan-Ge-Line had to ask herself, which she did out loud even though no one else was there, "Is it interference or intervention if you are trying to make things better for a people that were placed in a situation not of their making?" She thought, *Probably intervention, and direct intervention is the right thing to do, even though protocol says differently. Oh wait, Gabe said the old protocols are off. I guess I will exhibit flexibility of thought here.* Then out loud once again, "Flexibility. Yes. Sometimes we must be flexible in our thinking. And I am so flexible; I can bend way over backwards to help people." Evan gave a nervous laugh at her private little joke.

The Boss had previously decided to leave these people to their own devices. On one hand it made sense to use the available Order's resources for the greater good on Earth. On the other hand, it didn't seem right to abandon these people when they had been rendered helpless through no fault of their own. Evan caught herself with her next thought: *It isn't fair, but life isn't fair, is it.* Being fair to one another is the right thing, but life itself will deal with you any way it wants, and it seldom seems fair.

But now, because of the circumstances unfolding, Evan and her group were to guide these people towards an inevitable future. Gabe had told her to do whatever she thought needed to be done. The voyage from Earth had been long and during her time on watch she had plenty of time to consider her actions. There was also plenty of time before Earth's starships were going to show up, so there was no need to rush into anything.

Taking the cautious approach, Evan's crew had monitored things on the planet's surface and what they observed was troubling. The number of people in what she considered a commune was about the same as the number of people abducted by Tam. It was obvious they hadn't expanded their group beyond their valley. There were a lot of animals on the surface and some of them were rather large. When someone in her group screamed, Evan went over to the monitor and saw one of the commune members being killed and carried off by one of the animals. It was beginning to be clear why the commune was the size it was and why they remained in the valley. This was going to require a lot more work than expected to set things right. She would need to show these people a new path. Their ancestors were placed here through severe interference many, many years ago. Their survival as a people up to this point was starting to look more like a miracle than a plan.

Evan had their ship land outside the valley and they set up shop. They secretly watched the commune for nearly a whole season. What they saw as they tried to work out a plan was appalling. This day would be different.

Evan and two companions put on their antigravity backpacks and activated the panels that spread out from the packs. The three of them rose together and glided up over the valley walls into the valley that contained the commune. The usual routine for an Order member was to avoid being showy. While there was never an attempt to hide their size and to dress in the manner of the local population, floating in with the antigravity packs deployed and providing a faint golden glow around them was usually avoided. People sometimes got the wrong idea. Actually in ancient history, nearly everyone got the wrong idea. This was a case, however, where there would be nothing subtle about their arrival.

As they approached, one by one, each member of the commune stopped what they were doing in the fields and looked up. What they saw were three very large beings all dressed in white surrounded in a golden glow as they floated towards them with outstretched wings. The smallest one of these intruders was Evan at six feet two inches and 160 pounds. She seemed petite next to her companions.

Commune members stared in disbelief as these large beings settled to the ground and made the wing-like panels disappear. Minda was the first to speak, and before Evan could get out a word, she asked, "Have you come to take us back?"

That was not what Evan expected to hear; not at all. She and her companions were completely thrown off guard as they looked from one to the other. Hesitating, Evan could only respond using the commune's own unique language asking, "I am called Evan. What do you mean?"

There were no designated leaders in the commune, but Minda was standing in front and seemed to be assuming the role of spokesperson. "I am called Minda. You brought our people here to Gadan many seasons ago and left. Have you come to take us back?"

"Back where?"

"We don't know. You told our ancestors that this was Gadan and a new start. We were brought here from someplace else and then others like you came and they all left leaving us alone. Have you come to take us back?"

Evan was completely flummoxed. Gathering her thoughts she reasoned that while the commune's collective memories as a group started when they were placed here by Tam-I-El and his rogue teams, the story of their arrival had been passed on from one generation to another and that somehow turned into a belief that they would be returned to wherever they came from originally. "Why would you want to leave?"

"So we don't have to work and be eaten by the tandoo."

It became obvious to Evan that Minda thought she was here to save them from what Minda was calling tandoo, which must be the big animals seen taking commune members. *Well, this is awkward!*

It was true she was there to help, but to take them back? Was that even possible? If they were returned to Earth now, the results would be unimaginable. "We are not the ones that brought your ancestors here, but we are here to help you."

"What does that mean? Where are the first ones? Would they take us back?"

"No. You will never see the first ones again, so they would never take you back. We are here to prepare you for the arrival of others and show you how to live with the tandoo."

"We don't want to live with the tandoo. They take us."

"Okay, I said that wrong. I mean live here and not have the tandoo take you."

"How? Why not just take us back?"

Evan hadn't planned on being on the defensive and thought, *This isn't going well. It is a very good thing that these people have time to prepare.*

Trying to piece things together, Evan noted that everyone seemed well fed and extremely healthy, so that wasn't an issue. In fact, Evan was struck by how incredibly beautiful these people were. With everyone wearing the same basic clothing of short trousers, a vest, and no footwear, there was little question of who was male and who was female. Beyond the obvious, however, they seemed not to show any societal differential. In this brief encounter, all of these people calling themselves Gadans were acting the same except this Minda person. She was certainly the most forward one.

Evan didn't know what to do so she said, "We wanted to meet you. We will be back soon and will spend more time with you."

"Why?"

"To prepare you for new things."

Minda responded with, "You seem useless." Then she turned and walked away as the Gadans went back to doing what they had been doing before Evan showed up. Evan looked at her two companions, shrugged, and they flew back to their ship.

Back at their ship, Evan and her group laid out a plan, or at least the start of a plan. With the reaction they observed on this first visit, it was obvious any plan they might devise would most certainly have to change. But they had to start somewhere and it seemed logical to start with self-defense. Minda's people had no weapons and only stone and wooden tools that they devised to tend crops. The few implements that might have come with their ancestors had apparently been worn out or broken. It seemed that they didn't eat meat, as there was nothing that would kill any size of animal, let alone these big tandoo.

With tempered enthusiasm, Evan and her Order members set out to get things started. They felt liberated with the plan because they were allowed, actually encouraged, to be implementers, not just advisors. On the other hand, getting the Gadans to pay attention might be an issue they had never anticipated.

Trying to be optimistic, the Order members confirmed that self-defense against the tandoo should be the first priority. As a start, a selected group would be shown how to make weapons and how to use them. The weapons would be simple, but once the Gandans were trained in their use, they would be very effective. Later there would be gradual preparation for rejoining Earth's society.

But not all plans pan out. Within a week Evan did get the Gadans' attention and they were shown how to make weapons and how to use them, along with a few additional skills. But while they were preparing Minda's people to defend themselves, they forgot to protect their own ship. Their ship was outside the valley walls and while the tandoo only culled some people from inside the valley, anyone outside was considered "fair game." The tandoo banded together and raided the ship one dark night when the gangway was left open. Evan and her entire group were killed and dragged off. For Minda's people that resulted in no raids into the valley by the tandoo for a while, giving the Gadans time to learn how to use their new weapons while wondering why these strangers left them alone, just like the others had left their ancestors. The Gadans weren't surprised.

Chapter 22

Season Twelve (2157)

It was one of those special days in the cooling season of the year. The air was crisp, the sky was blue with fluffy white clouds, and the leaves of the trees were at the peak of color. All of this reflected off the stream alongside the path. On the path was Minda on patrol. While her job meant she needed to stay alert, it didn't preclude her from appreciating the beauty that was around her.

Minda stood at five feet six inches if measured by Earth standards, but here in Gadan, things were simply considered relative. "Oh, he is taller than so and so" or "she is lighter than so and so." There were no numbered scales. So in Minda's case, she was about average. Her blemish free skin was a light olive in color. Her hair was auburn and kept short, which seemed to enhance the slight slant of her green eyes.

With the chill in the air, Minda wore a coat of tandoo hide covering an extremely fit body. Fit because her job demanded it. It wasn't always this way for her people, but with the introduction of the bow and arrow twelve seasons ago, her people were no longer sitting back and waiting to be a food source for the tandoo.

The tandoo when fully grown were "very big." By Earth standards, that would be eleven to twelve feet in height and in the 650-pound range. They were at the top of the food chain on land and had, as long as the commune existed, looked to Minda's people as a food source. While the tandoo were certainly not brilliant in their thinking, they had just enough intelligence to allow Minda's kind to maintain a sustainable population level. The tandoo were also lazy, so they would usually seek an easy target. That meant the old and injured Gadans were usually the ones taken. For as long as anyone could recall, this was the way it was and while certainly not what anyone wanted, it had reluctantly been accepted as reality.

From the beginning the Gadans lived in caves, but as seasons passed they enhanced the entrances with wood from the trees in the forest. The caves provided protection from the tandoo and the sometimes very severe weather, so there was never really any thought of abandoning the caves for something else. The Gadans all lived within this one valley where the stream flowed down the center. Few ever ventured beyond the valley and those that did, never returned. Gadans were vegetarians, though that concept was nothing any of them actually considered. They grew crops and harvested from the forest areas. It never occurred to them to kill and eat an animal. Not even the fish that were in the stream. In the old days, everyone worked together to grow and harvest what was needed. There had been no distinction between male and female. Sticks and stones were the primary farming implements though there were a few worn out tools passed down from the "first ones." Curiously, no one seriously considered using these tools as a means to defend themselves from the tandoo.

The elders of the Gadans, those healthy enough not to be taken by the tandoo, would repeat over and over the story of the awakening. How one day, their ancestors had been born again. Carried here by some flying people referred to by the Gadans as the Bringers. The Gadans knew there was a past and there was a future unknown to them. The past was a previous life of their ancestors and someday they believed the present day Gadans would return to that life. In the meantime, the life they had was all they knew and they were to live it until that future day would arrive. The Gadans that were alive now had only the stories of how they had come to be. Many didn't believe the stories.

That all changed when three "very big" people literally flew into the commune. Though no one could count, that had been twelve seasons ago. These strangers wore all white and had long shoulder-length hair just as the Bringers were described in the stories. The first thoughts of the Gadan commune were naturally that the Bringers had come to take them back. There was disappointment when told that wasn't the case. As the people gathered around, Minda and the rest of the commune found a calm coming over them and started to listen to what was actually being said.

The leader of the strangers called herself Evan-Ge-Line. Even though she kept saying it, it still took almost a complete season to convince the commune that she wasn't there "to take the Gadans back." While the commune members didn't actually know what taking them back might mean, or where "back" was, it was believed to be a better place than Gadan.

While the Order protocol had previously allowed only guidance, the circumstances of the Gadans was unprecedented so stretching the rules was essential to prepare the commune for what was certainly going to be awkward. A hierarchy of some kind was needed where none had existed before, including a need to separate and define some specific duties. While it had been the practice that all able-bodied people worked to grow and gather food, cook, make clothing, tend fires, raise children, and do whatever else was needed, a separate group with only one task seemed prudent. While this wouldn't negate the eventual awkwardness, it would at least establish the Gadans as being more civilized and able to take some control of their immediate future.

Evan selected ten females for what would become the Protectors. Females were selected only because they were the most eager. Minda was the most vocal and readily understood what was being proposed and that it would change their society. By default, and reluctantly, she became the leader of the Protectors.

The first lessons were hard. Making the commune understand that they could live as equals with the tandoo made little sense to them. "The tandoo are big and strong. We are not."

"Yes, that is true, but what if you could stop a tandoo before it took you. Would you like to be able to do that?"

"Yes, that would be good."

"We are not saying you need to go looking for tandoo and kill them, but if they learned that if they came into your valley you could stop them, wouldn't they leave you alone?"

With some skepticism, Minda asked, "How do we do that?"

And that was the opening Evan's team needed.

"If you had a tool that could stop them, even kill them would you be willing to use it? Again, you don't need to go looking for them, but if you were to kill some, they would be less likely to return."

With the suggestion of killing put before them, there was a general gasp, which Minda put into words. "Kill the tandoo? We don't kill anything on purpose. That is not our way!"

"Again, we are not suggesting that you kill the tandoo just for the sake of killing them. We are suggesting that you take your place to be at least equals to the tandoo and show them that you also don't want to be killed."

Minda thought, *Well, that seems fair and it is something we have wanted,* but again asked, "How do we do that?"

"You need to build weapons and have some of your people learn how to use them. I would call them the 'Protectors.' Are you willing to be one?"

Minda didn't think about this for very long. At a minimum she wanted to know more so she said, "Yes."

Evan's Order members showed Minda and nine others how to take long, flexible tree limbs and bend them, attaching a cord made from a vine to each end. They then rested long straight sticks against the limb, held in place against the cord. As the cord was pulled back and then released, the stick was propelled forward with a force Minda and the others couldn't believe. Evan-Ge-Line had called this combination the "bow" and the flying stick the "arrow."

At first, the bow and the arrow were a bit crude and viewed mostly as a novelty. But as the ten designated Protectors practiced, they became stronger and much more accurate in their shots. It wasn't too long before the true potential of this weapon became apparent and refinements were made to suite the user. Minda now had a bow that was much more refined, with a smooth surface and tapered ends, that was as long as she was tall. It was powerful, which made her equally powerful. She worked to make her arrows straighter and fitted them with small fins on the end to make them go straighter. Minda thought this was something of a miracle and was very proud of her weapon, but at the same time was very ashamed. Today as she walked along the stream, her mind started racing. *Why did it take these strange people to show her how to make something like this? Why did they wait so long? It wasn't that difficult to figure out. She, or someone in the commune, could have come up with this. Was it just that they had all become used to the way it was? Shouldn't someone at some time have considered that life could be better? And where do these people go and come from anyway? Another valley?*

With all this thinking, Minda nearly missed seeing the tandoo that was waiting to reduce the number of Protectors by one. When she realized she wasn't alone, she grabbed an arrow from the basket at her waist, loaded it into the bow, and in one fluid motion pulled back and let it fly straight into the tandoo. It took three more arrows before the tandoo finally dropped. This tandoo had made the fatal mistake. While none of the Gadans wanted to kill anything, they had finally made up their minds to not allow any tandoo into their valley. If they were caught in the valley, they would be shot. While some tandoo had figured that out, this tandoo hadn't.

The next task was one Minda found disgusting, but necessary. The Gadans didn't like wasting anything. While they wouldn't eat a tandoo, the fur of the tandoo was warm and had become a prestigious symbol of the Protectors to be worn in the cold season, and as a bonus, a warning to the other tandoo when worn. Minda gritted her teeth, took her sharp stone from her basket, and went to work, being ever vigilant that another tandoo wasn't near by. Later the hide would be turned into a coat. The remains of the tandoo were left for the many scavengers that lived in the valley. The dead tandoo would serve a purpose.

So while Minda had done her duty, a perfectly good day enjoying her tranquil surroundings had been ruined. Killing and skinning a tandoo and now hauling her trophy skin back to the commune was not joyful, and it turned her mind to other thoughts. Other things Evan-Ge-Line had said were now coming to the surface of her thinking. Things that seemed like a warning but had no meaning. "We are here to prepare all Gadans for a reunion."

A reunion? What does that mean. I'm of Gadan. Our people know nothing else. But are there other communes? Should we look for them? Are they looking for us? Do these Order beings have a village and that will be the reunion? And why have these Order people not come back? They said they would teach us more. I want to learn more, but they have left us just like the stories of the Bringers we were told. Minda shook her head and stopped asking herself questions she couldn't answer as she realized that the more she thought about these things, the more anxious she became. She turned off these thoughts and focused on her heavy load and the effort to get back home. Minda decided that while this was work, it was a single task that could block out all her random thoughts. That was good!

Still, many times when she was alone, the random thoughts and unanswered questions would return. It would be many more seasons before Minda would have her answers—some of them anyway.

Chapter 23

New Crew (2157)

It didn't take very long for the UNSC Commission and Yvonne to decide what to do. Yvonne had never wanted to make decisions anyway; she was always leaving it up to Harlyn. Now that he was essentially demoting himself from director to vice admiral, Yvonne was in a tizzy, so she made the only decision she could. She resigned—this time for real. The commissioners listened carefully to the African Commissioner and when Gabe had finished, the vote was to proceed. Until he was to ship out, Harlyn was still the science director. Now with Yvonne gone, he was left to work out the details of the arrangement with the Trading Company. That didn't take long because everyone knew how it was going to turn out. Construction of the new ships had started that same year: 2153.

It would have been unlikely to change the vote, but "somehow" Gabe neglected to mention that the UAN was the silent partner in this enterprise. Gabe and Princess Charmy were eager to have the UAN more involved with space exploration and now with the UNSC gradually giving up power while the Trading Company was taking over more and more of the operations, Gabe and Charmy wanted to make sure Africa wasn't going to be left behind. They could see that while the Trading Company's financial resources might be stretched, it had vision and the UAN had plenty of cash to invest.

During the four years of the ship construction Katherine spent an equal amount of time with the ships based at Tau Ceti and on Earth. Star Ship Africa remained fully functional while Russia remained abandoned except for occasional visits from those on TCf.

By 2157 the Star Ship United States was preparing to go back to Prosperity. Many of the crew wanted to return as they could see riches beyond any expectations. For those that felt they had enough, it wasn't hard to find competent replacements that wanted their chance to be rich. Based on the studies conducted on Lehtolarite, it was a near certainty that the Star Struck Trading Company was going to be blessed with vast wealth. There was so much excitement that many had visions of a time in the future when perhaps another ship would be leased to the Trading Company just to support mining.

When on Earth, Katherine's focus was the recruiting of crews for the new ships Orion and Perseus. Some decisions had already been made, of course, such as naming Harlyn Jackson as Vice Admiral of Academics and Science. For Harlyn that meant he could finally live out his secret dream to be a true astronaut. He was thrilled.

With only two ships in this mini fleet, Katherine decided she would lean on the captains a bit more and forgo the need for a VAO.

Dakota would be the Gate Specialist even though he wouldn't have a lot to do until the other three ships brought the remaining Gate material and construction equipment. He'd be part of the teaching staff and try to focus on that task. Celeste would be going, as well as Astron Hooding. Everyone agreed, except Astron, that he would be assigned to Engineering as an apprentice while in shipboard school. Astron wanted to study design and the arts.

The Orion Captain was John Renaldo. John had been an operating engineer supervisor on British Commonwealth. He wanted to stay in the program, but felt he didn't want to face the long voyage back to Earth. He calculated the number of years it would take to complete the mission to Alpha Centauri from Earth and thought that would be just about right before he would need to retire. His physical characteristics were nothing outstanding, with an average height and weight. The only thing that seemed to set him apart was a Boston Red Sox baseball cap that he always wore, presumably to disguise his balding head. The fact that the baseball team had become a long-lost relic of the past made the hat truly distinctive.

At Gabe's insistence, Ur-I-El was named CASO and was assigned to Orion. Katherine saw no reason to object, though this added one more reason to be increasingly suspicious of Gabe's actions. Very few knew Uri wasn't human. There was little reason to make it public, though two things certainly identified him as an Order member. One was his impressive body. His muscles simply bulged and no one ever saw him exercise because he never did. The other thing was that he always seemed to be eating. Uri was small by Order member standards at six feet six inches and 235 pounds. His black hair had been standard Order shoulder length until recently, when he had it cut short so he might "fit in." It made little difference, however.

Some of Katherine's crew from Africa asked for a transfer as well. Lieutenant David Loring had been a shuttle pilot in the aborted attempt to salvage Russia. He had shown great skill transferring people between the shuttle and Russia even when he was less-than-comfortable with the assignment. For this mission he was promoted to Captain of Perseus as a reward.

Perseus CASO was Dr. Anna Giblin, whose specialty was ecology. Anna was tall, about fifty years old, and still attractive. She walked with some difficulty from arthritis because she refused any aggressive treatment with modern medicines "on principle." She had been made a widow at an early age and since then had dedicated herself to her research. Gabe, through the Trading Company, had recruited her and it seemed there was a specific reason. Katherine's suspicion meter went off once again and she would have considered Anna to be another Order member plant except Anna appeared to be normal. For Anna, the opportunity to study another planet was too good to pass up, so signed on.

Katherine found that it was easier this time to recruit competent crewmembers from the highest engineering ranks down to the lowest skill level. Word had spread fast about the potential riches that would come from the newly named planet Prosperity. Many who had tried to join the next expedition on United States decided that maybe another planet could yield the same promise, so offered their services on Orion and Perseus. Another appealing factor was the comparatively short trip. But even though Katherine could have filled the ships to capacity, she decided to limit the crew sizes to 6,500 each. That would be enough to get the ships to their destination and with the number of years before the other ships would show up, there would be plenty of time to complete the first phases of the Gate and explore.

On August 29, 2157 Star Ships Orion and Perseus left Earth's orbit and headed for the Alpha Centauri solar system with their specific destination, Proxima Centauri b: the terrestrial-looking planet circling the smallest of the three suns, Proxima. They would try to use the new ship design to their advantage and make the 4.3 light year trip as quickly and safely as possible. Everyone on the two ships was giddy with excitement as they settled in for the trip. Everyone, that is, except Uri. Uri was the only one in the mix that knew the Order's secret would be discovered. Combining that with his fear of the possible fate of his fellow Order members that had gone on before gave him a high level of anxiety. He hoped for the best, but was trying to prepare himself for the worst.

Chapter 24

SS Officers

Admiral Wu was not having a good day. In fact, he hadn't had a good day on this miserable voyage since he had been appointed Admiral. If it weren't for some competent officers busting their butt trying to keep everything running smoothly, the whole trip would likely be hopeless. Wang Fang, his so-called VAAS was useless; worse than useless because she was disruptive. Every time he tried to get her to do her actual job she made a big stink about it. When Wu realized she had delegated all her actual duties to the three ships' CASOs he was both annoyed and relieved. Annoyed because she wasn't doing her job, but relieved because he didn't have to deal with her anymore.

Fang essentially isolated herself with her lab assistants in her secret lab. It wasn't really a secret, but it might as well have been for the lack of any clear understanding of what the hell she was actually doing. All Wu knew was that she was working with some kind of microbes. When he tried to understand what she was doing all he got were snarky remarks like, "Oh you wouldn't understand." And when he insisted on an explanation, it was so overburdened with scientific jargon it was just babble.

Wu knew that any scientist that was truly smart could take any scientific topic they were working on and be able to explain the basics in layman's terms. It wasn't important for a layman to understand the minutia, but if a scientist could explain the basics in simple terms it proved they actually knew what they were talking about. Save the scientific words and phrases for other scientists. In Fang's case, however, she was the only scientist in the fleet in her field of inquiry so she was the only one, in theory, that understood what was being worked on. Her lab assistants only knew the specifics of their individual tasks, not the big picture.

The high self-esteem she had for herself seemed truly unjustified. But it was demonstrated regularly with her dismissive attitude towards everything that wasn't to her personal benefit. Wu considered locking her in her lab and sending food in through a slot in the door, but figured the lab assistants shouldn't be punished. Of course Wu had more to deal with than just Fang.

The captains and CASO's on all three ships had their hands full dealing with their own crew issues. Discipline was a huge problem. Almost everyone was doing their job, but not always to a very high standard. Everything always seemed to be in crisis mode. Making it worse, Wu knew that he had a few self-created heroes, but was at a loss as to what to do about it. To make themselves look important and to show how indispensible they were, they would create a crisis and then heroically save the day. "That part you need is no longer in inventory. You say you need it to keep the engine from blowing up? Wow, that's a problem. Let me see what I can do. I might be able work something out." Then, just at a critical moment, the "hero" located the critical component, which had been hidden away for just such an occasion.

The ships weren't clean. The food was okay, but the lazy cooks didn't go out of their way to make tasty food, and the Head Bar Tenders served up mediocre beverages saving the best for themselves and their buddies. This, in turn, made for more than a few disgruntled shipmates, which lead to fighting, which meant the brigs were getting crowded.

The two odd CASOs on South America and British Commonwealth were able to provide what seemed to be accurate calculations for the fleet turns to keep the ships on course. They also seemed to have the ability to quiet down any unrest when they found it. There just happened to be more unruly behavior than they could handle. And since they were focused on their own ships, China wasn't receiving much benefit from them.

Wu knew that feeling sorry for himself wasn't going to get the fleet back to Earth. Besides, he didn't really have time to feel sorry for himself and today was no exception. After a knock on the door, Wu said, "Enter," and in came VOA Earl Null, Captain Jie, and CASO Min with nothing even close to pleasant expressions on their faces. "Oh this ought to be just great," he said to himself as he watched them enter and close the door behind. "What's up?"

Earl said, "Admiral, you know we don't have the greatest cooks on board, right?"

"Yes," Wu said suspiciously. "So?"

"So some of the crew decided it would be a great idea to barbecue a couple of chickens out in engine room pod #2. And, well, it got out of control and they ended up with a fire setting off the fire suppression system."

"Seriously? Is that what happened? I thought that at least the engineering staff had a collective brain."

Min said, "It wasn't completely their fault. It was a few folks from the agriculture decks fed up with what the cooks were doing to their chickens. They convinced the operating engineers to let them set up a barbecue in exchange for a tasty meal."

"Brilliant," said Wu, "Just brilliant. Any damage?"

"Not really. Should we throw these clowns in the brig?"

"We should. Hmmm, how was the barbecue? Did it get ruined?"

Min thought this was a curious question under the circumstances, but answered, "I guess it was just fine. Apparently they managed to sequester it away before the fire brigade showed up, who by the way, were apparently treated to some of the food."

Wu stared at the three of them for few minutes, then he shook his head and laughed. "What a crew we have. Unbelievable. Tell you what. Transfer the guilty engineering staff to the water recycling deck for a month. Send the official cooks to assist on the agriculture decks and move the geniuses that came up with this barbecue scheme to the kitchen to oversee cooking. Tell them if they don't improve the overall meal quality, they will be sent down to the veterinarian deck to clean cages. Oh, and make this a secret."

"Why a secret?" asked Null.

"Because that's still the fastest way to get the word out to the rest of the fleet. Information always moves faster when it's a secret. If there is nothing else, dismissed. No, wait a minute. I have an idea. Earl, I want you to pick one Marine on each ship and give them a very difficult job. Pick from the best for this. Each of them should not wear anything that shows they are Marines, but they should wear something to make them stand out. You can figure out something. I want them to report directly to each CASO. They are to have the title of SS Officer."

Earl was a little concerned over this and asked, "You want Secret Service Officers?"

Wu smiled. "No, they are to be the Stop Stupid Officers."

Jie and Min looked at each other and shrugged, as Earl asked, "And what are these people supposed to do exactly?"

"They are to wander around the ships and if they see someone doing something stupid, they are to make it stop."

"That's it?"

"Yeah. Based on what you just told me and everything else we've been dealing with, I suspect this is going to be an exhausting assignment for our SS Officers." Then with his eyes staring at the conference room table and shaking his head, Wu said, "Dismissed."

Wu was correct, the three selected Marines were soon asking for help.

As Null, Jie, and Min left the Admiral, he sat back in chair, folded his hands and with his thumbs rubbed his lower lip. *It will be a miracle if we make it back to Earth at all,* he thought. *Why did I ever take on this job?*

Then he laughed at himself. He knew perfectly well why he took on this job. Why he wanted this job. It had nothing to do with the job or the title. He had made a deal to get away from Earth and unsavory characters that wanted his huge debt repaid. They couldn't reach him out here. Part of the deal with the UNSC directors, however, included a promise not to gamble on the trip. But, ironically, wasn't this trip the biggest possible gamble? In any case, he had wished to be free of his massive, mounting debt, and got his wish. What was that old expression? *Oh yes,* he thought, *Be careful what you wish for.*

Chapter 25

Breached (2160)

The Earth-bound fleet was now about halfway there in 2160. The first few years of the trip were anything but routine. Early on-the-job training by instructors, who themselves hadn't read the manuals, had unintentionally added to the less-than-relaxing experience. Too often the ignorant were teaching ignorance, which meant any time anything critical came up and a decision was made that resulted in a positive outcome, the standard comment was often, "Well, that's once in a row!" At least the mathematicians that had to calculate the skid steer turns knew what they were doing. Or at least it seemed that way. Wu was developing an ulcer.

Wu relied heavily on Earl, his VAO, as someone who actually did know what he was doing and ordered him to do whatever was required to get some semblance of competence on the ships. Earl had done that, making certain that those in Operations that took their job seriously were rewarded. These people were bumped in rank and those that were lazy or simply incompetent were demoted. While Earl promoted people, he was careful to avoid the "Peter Principle" so a competent person wouldn't get promoted to a level where they might exceed their level of competence. On the other hand, one engineering supervisor on British Commonwealth managed to get herself demoted so many times she finally ended up mopping floors, and she didn't do that very well either. Earl couldn't understand how she ever finished school and got the job in the first place.

As the SS Officers found more and more stupid things happening, Earl had the CASOs on the three ships set up refresher courses on everything, even though this was the responsibility of the VAAS. The CASOs were more than willing and more than competent. The two CASOs on British Commonwealth and South America had more than once proved their worth. They were remarkable. Any class these two taught had a waiting list. It had been a busy couple of years.

Now, ten years into the trip, a reasonable routine had settled in. Most of the crew, it seemed, had some realistic expectations and with that an understanding that they still had a long trip ahead of them. These people tried to make the best of it. The "secret"' of the barbecue incident on China and the new SS Officers helped with discipline, but still there were those that complained about everything putting a damper on morale. In the back of everyone's mind, of course, was that they were alone out in space and very much on their own. And while this was usually in the back of everyone's mind, it sometimes didn't take much for it rush right to the front. The CASOs worked hard to keep people busy, knowing that focus and busy hands would distract people from their precarious situation. It wasn't always enough, however.

For Wu, the weight of everything that was wrong was getting to him. Today, the weight was about to get heavier when Captain Jie and CASO Min came to see the Admiral with a new concern. "What's the problem this time?" Wu asked.

Jie said, "We're not exactly sure, but over the past couple of weeks, the animals have been acting strange. The service dogs in particular, especially the Labrador Retrievers. You know these guys are usually quite mellow, but they have become increasingly more agitated about something. This is most evident down on the lower decks. At the same time, we're receiving an intermittent signal from the hull integrity monitors indicating there may be a structural integrity issue. We can't pinpoint the location. In fact we're not sure it is one location."

Min added, "You know these ships are almost 100 years old. Do you think we might be approaching the end of the design life cycle of these things?"

"First off," said Wu, "I don't think there are any life cycle calculations on the ships. With most of hull material being carbon, I'm actually not aware of anyone ever considering anything like metal fatigue, but that doesn't mean it wasn't done or that it couldn't occur. It would be a little late to think about that right now, don't you think? Let's see if we can determine if there really is an issue and in the meantime, I'll ask British Commonwealth and South America if they are noticing anything odd."

"We already talked with Earl about this and he confirmed that British Commonwealth and South America aren't witnessing whatever is happening here."

"So what would be different over here?" And then, as if hit by an electric shock, Wu jumped to his feet and nearly yelled, "We have those little Mobile One guys on China and they thrive on carbon. I thought they were happy just 'breathing' our carbon dioxide, but maybe they find our hulls tasty." The room was silent for a minute or two before Wu continued with, "Get Kem over here and when he arrives get the bug ship crews in here. I want Kem to translate directly. The written word thing takes too long."

Within four hours' time all were in the Admiral's Conference Room. The Mobile Ones were surprised to be summoned by the Admiral, but, of course, no one could tell. With the Mobile Ones on the conference room table Wu wasted no time with pleasantries, "Have you guys been taking carbon from the ship's hull?"

After some back-and-forth creaking noises between Kem and the two bug ship Captains, Kem started to show concern. After more back-and-forth Kem said, "This is a rough translation but the answer is 'No, how stupid do you think we are? We wouldn't damage the one thing that keeps us safe! Maybe you should look to your own people.' And I won't repeat the derogatory remarks that went along with that answer."

Wu sat back in his chair with his hands folded and with his thumbs starting to rub his lower lip as he thought for minute. "Apologize to our little friends but I had to ask. Have them wait here and get our SS Officer in."

When SS Officer Stroud entered, Wu said, "Good morning officer Stroud. Thank you for coming, I'll get right to the heart of the matter. There is some concern that perhaps our ship's hull integrity might be becoming compromised. Any thoughts?"

Stroud looked at the Mobile Ones and said, "Am I to assume our little friends here are not the culprits?"

"Yes."

"Well then, no. I wasn't aware of any issue. But as I say that, I must note that one part of the ship I haven't been able to patrol is the Vice Admiral's lab."

Turning to Min, Wu asked, "I should have asked before. I don't suppose our VAAS has offered any thoughts, has she?"

"No" said Min. "Since she is supposed to be my boss, I did try to talk to her about my concerns, but all I got was 'I'm too busy, don't bother me.'"

This was Fang's usual response and as usual it really annoyed Wu. He decided it was time to get her to do her job and find out what was happening to the ship. And at the same time he needed to find out what the VAAS was actually doing with her time. If Fang was too busy to talk to her subordinates and too busy to talk to him, the work being done had better be important. Wu was fed up with her. It was time for a showdown.

Wu stormed into Fang's lab. As he entered, he had to admit that the lab set up in the cargo bays was impressive. The lab assistants all seemed to be busy doing something. All Wu knew was Fang's interest was in microbes, but what that meant had never been clear. He only had a general understanding of microbial diversity and with that limited knowledge he knew that microbes are everywhere. Some are good and absolutely essential, while others might have deadly consequences. Beyond that, he had only the vague understanding that Fang was on board to perhaps justify some aspect of the voyage but that it had little if anything to do with the actual mission of the starships.

The lab assistants noticed when Wu entered the lab, but kept working. Fang didn't seem to notice until Wu said, "So Fang, what are you doing exactly?"

With some irritation in her voice, Fang said, "You wouldn't understand. Why are you here?"

That typical response from this arrogant witch did not sit well with the Admiral and he let her know it. "First of all, I am your boss. If I don't know something, it is your responsibility to educate me if I ask. Directly related to that, if you were half as smart as you think you are, you would be able to tell me exactly what you are doing in lay-persons terms so I, or anyone else for that matter, would have a basic understanding. Secondly, you are not doing your job. You have relinquished responsibility to your staff. So, in order for me to justify in my own mind why you are here at all, I need a reason. Lastly, I have complete authority and if you piss me off, I can toss you into the brig for the rest of the trip and throw all this crap out into space. Am I making myself clear?" This was said loud enough that the dozen researchers and lab assistants in the room stopped what they were doing and watched the Admiral and VAAS.

Fang also stopped what she was doing, made a huge showing of a sigh, then looked at the Admiral and said, "We are manipulating a particular microbe so that it can more efficiently convert carbon into oxygen."

Wu went into panic mode as the puzzle pieces were coming together. "I pray to heaven you have this under control!"

Waving her hands as if this were nothing to be concerned Fang said, "Of course. What's the problem?"

"Did you forget our ships are made of carbon extracted from the oceans?"

Thinking for moment, Fang said, "Oh."

"What do you mean, 'Oh'?"

"Well, I actually didn't know what the ships were made of."

"I thought you were so smart that you knew everything. But apparently knowing anything relevant to your job or your surroundings is beneath you. So again, what does 'Oh' mean?"

Fang was now flustered and anything that resembled arrogance was gone. "I need to check something before I answer."

"You mean like now?"

"Umm, no, this will take a while."

The Admiral said, "It had better be a very little while," and left Fang's lab. As he contemplatively moved up to the bridge, he pondered the conversation he just had with the VAAS. The anxiety level increased with each step. His thoughts were all over the place. *What is that idiot doing? Who thought she was a good fit? Can I stop this before something happens? Is it too late? What can I do to put a check on this?* And with this last thought Wu had an answer. It was time to have a face-to-face with the three CASOs anyway, so he had Ere join the other two already on China for a breakfast meeting with the VAO and himself. He still didn't know the full story of Kem and Ere, but he knew they could eat, so plenty of food was set up in the Admiral's conference room.

"So, gentlemen and lady, I am a little in the dark on something and I need your collective wisdom to help me out. As we are aware, our Vice Admiral of Academics and Science has for all intents and purposes sequestered herself into her lab. Yesterday I was so bold as to ask her what she was working on. Did any of you know?"

Min said, "Well, as I said previously, I tried to talk to her but she was rather dismissive."

"Yes," said Wu, "But I got a little more information and now I have some concerns and that's where you all come in. She claims to be manipulating microbes that can convert carbon into oxygen more efficiently."

Earl seemed a bit puzzled when he said, "Convert carbon? Is that where the problem lies?"

"I'm not sure. It sure seems like it might be. I don't believe in coincidences so microbes that convert carbon to something else while we have a carbon-based ship that may be becoming compromised is certainly suspicious," said Wu. "But before I get all freaky about this, I want an independent review of what Fang is doing. She isn't going to like it, but I don't care and as I reminded her yesterday, I'm the boss. She is supposed to get back to me after checking something. I don't know what she's supposed to be checking, but so far I've heard nothing. Take with you whomever you need and go over that lab with a fine-toothed comb. Oh, Kem and Ere, you two seem to be able get people to open up to you, so make a point of interviewing all the techs. I'll tell the 'good' doctor Fang that she had better cooperate. It is time for a reckoning. Is the day after tomorrow too soon to get this done?" All the heads nodded and indicated agreement and all were dismissed after Kem and Ere each grabbed a couple more breakfast sandwiches.

When everyone had left, Wu poured himself a cup of tea and tried to get his emotions under control. *This is my fault*, he thought. *I should know everything that's going on in these ships.* He no sooner finished that thought when the ship seemed to scream in pain as it made a violent turn, tossing Wu and everything in the room to one wall. Then just as suddenly there was zero g force, indicating the ship propulsion had suddenly stopped. Somewhat dazed, Wu floated over to the door leading onto the bridge where the crew, also dazed, was trying to recover.

Wu's mind was fighting through confusion and he yelled, "Anyone know what happened?"

It took a full five minutes, an eternity it seemed, before the helmsman said, "We lost engine room pod #3 and the rest of the engines went automatically to idle mode."

"You mean engine 3 shut down?"

"No sir, it is gone."

Pushing himself over to the large portholes, Wu looked out and saw nothing but trailing cables where the engine room pod should have been. Off to the stern, Wu could see the pod perhaps a few miles behind where it suddenly exploded, sending another violent tremble through the ship. Wu, as well as everyone else on the bridge, was stunned.

Wu said to no one in particular, "There were forty people in that pod! Get me status reports as soon as you can."

Over the next hour status reports were brought to the Admiral. The CASOs from the other ships were still on board so they came back to the admiral's conference room. What they had to say was mind-boggling.

Sister ships British Commonwealth and South America were well out of sight before they understood what had happened. Both were calculating how best to rejoin with China. This would take some time.

The personnel tube that connected the engine room pod to the main hull had broken off at the hull and the area bulkhead doors had closed automatically. Still, another four people had been swept into space.

The operating engineering supervisor on the bridge was trying to rotate another engine pod into position so that symmetry could be regained for propulsion. Captain Jie reported to the Admiral, "We can't rotate any of the engine room pods. When number 3 broke loose it took a big piece of the slip rings with it. The best we can do is idle down number 1 and with 2 and 4 opposite each other we'll have some balance and control. The engineers are checking for damage and prepping for a startup, but a restart will take some time."

Wu made it clear he didn't want propulsion to start until there was some understanding of what was going on. With that order placed, the Admiral left Captain Jie and VAO Null in charge of operations while he turned his attention to the cause.

I have a bad feeling about this, Wu thought. *Losing an entire engine room pod like that seems like it could be a systemic issue. This doesn't feel like a one-off problem. And I'd be willing to bet our Vice Admiral Fang is responsible.* Then, he thought, *and that, unfortunately, is one bet I'd likely win!*

Two days later the ship was moving again and the senior staff was back in the Admiral's conference room. This time Fang was there as well, but she was uncharacteristically contrite in appearance.

Earl looked at Fang and said, "Do you want to tell him?"

Fang gave a quiet, "No. You tell him."

The Admiral took this as confirmation of what he had already concluded, and he was right.

Earl said, "Our friend here, has in fact, developed a microbe that attacks carbon and converts it into something else. Maybe oxygen, but right now, that doesn't matter. What does matter is that some microbes have mutated beyond what Fang intended and have made their way outside of a controlled environment. Some of the lab assistants had casually observed that some of the partitions, made with the same carbon material as the hulls by the way, had a powdery layer on them. They brought this to Fang's attention, but it was casually brushed off as inferior material. A closer look under a microscope, however, is showing microbial activity."

After a silent moment as this information sunk in, Wu said, "There is more, isn't there."

"Oh yes Admiral, you are correct," said Earl. "Fang's pet microbes did escape from the lab and they are now slowly converting our ship into oxygen as they eat away at it. That was what the hull integrity monitors were trying to tell us and why Engine room pod 3 broke away. It was because of the loss of structural integrity. It won't be long before we will have a holey ship, and I don't mean in the religious sense."

Ying looked squarely at Fang and said, "How long do we have?"

Fang answered, "How would I know?"

Furious, Wu yelled, "Because those damned microbes and anything they do are your responsibility. So if you don't know, you damned well better figure it out." Turning to Earl, Wu continued, "In the meantime I want everything in that lab sealed up and then ejected into space. That includes any partitions that even might have been attacked. No exceptions."

This got Fang's attention. "You can't do that. That's years of research. We're on the verge of a major breakthrough."

"That's a poor choice of words since it is your damned microbes that are breaking through the hull. Tell you what," said Wu, "We'll eject you with the lab through the next 'breakthrough' in the hull so you can continue your experiments."

"No," said Fang, and even more contritely added, "I'll just gather up our notes and computers."

Ere looked at Kem and both winced when Wu said. "Everything is to go. I mean everything including the clothes you wear and anything that might have made it into anyone's quarters. Got it? Earl, get started on this right away. Bring a couple of Marines with you. If you get any grief from anyone, have the Marines toss them into the brig. Fang is to be confined to quarters for now."

Admiral Wu and Vice Admiral Null knew this wasn't the end of it, but they were hoping to buy a little time so they could rejoin the other two ships that were now far ahead.

Over the next several months the powdery material first seen on the partitions was now starting to show up everywhere. By ejecting the worst of the interior partitions they hoped to buy some time. The hull was thick, but it was obvious that it was only a matter of time before the hull would be breached. When asked, Fang finally admitted she didn't know how to stop the spread. Controlling the microbes had never been a consideration.

Wu informed the other ships what was happening to China and ordered them to continue under the least possible acceleration; just enough to keep everything from floating around. He ordered slightly more acceleration, pushing the two operating China engines to their limits, so the ship could eventually catch up and a course was plotted. Five months later China caught up to British Commonwealth and South America.

With some creative engineering, China was able to get four engine pods symmetrically arranged and the three ships continued towards Earth. Anyone unfamiliar with the ships who looked at the fleet from a distance might not have noticed any changes in behavior. Inside, however, there was frantic activity. Over the next nineteen months after the first discovery of this destructive microbe, Wu implemented a gradual abandonment of the ship. Before the microbes reached the shuttle bay areas, Wu wanted everyone off to either British Commonwealth or South America. Deck by deck people were shuttled to the other ships.

Every effort was made to isolate the microbe to China so very little was allowed to leave the ship. Only two China shuttles were transferred as there was room for only one more shuttle on each ship.

Admiral Wu sent his final message to the UNSC headquarters from the bridge of China. The final shuttle trip was ready to take him, the Captain, CASO, and Fang over to British Commonwealth. Fang didn't report to the shuttle bay. Instead, via intercom, she told Wu that she was staying behind. The humiliation she was experiencing was more than she could tolerate. There were already breaches in the hull on the lower decks and it wouldn't be long before the engine room pods would be compromised. Fang would stay, stop propulsion and set the self-destruct sequence when the other ships were far away.

Wu agreed.

To the Mobile Ones, first accused of causing the problem, the microbe disaster was both frightening and fascinating. Frightening at first because Admiral Wu had falsely assumed the Mobile Ones were responsible and then even more frightening when they understood the human ship was being compromised. There wasn't much in the way of microbes on TCe, so that alone was interesting, but when the microbes were starting to eat Star Ship China, the Mobile Ones weren't sure what to make of it. It was with a great sense of morbid curiosity China was abandoned and the crew was relocated to the other two ships. There was concern that it might happen again, and the Mobile Ones were truly fascinated with the concept that one human, or a small group of them, could act so independently of the others. On TCe, all the Tall Ones think as one and constantly share virtually every thought with the Mobile Ones, so nothing like this autonomous activity would ever occur. It was fascinating.

It was also curious why any creature would want to convert carbon into oxygen. On TCe, oxygen was the problem, so why make more of the stuff? It was the carbon the Mobile Ones needed and they were more than happy to enjoy the relatively rich CO_2 content of the ships' atmosphere. They didn't need to eat the ship and were certainly smart enough not to eat something they needed for survival. They were insulted when it was suggested that they had created the problem. Adding to this, the Mobile Ones were confused when it become known that it was the humans themselves that had created the problem. Why would these humans make something that could destroy the same ships they needed for survival? Perhaps these humans weren't that smart after all. As hard as the Mobile Ones tried to gain a better understanding of the China destruction, there was no aspect of that disaster they could comprehend.

Chapter 26

Vocations

Orion and Perseus were making good progress to the Alpha Centauri system and were at the midway point in 2161. With the smaller crews there was more to do but very few complained. The kitchen staff seemed to be outdoing themselves and the Head Bar Tenders were producing some very fine beverages. Some crewmembers had started preparing for the journey's end by shifting into construction mode and practicing equipment operations on the simulators.

Astron, now twenty-five years old, had been assigned to engineering and had completed courses in mechanical engineering. It all seemed to come naturally to him. He was an excellent systems operator, instinctively knowing what to do at precisely the right time and performing flawlessly, but at the same time he had difficulty fitting in with the rest of the engineering staff. He seldom smiled, seldom entered into any conversation, and with his now fully developed size was a bit intimidating. Astron was six feet four inches tall and weighed in at 234 pounds. He did work out, a little— very little—but that could not account for his massive muscle tone and his huge appetite. No one in engineering knew about his father, so they all simply thought he was a freak of nature.

It wasn't that he didn't like the people he was working with. It was the fact he didn't want to be an engineer. He liked drawing, but also found a new interest that seemed to suit his nature. When off duty, he could usually be found with Celeste or he was down in the animal hospital. The service dogs, canaries, and even the tilapia fish farms needed attention. But it was the dogs that got Astron's attention, and it didn't go unnoticed by the veterinarians that the dogs always seemed to be happiest when he was around. He loved the dogs and often helped with their care.

Astron was considered part of Katherine's family so he was often at the dinner table when they were all able to eat together. One night, or more correctly, during the designated night shift, Astron said, "Can I ask something?"

"Certainly," said Katherine. "What's on the your mind?"

"Well, umm, I'm not sure you'll be happy with this, but I want to be a veterinarian."

Celeste just looked at her plate, but Dakota and Katherine looked at each other in surprise. Katherine said, "I thought you liked engineering. You're very good at it."

"I know, but I'm not really happy there. I like the dogs and they like me. They aren't judgmental, and this might sound odd, but I know what they are thinking and I can communicate with them. It just feels right."

There was silence for a few minutes before Dakota said, "Knowing what your father was capable of doing, I guess I'm not surprised that you have some unique abilities. I wouldn't have guessed this one though."

Katherine said, "Astron, we need you in engineering, but if you want to pursue your new passion that is more than fine. If this turns out to be an avocation rather than a vocation, nothing is lost. It would be interesting to know if you have this ability to communicate with critters other than dogs."

"I can talk with the parrots!" said a smiling Astron.

"Yeah, well, I can too," said Dakota laughing. "When Polly wants a cracker, I give it to her."

"Okay then," said Katherine, "I'll set this up with Harlyn tomorrow, but this will be in your spare time when not on the engineering shift. Got it?"

"Thank you," said an animated Astron.

"One other thing though," said Dakota, "What about your drawing? Are you giving that up?"

"No. I still draw. I like lots of things."

"Yes, I guess you do." Then before Katherine could stop him, Dakota added to the embarrassment of Astron and Celeste, "Including Celeste maybe?"

Celeste hadn't said much all through dinner, but now turned red and shouted, "Dad! Really?"

Dakota laughed, and Celeste went back to playing with her food.

Suspiciously Katherine looked over at the now very quiet Celeste. "You're unusually quiet."

"I've been thinking."

"Uh oh," said Dakota, "That's never a good sign."

"Very funny, Dad. I want to be serious."

"Oh dear," said Katherine. "What's on your mind?"

"Well, while Astron wants to get away from engineering, I want more."

"But you're already taking advanced science classes" said Katherine. "You don't like that?"

"I do, but when I was working with Dad on the old car, I really liked it. I actually want to design things, make them and then put them together."

"You've lost me," said Dakota.

"I want to take some shop classes. I want to be a machinist and an engineer—a mechanical engineer. The advance science classes I've taken will help, sorta, maybe."

Katherine scowled at Dakota. "This is your fault. You're the one having her up to her elbows in grease and oil with wrenches and screwdrivers." Dakota squirmed.

Turning to Celeste Katherine said, "Seriously honey, if that's what you think you want to do, it's fine with me, but your father is grounded. He's not allowed to leave the ship for at least a year." With that said, Katherine and Dakota couldn't help but notice Celeste and Astron were beaming at each other across the dining table. This was anything but a spur of the moment conversation on their part.

Katherine, pondering this vocation discussion, decided she was going to talk with Uri to try and get a better understanding of the Astron's abilities, especially the ability to relate to different species. *Is this ability something Order members have?* The answer, she would learn, was "no." Uri's people had the ability to communicate with any being that had a high level of self-awareness by intuitively understanding language meaning. But Uri had no idea of what Astron was claiming with respect to the dogs, or even what to think. Uri would send a message to Gabe to see if he might be able to shed some light.

Chapter 27

Arrival (2165)

The new design for the starships was greatly appreciated by those on board. The turns going from acceleration to deceleration and back again were so much smoother with the orb-shaped center sections of the ships rotating to help compensate for the centrifugal force during the turns. This, combined with some heavy calculations for each cycle, sped up the trip even more.

On November 4th, 2165 Orion and Perseus went into orbit around Proxima Centauri b. Katherine had reports from Captain Renaldo that there were indications of life forms on the planet so Katherine was anxious to get a better understanding what that might mean. Certainly the planet looked great. It seemed very Earth-like, as had been predicted, but these predictions didn't extend to what kind of life might be on the surface. Based on what the UNSC expeditions had found on other planets, Katherine wasn't going to get too optimistic. Not yet anyway. Still, it would be a shame just to turn around and return to Earth.

Standard protocol was implemented, with the shuttles flying surveillance over the planet at increasingly lower altitudes. If there was a sophisticated society on the planet, they should notice the shuttles, and if they were hostile or overly protective, some sort of interception might result. There were none.

Early reports were interesting. There was definitely a diversity of life on the planet. Some land animals were seen and some were huge, bear-sized critters. They seemed to be just about everywhere, but not in any dense concentrations. But what really got the scientists' attention were some smaller animals and birds that looked like Earth species. How could that be?

Katherine and Harlyn knew that Uri, as a member of the Order, had some special knowledge of things so she asked him to come to her conference room. "Uri, the surveys are showing some rather peculiar results. Among other things, the scientists think there are mammals and birds that seem to be the same as what we have on Earth."

Uri said, "Interesting."

"Is 'interesting' all you have to say?"

"For now. Complete your surveys, but before there is a landing we will need to talk. I predict you'll be finding something even more interesting."

"I thought you were here to help. That isn't much help. In fact you are not helping at all. You are just adding to the mystery."

"I know," said Uri, "But I have my instructions. Trust me when I tell you that much will be revealed in due course."

Katherine sat back in her chair with her fingers laced and looked at Uri for a few minutes before saying, "There is something going on with your so-called Order. I was led to believe from Admiral Dodson that there is a handful of your kind and that occasionally someone in your Order would provide some advice to help us get past some major issue. From my experience since we set up shop on TCe, more of you are joining right in and becoming much more proactive when something comes up. I know you, and I mean the Order, was responsible for locating Lehtolarite, getting these two new ships built, getting the UAN back on track and I suspect a bunch more. Now I know that somehow you know something about this planet. But you're not going to tell me."

"Maybe." said a smiling Uri. "If I knew something that I thought you needed to know now, I would tell you."

"So which is it, if you *knew* something you'd tell me, or is it you know something but won't tell me because I don't I *need* to know?"

"Yes."

"Okay, wiseass, you can leave now." And Uri left with the Admiral thinking, *He is being really weird; more so than usual.*

Eight days later Katherine was on the bridge when Harlyn said, "Admiral, I think you need to see this."

As Katherine approached and looked down at a monitor, she asked, "So what am I looking at?"

"What we are looking at is coming from Orion shuttle 2. We actually just found two things. Look over here. We think that round thing is some kind of ship."

"Wow, you're right. It looks like one of those fuzzy shots of what was supposed to be proof of flying saucers in the 1900s."

"I agree," said Harlyn, "But wait until you see this."

Katherine looked closely as the shuttle made multiple passes over the next valley and finally said, "That looks like people down there. Like us!"

"Yes, it does. We haven't seen anything like this anywhere else yet. Just here."

Katherine looked up and stared at Harlyn. She then said, loudly, "Did you just agree with me? Those are people down there? How did they get there?"

"Umm, I have no idea. Maybe that flying saucer thing?"

Katherine said, "A flying saucer? Yeah, right." Then after a pause said, "Is there a town or something?"

"We saw some fields and these few people. We didn't see anything indicating technology, so I'm guessing none of these people, if that is what they are, flew any flying saucer here. It is difficult to tell from the flyovers."

"Cool it on the flying saucer already. At least until we look at it. Did you see anyone near the saucer?"

"Nope. And we flew a shuttle over it few times thinking someone or something might emerge. But nothing."

Katherine asked, "What about that village or commune or whatever it is. Did they see our shuttle?"

"They must have."

Katherine was about to ask some more questions, but stopped and instead thought, *I'll bet that Uri knew about this. He's getting to be really annoying.* But she simply said, "Get Uri in here."

By the time Uri got to the bridge, Katherine had worked herself into a boiling caldron of indignation and let it loose. "Uri, you better tell me what is going on. First we saw wildlife that should only be on Earth, then we see what looks like a flying saucer, and now we see people down there. Or are they something else? I want straight, no BS, answers and I want them now."

Uri glanced around the bridge. Everyone was looking at Katherine and him. No one recalled ever seeing the Admiral this angry. Uri said, "Here?"

"Right here, right now!"

Uri took a deep breath and looking down at Katherine, who seemed to be looming over everyone, and said, "Those are people. Their ancestors were brought here in the 1970s by a group in our Order that defied all of our rules."

With the entire crew on the bridge staring with their mouths open, Katherine said, "What? Why? In that ship?"

"Some thought that life on Earth was doomed from what appeared to be the coming of a nuclear holocaust. 400 people were brought here as a safe haven with the notion of saving some of humanity."

Katherine wasn't sure what to say but managed to get out, "This is unbelievable. Not just from the standpoint of how you got them here, but that your people would do something like this. This is outrageous. I need to think about this before we do anything."

"Umm," said Uri, "There is a tad bit more information you need to have while your thinking. These people have no memory of Earth. They have no known history prior to their ancestor's arrival. When it was becoming apparent the Earth ships were going to come here, an advance team was sent out to prepare these people for your arrival. It had been assumed that all five star ships would leave Earth together. Obviously, the plan changed, but this is probably for the best—having two ships as an advance group."

Then with a big sigh, he went on with, "We, meaning my people, aren't sure what happened, but communications with this advance team stopped suddenly. I believe that ship you found outside the valley was their ship. There were seven on board and now I am thinking they were lost somehow early on otherwise I think we'd see more advancements down there and there would have been some contact. I suppose my people could have just joined, but it is doubtful. The instructions to the team were to prepare that group down there for your arrival, but I honestly don't know how far they got. I assume you'll be going down to meet them. I don't know what their reaction will be when they meet you. I certainly don't know what you should expect either."

The stunned look from everyone on the bridge told Uri he needed to stop talking for now, so he just said, "There is more, but it should wait until you have considered this part."

Chapter 28

Tandoo Encounter

Katherine had too many things to consider; too many only because there seemed to be conflicts. It was gradually becoming clear Uri wanted a happy ending, but was also either reluctant to tell Katherine everything or really didn't know. Katherine decided she would do what she thought would be the right thing to do and if Uri had other ideas, he would tell her. At least she hoped Uri would tell her.

Putting the local human population aside for a little while would allow her to sleep on the idea of how to approach them. In the meantime she decided that one shuttle under Anna Giblin's supervision should continue to fly over the valley and learn as much as possible. Four shuttles were to survey for an ideal wormhole gate location. That was, after all, their official assigned mission. With the equipment and supplies on board, it was thought she could find the ideal location and get construction well under way before the other three ships showed up with the rest of what would be needed. This was supposed to be a more relaxed way to get to the end product, a new Gate, on line. Katherine didn't feel very relaxed, however.

The sixth shuttle would be used for still another distraction from the issue of the local population. A landing party with Katherine, Uri, Harlyn, and six marines would examine the Order's seemingly abandoned ship. Uri had expressed deep concern for the fate of his friend Evan and her companions and wanted to get to their ship as soon as possible to try and get some answers.

The shuttle landed 100 meters from the ship, which, Katherine admitted, looked a lot like a saucer—a flying saucer. The saucer's deployed ramp and open hatch looked ominous. There was no sign of life, not even footprints coming or going in the considerable dust and dirt on the ramp. Uri said, "I don't have a good feeling about this," as they cautiously walked up the ramp. Katherine was glad she had the foresight to include a few Marines in the landing party. Two remained with the shuttle and pilot. Two were left at the foot of the saucer ramp, and two were with her, Uri, and Harlyn. All had their weapons at the ready. As the five went up into the ship it became obvious there had been a struggle of some kind in the past. While the ship looked like it could function, there were loose items scattered around, obviously out of place, and there was some ripped white cloth with dark red stains. Uri silently looked around then said, "I need to leave. I'll come back later."

Katherine, Harlyn and the two Marines probed around the ship, being careful not to push any buttons or pull any levers. When they entered the stasis chamber room, Katherine knew immediately what it was. She had seen the stasis chamber on British Commonwealth that Raman had been in when he was rescued back in 2113. The six in this room were just like that. In other parts of the ship the controls and the mechanics that could make the ship operative were unfamiliar to Katherine, but it seemed obvious in general terms what their purpose might be. But she smiled to herself as she certainly knew she wasn't going to fool herself into thinking she could fly the thing.

Over the next hour or so, while Katherine and her party were poking around, Uri remained outside with the other two Marines. Suddenly with no warning, Katherine's survey quickly ended when they all heard shots from outside. She looked at her three companions and the four of them ran to the boarding ramp. Once outside she saw Uri trying to communicate with huge animals. Apparently the two outside Marines had fired warning shots to get the attention of these intruders; five of them. They looked to be about eleven or twelve feet tall standing on their two hind legs. They were covered with a kind of black and brown fur and looked like they weighed over 600 pounds each. Their eyes were huge red orbs. Their front legs, or arms, or whatever, were massive, with what looked like three fingers and two thumbs for lack of any other description. Displaying some sharp-looking teeth, these creatures were quite scary.

From the look on Uri's face, attempted communications weren't going well. Everyone that knew anything about the Order members knew they could communicate with any intelligent species. It wasn't that they knew every language; it was the ability to understand the means of communication, such as words, as something connected to an individual's mind. Uri was no different. With just a few sounds, like words, Uri could "learn" the language.

The key to this kind of communication was interacting with an "intelligent species" and in this case that was a problem. When Katherine came out of the ship, Uri said, "These creatures are dumber than dirt. They make a Labrador Retriever look like Einstein in comparison. I think the only reason they have survived as a species is that they are bigger than anything else that might be around. Anything smaller is considered food to them. Word got out, and I'm being generous with the use of 'word' here, that we were here and these five decided to help themselves to a free lunch. The Marines firing startled them, but I think they'll recover."

And just as Uri was saying that, two of the creatures lumbered toward the landing party. The two Marines that were with Uri asked, "What shall we do?"

Katherine said, "Shoot to wound."

The two creatures were each shot once. One was hit in the leg and the other in the shoulder. Both started to bleed a purple substance. They stopped for a minute as they looked at the wounds as if they were bug bites. They then started forward again, but this time, the four Marines let them have it and they dropped. The other creatures turned and lumbered off.

Marine Sergeant Green said, "That was unfortunate, but I think we all know what happened here before and we weren't about to allow a repeat performance. Not on my watch anyway."

"Thank you Sergeant," said Katherine. "I don't see that you had much of a choice." Then turning to Uri she said, "Can you close up the ship? I want to leave now and see where these creatures are going. We'll leave the bodies alone. Maybe their buddies will come back for them."

The Marines at the shuttle had seen the action at the saucer and were on high alert when the landing party made it back. The pilot needed no prompting to take off and did so before everyone was seated, to the annoyance of the passengers. When airborne, they followed the creatures into a hilly wooded area where sight of them was lost. Later on, they would learn that the creatures were called "tandoo" in both the singular and the plural.

Chapter 29

Gadan

Back on board Orion, Katherine was considering the encounter with the tandoo. She was curious how the human commune had been able to survive. The best way to understand that interaction, she decided, was to go to the source, which she would do shortly.

As a whole, the planet itself looked wonderful. It was so much like Earth once was; lush greenery, clear waters, and clean air. According to Uri, that was why people had been brought here in the first place. It had seemed so ideal that this fellow Tam-I-El who brought them here had called it the Garden of Eden.

Certainly first impressions were playing a lot on Katherine's mind and these first impressions indicated strongly that the goal should be having minimal impact on this planet. It seemed that even though this Tam-I-El and his gang had introduced several kinds of non-indigenous species, the impact thus far seemed limited. But a whole new wave of people following the construction of a town and wormhole gate could be devastating if not done properly. *Whatever that is*, thought Katherine.

It didn't escape her that there was, in fact, indigenous life here that needed to be protected both during Gate construction and later from the possibility of too many people moving in from Earth scouring the landscape for resources. *Though*, she mused, *those big furry creatures we ran into might be an exception. This was going to take a lot of thought and careful planning. Anna and her staff are going to have a lot of work ahead of them.*

On the planet's surface, Minda was on patrol, once again enjoying the natural world around her. A sound caught her attention, one that was almost familiar, but not. She slowly pulled an arrow from her basket and loaded it in her bow, ready to pull back and let it fly if necessary. The sound was from overhead and as she looked up she saw what looked like some kind of silver bird. But this bird was making a thunderous sound and leaving some kind of trail behind as it moved. Minda watched, fascinated, until it disappeared from sight. Soon, however, the bird returned but it seemed to be a little bigger. This was very odd.

When she returned to the commune center, everyone was talking about this strange bird and asked Minda what she thought. "Why are you asking me?"

"You are the Protector leader. It is big. Is it dangerous?"

Minda had never been in a position like this so said, "What do the elders say?"

"They say 'ask Minda.'"

Great, thought Minda. *Because I said something before I ended up as the Protector leader. Now I'm supposed to know everything.* She thought for a minute and then, remembering what had been said about a reunion twelve seasons previously, got uncharacteristically flippant and said, "Oh it must be the ones that will bring us back." If she only knew how close she had come to the truth.

"Oh," was the response. "The time has come?"

Now irritated, Minda said, "I don't know! I just made that up."

On Orion, however, Katherine was actually thinking about a reunion. Uri had filled in Katherine on as much as he could about the origins of the commune. Without providing any explanation of how he knew some of these details, he told Katherine about the Gadan society and even how they came to be calling the center of the valley where they spent most of their time by the name Gadan.

Uri told Katherine that since each person originally brought to the planet spoke a different language, they developed their own with a mixture of words from each society. They had been told they were in the Garden of Eden, which of course meant absolutely nothing to them since their memories had been erased. In a relatively short time, "Garden of Eden" morphed into "Gadan." Gadan then became their name for home, or where they lived as a group. Getting beyond the reason they were there, Katherine could only think, *What an experience for these people. Literally starting with only new memories and they don't even know it. Wow!*

Katherine called a senior staff meeting. "We will introduce ourselves to the locals tomorrow." Filling the staff in on what Uri had said, Katherine went on, saying, "When our people first went beyond our solar system to Epsilon Eridani we found a civilization that was very different than ours. When we went to Tau Ceti we found intelligent life that no one could have imagined, except maybe in a science fiction novel. And we found a second planet there that could be considered perfect except no one can leave. I'm only saying this because even though we now understand that what we have below is a society of fellow humans, we have no idea how we will be received. I am hoping for the best outcome, but we must prepare for the unexpected.

"At this point, they must have noticed our shuttles flying overhead, and maybe even our two ships in orbit. While that might generate curiosity, it will be nothing compared to our entrance. So we will land at the far end of the valley. The shuttle pilot will stay with the ship with some armed Marines. Uri, Harlyn, and I with two additional Marines will walk to the concentration of caves that they seem to use as homes. From that point on, I have no idea what will happen. I'm a bit nervous about this.

"Anna, while we're introducing ourselves to these Gadans, I'd like you to stay near the shuttle and gather samples of whatever might be in the area. But—and this is a big one—isolate everything you gather to eliminate any possibility of contamination. We don't want another TCf type incident."

The next day, Katherine and her landing party went down to the surface. From an environmental standpoint there were no surprises. Her previous landing to scout out the Order's saucer found the environment to be quite nice and so far, Anna hadn't found anything to be worried about. Still the order of the day was, "Proceed with caution." The landing party couldn't help but enjoy the fresh air, especially after breathing recycled air for the last few years. The temperature was hovering around 20 degree Celsius, so only a standard lightweight uniform was necessary. The sun was shining and the birds were chirping, so she supposed this could easily be considered the Garden of Eden. They walked for about an hour and never saw another soul until they entered the clearing where most of the activities of the commune were carried out.

About a dozen Gadans saw Katherine and her party all at once. As Katherine and her party stood still, these Gadans were joined by others, and as a group, the Gadans slowly moved towards the strangers. The Gadans were nearly all dressed in sort of dark brown cloth shorts and what looked like a vest with a single cinch above the waist. All were very handsome people, and their dress was especially fetching on the women. A few Gadans wore a kind of footgear that was apparently made from a large and very thick leaf laced with the thin vines that seemed to be used for everything. This was obviously warm-weather attire and Katherine's party wondered about what people wore in the colder seasons. Cleanliness was obvious, except for the people that had been working the crops who displayed appropriately dirty hands and knees. Everyone's hair was the same length, short of the shoulder, and was unexpectedly combed, but with what wasn't evident.

Later when the seasons changed, the question of winter wear was answered. Footwear was enhanced with layers of cloth wrapped between the "leaf" shoes and feet. Shorts and vests were added to in layers, but as the weather got even colder, more time was spent in the shelter of the caves. Fires that burned continuously out-of-doors in the warm seasons were moved to the mouths of some of the caves. One very large cave had a natural opening in the roof deep inside and it was here that one fire was always kept burning and most food for the compound was cooked. Even deeper in the cave was where much of the food grown and collected during the warm months was kept. It was natural refrigeration, though the Gadans had no real concept of refrigeration. They just knew it kept food from spoiling.

If there wasn't the natural need to relieve themselves, the Gadans likely would have stayed in the caves throughout the cold seasons, but nature calls did force them outside where the Gadans had prepared rotating designated areas for "relief." Interestingly, they had learned, or had been taught by Tam's people, to allow the waste to compost and then be recycled into garden areas as fertilizer. They seemed to have relearned Earth's early techniques for soil enhancement.

There were a couple of women wearing the same style clothing, but made of some kind of leather. These women were carrying very long bows and looked like they could break a tree in half with their bare hands. They projected quite the image. If the Marines hadn't been with her, Katherine might have been intimidated.

To break the silence, Katherine said something completely dorky she had heard in a movie someplace, but it somehow seemed appropriate. "Greetings from planet Earth. We come in peace. I am Admiral Katherine Hickey."

One very attractive woman with a big bow came right up to Katherine and spoke. Katherine heard a few words that sounded like French, Spanish, Chinese, and even English. In total it made no sense, which wasn't unexpected based on what Uri had told her. Uri translated Katherine's greeting and the response saying, "This women is called Minda. She is the head of the Protectors. She wants to know if we are the people that will take them back."

"Take them back?" asked Katherine. "Back where?"

"They have only the stories about large people bringing their ancestors here many seasons ago and they believe that someday, they will be brought back from where they came. It is supposed to be a better place than here, where they don't get eaten and they don't have to work. I think it is safe to say, they are referring to Earth."

Katherine said to Uri, "Didn't you tell me your so-called advance group in the saucer was supposed to prepare these people?"

"I'm only guessing, but maybe they didn't get far along with the mission before…" and Uri's voice trailed off.

"You said these people are eaten?" Katherine said with shock. Then said, "You didn't get all that from those few words."

"Well, no, not exactly. The creatures we saw at the saucer are called tandoo. They are the ones that come and take people away and…" and again Uri's voice trailed off.

"Hmmm. Just tell this woman, what did you call her, Minda? Well tell her 'maybe.' And maybe others will be coming here."

Uri said so, and everyone around became animated. As people settled down, Minda moved closer to Katherine, stared down at her, and through Uri, asked, "Do you want to have some food?"

That was a relief, so Katherine said, "Yes."

It soon became obvious that the guns the Marines held were a major source of curiosity for the Gadans. The Marines never put the guns down, instead ate with one hand. To the Gadans the guns seemed to serve no purpose, but they were obviously quite important to these two strangers.

The food set before them was amazing. Vegetables, fruits, and nuts of all kinds prepared in numerous ways; baked, boiled, and roasted. There were even some kinds of breads. Many of the vegetables weren't recognizable to Katherine so she assumed they must be indigenous. Others were very familiar, like beans and squash.

When she tasted the beverage served to her in a gourd-turned-cup, she had to laugh—and did so to the delight of the Gadans in attendance. Apparently humans everywhere figured out how to make an alcoholic beverage. Katherine didn't know what she was drinking, but it was good and it definitely had a kick to it. As she dined and drank her drink, she wondered, *What am I do to with these people?*

Chapter 30

Demonstrations

The feast shared with Katherine and her small entourage seemed to make any feelings of trepidation disappear. All were enjoying the beverages and were feeling rather mellow. There wasn't much talk as the Gadans were expecting more to be shared from the strangers. Katherine's people, on the other hand, weren't sure what they should be sharing. Finally, it was one of the Marines that broke the ice. Sergeant Green slung his gun over his shoulder and slowly gestured to Minda indicating that he would like to touch her bow. Minda looked at him, then her bow, then back at the Marine. With some apparent reluctance, she handed him her bow. The sergeant next smiled and indicated he'd like an arrow while he pointed to a tree that was probably a hundred feet away. Minda obliged.

Sergeant Green was no weakling, but he struggled to pull the cord back. When he did and let the arrow fly, it fell short of the tree. Everyone laughed, including the luckless Marine.

Minda took the obvious challenge, loaded an arrow, pulled back as if it were nothing and let loose. The arrow didn't just make it to the tree; it hit dead center in the trunk and the penetration was impressive.

Katherine looked at the sergeant and said, "Were you trying to make Minda look good? If so, you succeeded."

"Trust me when I say, that bow is powerful. All I can think of is the old English long bowmen that could strike fear in any enemy they faced. The draw weight of that thing has to be close to 150 pounds. These women with the bows are for real. I am impressed and embarrassed at the same time."

But Minda had more in mind. She said something to one of the other women with a bow. This woman grabbed an uncooked squash, walked 100 feet away, and tossed the squash into the air. Before anyone realized what was happening, Minda let loose an arrow that went through the squash as it was falling back down.

The sergeant was feeling somewhat insulted now, and wanting to redeem himself said, "Admiral, would you permit me to fire off one round with the gun? They are obviously curious about these weapons."

Katherine considered this for a minute and almost said, "Go ahead," but changed her mind and said instead, "No. I don't think that's a good idea right now; maybe some other time. I do have another thought."

"Yes ma'am."

The Gadans used fire to cook their food, but Katherine wondered how they got one started. It must be a chore. From what she could tell from the pile of ashes under the fire, once a fire was started, it might be moved to other locations, but efforts were made to keep at least one fire always going—a perpetual flame. With that in mind, she said to her downcast Marine, "Do you have any matches on you?"

"Yes ma'am. Why?"

Then smiling at the sergeant said, "So why do you have matches? Never mind. Gather some material together and light a fire. I want to see the Gadans' reaction."

With much curiosity, the Gadans watched the sergeant gather up some dried leaves and twigs and formed a little pile in the form of a miniature teepee. When done, he motioned people to gather in a circle around this little structure. The Gadans seemed to think this Marine was performing some kind of ceremony. In a way he was.

With exaggerated movement, he slowly pulled out his book of matches, broke off one match and showed it to the circle of people. Then he struck the match and lit the fire. The reaction was one of disbelief. Minda, always the brave one, asked, "How do you do that?"

Sergeant Green, feeling somewhat vindicated now, showed Minda the matchbook, broke off another match, and showed her how to scratch the "red" part against the "black" part, which she did. The match lit and she immediately dropped it to the ground. She stared at it until it went out and then tried to force the matchbook back to Sergeant Green. He closed her hand over the book and through Uri said, "It is a gift to you."

Harlyn had noticed that food was prepared using a sharp stone for cutting and from this he saw an opportunity. Carrying a pocketknife was a habit he had from when he was a teenager. The beverages he was drinking made him feel very generous, so he took the knife from his pocket and showed it the man that appeared to be the most senior member of the group. Harlyn opened the knife and cut one of the uncooked squash with it, impressing the senior Gadan. Harlyn touched the blade indicating it was very sharp, and then he folded it back up and gave it the Gadan who smiled at Harlyn appreciably.

"Okay," said Katherine. "No more gift giving today. Uri, tell our hosts that we will return very soon, but that we need to leave now." And they stood as one and walked back along the trail that had led them to the commune.

What Katherine didn't know was that Minda had followed them quietly and undetected. Minda watched the strangers enter a shiny structure. When it lifted off the ground she realized it was the silver bird that had been flying over the commune. *Surely*, she thought, *these are the ones to bring the Gadans back.*

Chapter 31

Issues (2166)

Once again back on board Orion, Katherine met with Harlyn and Anna, but not Uri. Katherine realized there were more issues than they had initially considered. When they were getting ready to leave Earth, the plan was simple. Go to this planet, find a place to build a wormhole gate, start construction, and when the other ships showed up, finish the Gate and start moving some people in! Nothing to it!

But Uri had laid out a bizarre scenario of people being abducted and taken to this planet many years ago. He assured her it was true. "However," he had said, "These people were left in a primitive state and the subsequent generations haven't progressed very far." It didn't take a genius to realize this was an issue with no clear resolution.

The more Katherine was learning about the planet, the more issues were presenting themselves. While she shared many of her thoughts with Dakota, he was focusing on the potential Gate location so he wasn't in this meeting. Uri only wanted to discuss the Gadans, so for this meeting he wasn't included. It was just Katherine, Harlyn, and Anna.

Katherine started the conversation with, "Our mission in the broadest of terms was to establish a construction site and start construction of the Gate. It doesn't seem that simple anymore."

"Agreed," said Anna. "Everything I have seen of this planet so far tells me it is very special. In good conscience, we shouldn't allow it to be ruined. By the way, what are we calling the planet? It seems like it should be called something other than 'the planet.'"

Harlyn said, "How about Sanctum, meaning temple or retreat? Seems kinda appropriate to me."

"Okay," Said Katherine, "Sounds good, Sanctum it is, at least for now. Can we move on to more pressing issues?"

"Sorry," said Anna. " Actually the name fits, depending on how we treat it. And I suppose why the Gadans were brought here in the first place."

"What do you mean?" asked Harlyn.

"Well, the ecology here seems rather well balanced. It would be a shame to introduce anything that could mess it up."

Katherine just listened to the banter.

"But things have already been introduced," said Harlyn. "We have a number of animals that were brought from Earth a couple of hundred years ago, including humans."

"Yes, that's true, but it seems to have remained at a small scale. Though I admit, it is because the locals—and by that I mean these tandoo creatures—have kept it that way."

"I don't know," concluded Harlyn. "It seems to me we could do something significant here even with protective restrictions. And until we look more closely, who knows what some local attributes might be beneficial back on Earth?"

Katherine said, "Like what?"

"I'm not sure exactly. Not yet anyway. But I couldn't help but notice how incredibly healthy all the Gadans happen to be."

Katherine gritted her teeth and said with a menacing voice, "You don't suppose it might have something to do with tandoo killing the weak and old Gadans do you?"

"Yeah, you have a point, but it seems to go beyond that. With permission, I'd like to put a study team on the ground. I didn't see a lot of children and very few older people. I don't think we can attribute that completely to the tandoo."

Anna said, "I like the study team idea. I'd like to lead the group."

"I hesitate," said Katherine, "only because of the tandoo. That said, pick a small team and it must include a Marine guard. Hopefully the tandoo learned a lesson from before and will leave you alone. Now I realize the presence of the Gadans was a surprise and have properly become a focus of ours, but we do have the primary mission to build a Gate. Once constructed, perhaps all other issues will fade away, including what to do about the Gadans. So, we need to get a settlement down there and start the Gate construction. I've asked Dakota to try and pick an area that is naturally isolated, like another valley, but hopefully not on the other side of the planet. Eventually we need to lay out specific guidelines for interplanetary travel between Sanctum and Earth. That is to say, I agree that we don't want to disrupt the plant's ecosystem any more than is absolutely necessary. I need to talk to Uri some more. I don't think he has shared everything he knows. What else?"

And as if that were a signal, there was a knock on the door and Captain Renaldo entered the room. "Excuse me Admiral, but I think you need to see this," he said as he handed her a note.

Katherine read the note and said uncharacteristically, "Shit."

With Harlyn and Anna staring at her, Katherine said, "This is from the UNSC. It's not clear how old the actual message is because of the time it took to reach headquarters from Admiral Wu and then from headquarters to here, but it seems Star Ship China is gone. It seems that the Vice Admiral was doing experiments that went out of control, resulting in the ship's loss. Most of the crew was safely transferred to British Commonwealth and South America. Important to us, is the remaining two ships are trying to make up for lost time, but that still leaves them one ship short to carry everything we need to complete the Gate."

Harlyn repeated Katherine's initial response, "Shit." Then, letting it sink in for a few minutes, seemingly out of the blue he said, "I wonder if there is time to build another ship?"

Katherine looked at the note again and said, "Were you reading over my shoulder? It seems that's exactly what the UNSC is planning to do. It appears, however, there is a catch. They could build a new ship, but the critical control modules for the engines aren't on Earth. They only have one. We have all the spares here."

With a sigh Harlyn said, "Ouch. It never occurred to me that this might happen when setting up for this mission. I just wanted our ships to be as well equipped as possible."

Anna said, "Look I know this is way out of my field, but couldn't they use that one unit and reverse engineer to make more?"

Harlyn answered with a very quiet, "I honestly don't know."

Katherine looked at the note again, winced again, and said, "How can one little note make such a difference? It also says that Sharon Hooding has died at the age of eighty-five. Apparently it was very sudden and happened while she was at work." Katherine looked up and added, "She was an amazing woman. She experienced a life few can comprehend. I really liked her. And now, I'm going to have to tell Astron. This is not going to be pleasant." And once again she said, "Shit."

Chapter 32

Sanctum Ecology

While most of the crews of the starships Orion and Perseus were naturally focused on a Gate construction location, Anna Giblin and few of her staff started to focus on the Sanctum ecology. There were more than a few things she was interested in, though some would take many years to even partially understand.

The fact that there were three suns in the solar system would certainly have an effect on the planet with the most obvious of the three, of course, being the one around which Sanctum orbited. But if they were all lined up would that affect the weather or even the overall climate? Maybe, but certainly the flora and fauna did not seem distressed.

Weather patterns needed a lot of study. Katherine had weather satellites deployed, but the fleet's meteorologists were increasingly perplexed as storms seemed to materialize out of nowhere. Mathematical models developed to predict Earth's weather were useless here, forcing the meteorologists to think for themselves and they were not finding the task easy. They became convinced that the storms could get very nasty, so cautioned Katherine and Dakota to pick a Gate site that might offer some protection. It would be evident later that the term "nasty storm" wasn't a strong enough term when compared to some of the actual storms. They would learn later this was why the Gadans used the caves for dwellings.

The ring around the planet was also fascinating. Unlike Earth's moon, which affected the oceans tides, it wasn't immediately clear if the shifting of the ring relative to the equator had a different effect. These thoughts stimulated curiosity, but they weren't Anna's area of special interest.

One of the areas Anna wanted to better understand was the introduction of species from another planet into, as far as she could tell, a stable ecosystem prior to their introduction. Katherine provided Anna with a shuttle and crew so her studies could be over a broad area, eventually covering the entire planet. This wouldn't come close to providing all the answers, but it might at least clarify the questions.

The most obvious change with the introduction of Earth creatures had been with the tandoo, who soon developed a taste for people. That wasn't their only food source, of course. It couldn't be. There seemed to be tandoo everywhere, except at the extreme poles. The tandoo varied in size and color from region to region, but not much. They appeared to be lazy omnivores taking advantage of whatever food source was in the region they occupied without expending unnecessary energy. They were definitely at the top of the food chain with no obvious natural enemies. They lived in loose packs, or groups, and didn't go out of their way to find shelter.

There were other mammal-like animals. Many were grazers, explaining some of the open grass area. Others were ground and tree dwellers not unlike Earth's squirrels and other rodents. Nothing looked or acted like dogs or cats.

The seas had unusual creatures, and with some imagination they could be considered fish. Most either crawled along the bottom or floated up and down. Swimming creatures seemed few, and Anna's team thought they were more mammalian—like a dolphin or a whale—than ichthyologic, like a fish, but the physical appearance was certainly different.

Birds, or flying creatures, were really interesting and a little confusing. Confusing because when Tam-I-El brought humans to Sanctum, he also brought some other animals. Some species didn't survive the trip and others couldn't adapt and died off quickly. Birds, for some reason, did survive and adapt. However, it appeared they interbred almost from the beginning with native bird-like creatures so it was now difficult to tell if some of the flying creatures were indigenous or not. Captured animals and DNA testing would eventually solve the puzzle, but for now, it was assumed that the flying creatures that looked like birds were, in fact, birds. The other flying creatures seemed to be more mammalian, like Earth's bats.

There were bugs of many types. The flying kind could be very annoying, often swarming and landing on people, getting in the ears, eyes, and nose, but Anna's team didn't notice any bug bites. The crawling varieties were of many sizes, including some as large as a weasel. These were pretty scary looking, but also seemed harmless.

Anna found Sanctum had a wide variety of vegetation. There were trees, large and small, and though each species was very different, all seemed to share the characteristic of having some kind of fruit or nuts. The Gadans had determined what was edible in their valley, but there were many other varieties outside that valley still waiting to be tested, or tasted. In Gadan, vegetable seeds from Earth had been planted, but there were also native vegetables that were consumed, and they were quite delicious.

The bottom line for Anna, after a just a couple of months of study, was conclusive. She told Katherine in a staff meeting, "I know there is a lot more work to be done and it will take years and many resources if we are to have any kind of understanding of the Sanctum ecosystem. What I have determined with these early studies is that the conclusions made by that Tam-I-El, as far as this planet is concerned, were correct. This planet isn't perfect, but it is damned close and we should make certain it stays that way."

"What do you have in mind?"

"Well, first of all I suggest we keep any discussion of the Gadans as a separate topic from everything else; at least for me and for now. That is certainly an important subject, but I'd like to focus on the planet as a whole. I'm not sure that building a Gate will be good for Sanctum in the long run, but I'm not going to suggest that we forgo Gate building."

"Good, because that wouldn't happen. We are going to build the Gate."

"I know that. I'm not naïve, but I am going to suggest in the strongest of terms that we set limits on everything we do here so we don't destroy the planet. It wouldn't take much to ruin the good thing we seem to have here. Strong, passionate leadership is a must."

"Okay. Suppose I agree. There seems to be an ever-expanding list of conflicting issues to consider. I doubt there will be a simple answer. If we lay out everything each competing interest might have, I'm hopeful that compromise solutions can be found without compromising the planet. To be clear, Anna, I share your concerns." After a moment of thought Katherine continued with, "You know, Admiral Dodson once told me something that has served me well. He said, 'Katherine, remember to lead, follow, or get out of the way.' In this case I'm going to get out of the way for now and let you take the lead." And then smiling at Anna, she added, "For now anyway. Put together another small task force to develop a long-range plan. Start with a list of every issue or potential issue that might need to be addressed. The list needs to be a living document to be expanded as new thoughts emerge. Leave nothing off even if it seems obvious. We can cross things out later. Top on the list is the Gate operation and a financial return on the investment in this enterprise. As much as you'd like to ignore the Gadans, you must include that issue as well. Other words of wisdom I received were obvious as well; 'you can't change a plan if you don't have one.' Once you have the beginnings of the list, start on a plan." Smiling, Katherine added, "Do you need more than an hour?"

"Very funny. In my spare time can I do some research?" And Anna left without another word.

Katherine sat for a minute thinking, *I like Anna. She's smart and caring. It will be interesting to see what comes out of her little task force.*

One result that would come out would be a surprise to everyone!

Chapter 33

Bird Island

Dakota, following his wife's guidance, did find what he thought might be the perfect location for the Gate and the required support settlement. It was a valley not very far from Gadan, at just about the 45-degree latitude, which would take advantage of the Sanctum's magnetic poles. There were plenty of trees for building materials, and unlike the species found on TCe these trees apparently weren't thinkers. The major drawback was that there was considerable wildlife, including the tandoo, who were quite abundant.

Katherine talked it over with Dakota and they agreed that this likely didn't fit into the category of minimal impact, so it was on to plan B. Actually for Dakota, it was closer to plan X based on all the sites rejected thus far. In any case, plan X was an island approximately twelve miles off the coast in one of the major saltwater seas. From the shore, it was another thirty miles to Gadan. With a nearly circular shape and ten miles in diameter it would fit the bill for the Gate. Elevation-wise it seemed safe from any major storms, though there still wasn't enough information to know what kind of weather might be expected. The island was mostly sand and gravel making for easy digging, but with a relatively high water table in these soils, tunneling was going to be a challenge. The number one plus was that only birds were calling the island home, so it was given the not-so-original name: Bird Island.

In spite of many conversations with her staff including Uri, there was still no decision on what to do about the Gadans, so Bird Island offered the additional advantage of being far enough away from Gadan that they might never know about the Gate if they ended up being left alone. A disadvantage was the likely need for some boats in the future, something that was neglected, for some reason, when packing for the trip. In the meantime it didn't matter, as the shuttles would simply go back and forth from the ships and Bird Island.

So now, after nearly seven months in orbit around Sanctum, the shuttles were finally bringing the construction people and supplies down to Bird Island. For most of these people it was their first taste of the planet, and they liked it. First tent camps were set up, then some more permanent structures were built, including shops and a small manufacturing plant to make bricks and cement products. Next was better lodging, with a waterworks and a sanitation facility. A solar farm and wind turbine were set up for heat and power for the settlement, with major power to come later from spare starship engines when they were eventually brought down.

Even with the many resources on the ships required to build the support facilities, a little less than half of the Gate complex could be built. So it was that by the end of 2168 Bird Island settlement was established; a community of roughly 4,000 had done as much as they could and where now waiting for the next wave of supplies. With time on their hands, the taverns and bars were busy, boats were built for recreation and to reach the mainland, and sports fields were built.

Dakota, Celeste, and Astron were anxious to bring a certain large box down to Bird Island, but that was put on hold when the idyllic weather was taking a turn and the first "nasty storm" hit. The Gadans had said there were big storms at times and that was why they hadn't abandoned they caves. But "big" was one of those relative dimensions used by the Gadans, so no one knew what "big" was. The residents of Bird Island soon found out.

Over a period of days a weather system monitored from the orbiting ships grew larger and larger until it was the size and ferocity of the biggest storms on Earth. The eye of this mammoth storm was hundreds of miles across and aimed right for Bird Island. The storm surge was massive, but the settlement was high enough that the surge only affected the marine facilities that had been built. For two days Bird Island suffered with driving rain turning to snow, blasting with a fierce wind of over 200 hundred miles per hour. The storm destroyed much of the settlement and killed over 500 people. Most of the heavy construction equipment made it through, only because it was so heavy. Harlyn suggested to Dakota, "Maybe that's why there were only birds on the island."

The storm was devastating. The loss of life was the worst of it, but it couldn't be overlooked that many of the resources used to build the settlement were gone. Much of the damage, such as the destroyed wind generator, was beyond repair. Contingency plans to utilize local resources had to be drawn up. Word was sent back to Earth with a list of what had been lost. Back on Earth, anyone that had any interest in Sanctum went into a panic mode. It became more important than ever to somehow complete the newest Star Ship Centaurus.

Despite previous notions that the impacts on Sanctum might be negligible by keeping almost everything on Bird Island, it now became apparent that a mainland support facility had to be built to help rebuild what was lost on the island. A small valley was selected about midway between Gadan and the shore facing Bird Island. This valley also had caves, which were now looking pretty good to the newcomers. Tandoo and other animals were in residence, and reluctantly they were "asked to leave" with considerable prodding by the Marines. Though they left, they keep coming back for months, occasionally picking off a helpless worker. Using the logic employed by the Gadans' Protectors, Marines would kill an attacking tandoo. As dumb as they were, the tandoo eventually got the message and didn't venture too close.

The purpose of this settlement, named Mid Way, another not-so-clever name, was to manufacture building materials. As such, only 275 people settled in at first. Solar panels, lumber, and masonry units were made here and transported to the coast. It was here at Mid Way that Dakota's big box was brought down. Celeste and Astron attacked the box with hammers and crowbars to the amusement of the tradespeople on site. What onlookers finally saw was the 1914 Model T Ford that had been disassembled and packed away. With much pride, Dakota watched Celeste and Astron unpack the machine parts and put it back together.

When Katherine realized what was going on, she marched up to Dakota in front of a large group and said, "Are you kidding me? You brought that stupid thing here? What do you think you're going to use to make it run?"

"Oh come on sweetie," said Dakota in his most syrupy voice. "This will be the only car of its era to be driven on another planet. Don't you think that's cool? Anyway, I did make a few modifications. I convinced Suzanne Lehtola to give me some Lehtolarite; just enough to modify the car for power generation and storage. The engine was replaced with an electric motor. You have to admit this is awesome."

"Sometimes Dakota, sometimes!" stammered Katherine.

"Sometimes what?"

"Sometimes, I don't know what." Then looking at Celeste and Astron who were obviously trying not to laugh, Katherine said, "And you two conspirators better not laugh." They didn't, but the gathered group did.

Chapter 34

Elixir (2168)

Katherine decided there was nothing to be gained by worrying about the fleet heading towards Earth. She would focus on what she could control and adapt as required. If she worried about things over which she had no control, she would be less efficient. And if she became less efficient, she would have even more to worry about. When she had more information she would adjust. At least that's what she told herself. Right now, she had Bird Island and the start of a Gate. There was also Mid Way as a more protected settlement. Those seemed to be as under control as possible.

Anna had been permitted to set up a study on the Sanctum's surface. Her assigned shuttle had been packed with researchers, Marines, tents, camping equipment, and of course, research equipment. A field lab was now set up to analyze air, water, and soil samples. That also seemed to be under control, though the answers to questions Anna and her team would generate were certainly unknown and therefore everything could get out of control at any minute.

Reports from the survey team mostly confirmed what they all thought they were observing from a distance. The air was very close to what everyone was used to, except it was fresh. Nothing like the recycled air found on the ships. The soil was extremely rich in nutrients. There were some bacteria and microbes that weren't familiar to the scientists. But under close examination, they didn't seem to possess any attributes that might be considered harmful. That alone was interesting, if not puzzling.

When Bird Island was being developed, there was obvious curiosity about what might be in the water and some with a penchant towards fishing did their own form of exploration. These "explorers" discovered that anything shiny would attract some interestingly weird creatures. Pictures were taken, but all decided that catch-and-release was the best way to go once the fishermen saw what was on the end of the line.

Anna's study group was far from any sea, so for now her work was focused on terrestrial attributes. The current field lab was set up near her shuttle on a grassy plane. A good-sized stream ran between the field lab and a tree line. The forest from a distance looked very much like one might find on Earth, but a closer look at individual trees made it clear that these were something quite different.

The differences were very subtle, so it took a couple of days before a very observant technician said, "Those trees next to the stream are different from the rest. They bend over and dip branches into the water and then straighten up. It is so slow I wasn't sure at first, but watch."

It took hours, but sure enough trees were slowly bending into the water and straightening back up. Not all trees did this at once and it was so slow and subtle that if no one was paying attention, it looked like there were simply some trees bent over. They were, however, taking turns with perhaps 15 to 20 percent of the trees with branches in the water at any one time.

When this curious behavior was pointed out to Anna, she immediately assigned a small team to watch more closely. Caution was given when the Marines assigned to guard the team noticed that there were "eyes" watching from the forest—big eyes.

An attempted analysis of the stream waters was confusing. It was water and it was clean, that was certain. It was almost too clean to be for real. There were some minerals probably from the streambed, but there were absolutely no nutrients at all. Something should have washed in from the riverbanks, someplace. One of the lab assistants, Paul, put on a pair of shorts and waded into the stream to about waist deep and reached down to grab a sample from the riverbed. Only his head remained out of the water. When Paul had a good-sized sample of gravel he came out of the water and marched over to the field lab. Under the microscope, there was nothing to see except some unidentified minerals; very clean minerals.

Anna was puzzled. And as she stood thinking, she absentmindedly looked around until her eyes fell upon Paul. He was still wet from his little excursion and was standing with his arms outstretched, seemingly studying his limbs.

"Is something wrong?" asked Anna.

"No," said Paul. "Nothing at all, but there should be."

"Huh?"

"Well, setting up this lab was a little more effort than I'm used to and my muscles were a bit sore."

"And?"

"And now they're not. I feel great. Just wet, that's all."

Anna thought about this for a minute, and then asking in general to everyone, "Has anyone else noticed anything like that?"

One of the Marines standing guard said somewhat sheepishly, "I guess I did. When I went to the stream with Paul, I grabbed a drink."

"That was pretty dumb," said Anna. "Didn't I tell everyone to stick with the supplies we brought with us?"

"Yes ma'am, but everyone said the water was clean and it looked so good. Sorry."

"And?"

"Well, I did eat something for lunch that perhaps wasn't the best. I had an upset stomach and a small headache. But when I took a drink from the stream water, I felt fine, almost right away."

Anna was baffled. She thought, *There is nothing we can detect in this water, but there must be something. What the hell is going on?* Out loud she said to Paul and the Marine making them a little nervous, "You two are to stay away from the water. I want to know about any changes you feel or think you feel. Got it?"

Not certain what, if anything, she'd discover, she asked Katherine to have a shuttle crew gather water samples from as many locations as possible to note everything in the vicinity, such as temperatures, foliage, any wildlife; anything and everything. On the ground, Anna sent a couple of lab assistants with a pair of Marines upstream beyond where the trees were next to the water.

Over the next few days, the field lab found itself very busy. All samples were analyzed trying to find a pattern. Spectral analysis did show some differences with the most striking differences being in any area where the dipping trees were located. What the analysis didn't reveal was likely the most important, as nothing was identified in the section of the stream where there were the dipping trees. Something seemed to be there, but there was no data for comparison so specifics weren't identifiable.

Paul and the thirsty Marine were showing no ill effects after a few days, so Anna thought, *No guts, no glory,* while telling her staff, "I'm going to try something." And with that she grabbed an empty bottle, went over the stream and filled it. Back at the field station, she made a big sigh, looked at the bottle, and drank a long slug of water. Everyone watched this rash behavior of their leader wondering what would happen. Anna rolled her shoulders, lifted and stretched her right leg, and then did the same with her left leg. With a huge smile, she said, "I have no arthritic pain. This is amazing."

What was even more amazing came much later when the chief medical doctor said, "I see no evidence of any arthritis at all. None!" It was becoming clear now that one reason for the Gadans' apparent good general health was the water they drank.

The water was some kind of elixir. Still, long-term evaluations of the effects were required to make certain there were no bad side effects. Volunteers were recruited from the ships' crews for a controlled study. It wasn't hard to find volunteers that suffered from the mildest of maladies to the most severe. Each subject completed forms with dozens of health questions and then underwent intense medical evaluations before and after drinking the water. Initial results were amazing, but in the parlance of researchers they only said, "Fascinating." Most health issues disappeared except for those with the most serious medical conditions, but even these people found some relief.

Over the next several months, more studies were done using the water at the field station site and at other locations that looked similar. While the results were a puzzle, there were consistencies. The "elixir" waters were the same wherever there were dipping trees and a specific, but yet unidentified, mineral was found in the streams. Waters from above these specific conditions showed no beneficial effects and the same was true of waters found hundreds of yards down stream. Adding to the curiosity factor was that only streams up to a yet-to-be-defined flow provided the elixir. Rivers, ponds, and lakes did not.

Anna didn't want to ruin a good thing, but her scientific curiosity forced her to harvest a small dipping tree branch and a few leaves. Nothing detrimental to the tree was noticed. Detailed analysis of the leaves and streambed gravel seemed to indicate that the trees were extracting something from the water while the gravel was adding something, probably from erosion as the water flowed over. What was being removed and what was being added would take many years to determine. This was an exciting puzzle that Anna was anxious to solve. But it had to be solved without destroying the source in the process.

Harlyn was just as curious as Anna, and also wanted to protect the source. But he was still very mindful of who was funding this expedition. He couldn't help but think, *Wouldn't this be something if we can bring the stuff back to Earth? The Trading Company would certainly reap a huge financial reward.*

Chapter 35

Reality Check

Uri, Anna, Harlyn, Dakota, and Katherine had a decision to make. Katherine had been procrastinating, but the Gadans issue couldn't be put off forever. While any decision made could be reversed, something needed to be done at some point, and that point had been reached. The issue was what to tell the Gadans. Their entire history and beliefs were based on the one concept of going "back."

"Back" was vague, but somehow it was believed that where their ancestors had come from was a much better place than where they were now. Katherine wasn't sure that was true. In fact she felt just the opposite. True, Earth was very different than Gadan and it had been home to their ancestors, but could it be their home now? Where Gadans had fire, bows, and arrows as their highest level of technology, their now distant relatives of Earth fly from one solar system to another. But was it better?

The Gadans occupied a very tiny portion of Sanctum, but to the crews of the starships, their commune looked very pleasing indeed. It seemed as though all the things mankind had come to consider essential just weren't important here. Perhaps that fellow Tam-I-El wasn't that far off when he called it the Garden of Eden. And in the case of the Gadans, perhaps ignorance was bliss.

Katherine started her meeting with, "I believe it is time for us to decide what to do and/or what to tell the Gadans. The UNSC knows of the Gadans by now, based on messages sent earlier, but the UNSC doesn't know the Gadans as well as we do so even if they were to give us a directive, it could just as easily be wrong as right. We need to do something and we shouldn't put it off any longer. I am quite mindful that we can change whatever plan we come up with, but once again, we can't change a plan if we don't have something to start with.

"The way I see it, we can try to prepare them for an eventual trip through the wormhole gate back to Earth. We can try to tell, or even show, what they can expect to see. I think that scenario could be overwhelming. Even if that were successful and they went through the Gate to Earth, where would they go? For all intents and purposes, the Gadans are their own race and have their own culture now. They have zero attachments back on Earth.

"We could tell them they can't go back, but is that acceptable? Who are we to judge? We could also do nothing and just walk away. However, while we didn't create this problem, it doesn't feel right to me to just walk away. We could show them some things and perhaps provide them with some things to bring their society up a notch or two. Uri's people did that by introducing the Gadans to the bow and arrow. I don't know how far things would have gone if the tandoo hadn't become a factor, but I think it is safe to assume the Gadans would have at least received some additional guidance. What are your thoughts? Uri, it was your people that created this mess in the first place. What do you think?"

With a big sigh, Uri said, "Yes, some of our people were responsible and they were punished. I'm not trying to justify what they did, but their intentions weren't evil."

Anna said, "Perhaps, but sometimes the best of intentions have dire consequences. In this case, the consequences were recognized, yet the rest of you just walked away. In my mind that seems quite unconscionable!"

Uri, starting to feel the need to be a little defensive said, "Well no. It seemed that they would be able to thrive here. Sure they had no memory, but they weren't stupid either. And you have to admit, it's pretty nice here and all the Gadans work together in harmony."

"Yes," said Harlyn, "if you overlook the fact that the tandoo have made the Gadans a food source."

Uri winched at that, saying, "Yeah, okay, that likelihood wasn't anticipated."

Katherine said, "It might have been noticed if your people hung around, don't you think? Anyway, enough blame game stuff, we need to focus on today, not past transgressions. What should we do?"

Dakota, seemed not to have been listening and was instead doodling something on a scratch pad. He started mumbling without looking up, "We don't have to be that rigid, you know. It isn't all one way or another; perhaps a hybrid solution of some kind would be best."

Katherine didn't say anything, but was smiling inside because she knew how Dakota's mind worked and how he was piecing things together.

"Could you be a bit more specific?" asked Anna.

"Well, we are building a little village about halfway between shore and Gadan. It really isn't a long distance, but since the Gadans don't leave their valley, we could be just over the ridge and they wouldn't be any wiser. I propose that the Gadans be told that it isn't time to go back—that the time will be in the not too distant future. Since they don't really measure time the way we do, it can be left vague. Tell them that we have a settlement some distance away. They don't need to know that it is a new one. Tell them we want to share with them some things we know that would help them until it is time to go 'back.' Maybe we could have some kind of school. If nothing else it would be nice to communicate without translation all the time. Maybe we could start a little trading for some of their foodstuffs.

"During the sharing period, which I would say might be bit a longer than the time it will take to finally finish the Gate, we thoughtfully enlighten them. It would be a huge step, but when we think the time is right we could bring a few of the Gadans that we think can handle it back to Earth. The Earth Wormhole Gate in South Dakota is still remote, so the initial culture shock on the other end might not be too overwhelming. We'll need to judge the timing, but we could eventually get these brave souls to a city. I suspect they might be more than willing to come back to Gadan and tell the rest, 'we have it good here.' Or maybe not. At that point, I think the proper path might be obvious. In the meantime, I think we need to lay out a plan for us on Sanctum. And by that, I mean all of us that are here and those that might come here."

Anna said, "I agree with everything you said, but my personal interest is still the potential impact we could have on the planet. It's a huge concern, but with an eye towards good stewardship starting with us, it could be done. What I'm thinking is something like the controls that were used on national parks before so many were ruined by bad management."

Harlyn, said, "Yes, but there is still the unfortunate reality that we need some way to generate some revenue. Remember, it is the Star Struck Trading Company that is funding this adventure. The company needs to at least cover costs. Do you think the magic water you dubbed Elixir can do that?"

"Maybe."

Chapter 36

Truth

"Uri," said Katherine, "This is going to be difficult. You've been rather silent on this but I know you have been thinking about this for far longer than me. Probably since before we left Earth. And I'd be willing to wager this entire issue of the Gadans was why you came."

Katherine and Uri were in a quiet corner of the main lounge and were on their second pint of ale. Actually, Katherine was on her second pint, while Uri was on his second pitcher, as usual. "You got me, Katherine. Obviously, well I hope it's obvious, I want to be as helpful in any way that I can. The rules of the Order are off so I am free to offer more than suggestions. But my number one assigned mission was to find out what happened to the advance team sent here to prepare the Gadans for this reunion. Depending upon what I found, I was to assist in any transition. I had great expectations that the Gadans would have their bags packed and be ready to go."

"Well, they don't have any bags and if they did, it sure doesn't appear they have been packed. They do seem eager to go, but they certainly aren't ready."

"I can't argue with that," said Uri. "This is nothing close to what I had hoped for. I had visions of my people teaching an eager people about Earth and how they came to be. It never occurred to me that the Gadans hadn't expanded beyond these valley walls and become the dominant species. It might have occurred to me that something happened to the advance Order team, but somehow expected, or hoped, I'd learn they had simply been unable to communicate."

"So what are you telling me?" asked Katherine.

"I'm telling you, I don't know what to do. However, the default is usually the truth."

"And as I see it, telling the truth to the Gadans means 'you're not going anywhere, not now anyway.'"

"Yes," said a very contrite Uri, "Probably not in those words, however."

Katherine quaffed down the rest of her ale, looked at Uri for a minute and said, "I was hoping for a bit more from you." Then she got up, leaving Uri feeling very small.

It took a few days for Katherine to decide exactly what she would say. The truth would be the proper thing, but how much truth would be appropriate at this point? She had been making periodic visits to the commune, each time learning a little more about how the Gadans were living and what kind of conditions were encountered each season, realizing that it was the seasons they used to measure time.

Anna had been along a few times and asked if she could take samples from the stream that ran through their compound. She found that just like other streams sampled, this one had the dipping trees and the riverbed had the same gravel base. After conversations about how and what the Gadans cooked and drank, it became apparent they had become wise to the benefits of the water taken from a specific section of the stream. The Gadans also learned that the beverages they made only had an alcoholic content if the water was taken from above the section of the stream that had the dipping trees. Anna added that tidbit of information to her puzzle.

Katherine had been hinting on previous visits that her people were not the ones that had brought the first Gadans to the valley. Today was the day she would be more direct.

Minda and two of her Protectors were, as usual, the first to notice the big silver bird fly in and land in the distant section of the valley. She had been keeping the knowledge of this bird that took these strangers away to herself and her fellow Protectors. She had told them to be careful. "That silver bird needs to be watched. It eats those people, but it doesn't. And different ones come out of it. If it decided to be angry, it would be worse than the tandoo."

This day, when the shuttle landed, Minda and her two companions walked out of the woods and confronted Katherine, Uri, Harlyn and two Marines as they emerged. "Damn," said Katherine. "I suppose they would see this eventually."

Minda wasted no time saying, "How do you control that bird? It eats you, but it doesn't."

Harlyn said "What?"

Katherine thought for minute, then laughed saying to Harlyn, "They never saw a machine before. The shuttle flies and the only thing they've seen that flies is a bird. We go in and out of what looks like a mouth. That's a logical question, don't you think?"

"I guess," said an unconvinced Harlyn.

Katherine thought for a moment before saying, "Uri, ask them if they want to go inside."

He did and after talking it over, all three Protectors said "yes" and proceeded up the ramp with Katherine. Once inside, Minda had no idea what she was looking at. Harlyn tried to explain. "This is a machine that we use to fly from one place to another."

"What's a machine?"

How do I explain this thought Harlyn, but after few minutes said, "You have a bow that shoots arrows. The bow is made from a branch and a vine. It is a machine that shoots the arrow. This is a machine that has many more parts made to fly."

Minda and her two companions were overwhelmed and said, "We want to leave."

They all left the shuttle and started for the commune. Minda and her companions stopped several times and looked back at the machine showing a high level of anxiety. Once out of sight of the shuttle, the three Gadans kept glancing at Katherine's group. The Marines noted the Gadans were holding their bows in a less than relaxed posture with one hand twitching next the basket of arrows at their waist.

As previously, the Gadans in the commune stopped what they were doing and surrounded the outsiders. Minda said something to the Gadans that Uri didn't quite catch and it was obvious there was increased agitation. Minda said, "Is that machine taking us back?"

Katherine took a big breath and exhaled before saying, "No. We are not the ones to take you back. We have a commune like yours in another valley. We existed not knowing of the Gadans until you first saw our silver birds." Katherine knew she was mixing in a few things that were misleading with the actual truth, but an all out truthfulness wouldn't be understood or believed. "Some seasons from now you will be able to go back as will we. But I tell you truthfully, you are not prepared for what you will see and may not like it. In fact there are very many people back there that would prefer to be here. You may not understand, but I can tell you that what you have here is very special, especially now that the tandoo stay away."

Minda said, "Who will take us back?"

"I don't know that answer," said Katherine. "Why do you want to go back?"

"Because it is wonderful and it is where the first ones came from."

Harlyn said, "There are many wonderful things there, but there are also many evil things. We will show you as much as we can so you can prepare to go back if you want. Can you trust us?"

"Maybe."

Chapter 37

Next Step

Telling the Gadans that they wouldn't be going "back" any time soon was the first step. Katherine wasn't sure how the next step was going to go, but it was time to find out. It was Anna that suggested that having a party of Gadans leave the valley on foot with an escort might be the best way to get started. Flying them out in the "silver bird" would be simply too much to handle at once. Let them walk and slowly move to Mid Way.

And so it was. It had been announced days in advance that Gadans selected by the commune would leave the valley with the strangers and walk to the their commune called Mid Way. Fortunately, no one asked what it was midway to. Not surprising, Minda was the leader of the Gadans for this journey. With her were two other Protectors and two Gadans considered elders. There was some anxiety among the Gadans because no one had ever left the valley and returned. It was always assumed that the tandoo got them—a correct assumption.

Katherine had elected to stay at Mid Way to prepare for the Gadans arrival. The party selected to escort the Gadans included two armed Marines, Harlyn, Anna, Uri, and Astron. The plan was to walk to Mid Way, which would take most of the day, stay two nights, and return. Everyone expected to encounter tandoo once out of Gadan and they weren't disappointed.

Once outside the valley walls, they could feel the eyes watching from the trees. The party was perhaps five miles from Gadan when six tandoo blocked their path. Astron, moved towards the group and started making unintelligible sounds. Uri was fascinated with this scenario because while he could easily communicate with creatures of high intelligence, he was unable to communicate with creatures as dim-witted as the tandoo. It appeared as though Astron could communicate with the tandoo, and perhaps Astron being half-human had something to do with it. This was new to Astron as well, but somehow instinctively he knew he could do it.

The Marines and the Protectors remained on guard, uncertain how this confrontation was going to play out. Astron made sounds and the tandoo seemed to be responding and were moving off. But from behind the party was another group of tandoo moving up. Minda and her other Protectors immediately loaded their bows and sent arrows flying. At the same time, the two Marines fired single rounds, each dropping two tandoo in the their tracks. The rest of the tandoo fled, including three with arrows protruding.

This was the first time the Gadans had heard gunshots and were stunned to see what had happened. The Marines, including Sergeant Green who had been embarrassed by Minda when they first met, all smiled at the Protectors and everyone relaxed their weapons. Sergeant Green was especially pleased now that he had finally been able to demonstrate his weapon.

Anna was upset that there had been a killing, but understood the need. "I hope," she said, "that will be the last killing."

"Actually," said Harlyn, "I'm not sure any tandoo were killed. Look. One of the ones shot has got up and is leaving. Maybe the other one is alive as well, but I'm not suggesting we go check for a pulse. Let's move on."

For the next couple of miles, Uri was busy translating between the Marines and the Protectors. The Gadans, overcoming their initial surprise of the gunshots, were now very curious about the guns and the Marines that used them. Sergeant Green, increasingly enamored with Minda, was hoping that she might now show something other than the cool recognition that he even existed. As the conversation escalated about weapons and the tandoo, there was definitely solid evidence of a thawing, much to the obvious pleasure of the sergeant.

Perhaps, thought Harlyn, *that encounter with the tandoo was a Godsend.*

The rest of the trek was uneventful as far as wildlife was concerned. There were some streams to cross, some very thick underbrush to get through in places, yet other areas were strictly tall grass. Only Harlyn was having difficulty keeping pace as he was the only one in the group that wasn't used to so much physical exercise.

As they approached the Mid Way defenses, the Gadans became more animated. Minda thought, *There really is another commune.* And as they got even closer she thought, *They certainly live differently than we do.*

The Gadans obviously noticed more Marines along the defensive barrier as well as the actual barbed wire defense barrier itself. *What is this stuff?* Minda thought. *It looks like some kind of vine with sharp points and it is very hard.*

In the village, there were buildings unlike anything the Gadans could imagine. And in some of these there were people making things. There were all kinds of things the Gadans had never even imaged might exist. Outside the village, Minda could see some more of those silver birds. *This is amazing,* she thought, *How did we never know about this place?*

Katherine came to greet them and brought the party to a central area with tables and benches. On other tables there were plates filled with food and pitchers filled with beer, tea, and ice water. Uri offered caution on the beer. Though the Gadans had their own alcoholic beverage, beer was something different and it wouldn't be good if they got too carried away with consumption. That didn't stop Uri from showing them that he was certainly familiar with the stuff and poured himself a very large glass. After all, he hadn't had much to eat today and he was thirsty.

Minda and her party did take food and drink, even things they didn't recognize, and sat down. There was a great deal of small talk to which Minda only half listened. She was fascinated with everything she saw. *These people seem very busy, but what do they do?*

The party went on into the night. As the beer started to loosen people up, the Marines and the Protectors started to become very friendly towards each other and Katherine warned the Marines, "Now is not the time, and you know exactly what I mean."

"Aye, Aye, Admiral," said a somewhat disappointed Sergeant Green.

The next day Katherine said, "We have some gifts for you. Things we believe will make your work easier." With that she presented them with shovels, hoes, knives, and saws and then showed the Gadans how to use them. "But you don't need to carry this back. We will bring them to you in the silver bird."

Minda said, "What can we give you that you don't have?"

"Some of the food you grow and gather that you don't need would be more than a fair exchange."

When the Gadans were back home, they had some amazing stories to share. While they didn't understand much of what they were shown, it still made a significant impact.

From Katherine's perspective she shared with Dakota that, "I'm positive they were overwhelmed. It is going to take a long time before they are even close to being shown Earth. We certainly shouldn't be bringing up the Gate any time soon."

"I absolutely agree," said Dakota. "By the way, did you tell Harlyn to do an exam on any of them?"

"No. Why?"

"Well, he did get permission to have our medical team look one of them over. It wasn't very thorough, but from a cursory exam, that particular Gadan appears to be well into his fifties."

"That can't be," said Katherine. "Just look at him. He can't be more than, well, maybe late thirties. Makes me wonder about the Protectors."

"Yes. This place gets more and more fascinating, doesn't it?"

Chapter 38

Picnic

With the Bird Island Gate complex essentially on hold until the rest of the ships arrived from Earth, and the village of Mid Way being refined with no special urgency, people had more time to enjoy their surroundings. Katherine's mandate that everyone take one day off for every six days worked wasn't hard to observe. As on Bird Island, Mid Way now had a temporary non-denominational chapel being constructed and many actually went to religious services, including to the surprise of some, Uri. Katherine made certain that those that wanted to spend time on the planet's surface were given the opportunity. With about 3,000 people currently on Bird Island and now about the same number at Mid Way, that left about 6,000 still on the two ships. To the casual observer, that was a lot of people, but with the many shifts required to keep everything running it really wasn't.

The number of shops at Mid Way covered all the manufacturing needs to complete and fortify Bird Island's non-Gate related structures from violent storms. As more equipment was brought down, the shops were becoming more and more sophisticated. A sewer system was being built using the latest technology to remove all contamination and nutrients in the "used water," just like on the ships. Mid Way, just like Bird Island, was beginning to feel like a hometown.

The Marines had set up a defensive perimeter to keep the tandoo out, but no one had seen one since they started building the village. People were feeling very relaxed including Celeste and Astron. They were now thirty and thirty-four years old respectively. They had been friends since they were very small, and while they each still considered each other as just a friend and said so when asked about their relationship, everyone could see that it wouldn't take much to move on from "friend" to something much more. Celeste and Astron seemed to be the only blind ones.

Celeste wasn't petite. She was nearly a foot taller than her mom and was very attractive in every way. That is, once the oil-stained machine shop coveralls she often wore were shed in exchange for a more dignified look. Astron would often say, "You do clean up well."

Today was their day off and they had something special planned. They were going to have a picnic with two of their friends, Ben and Carol, who planned to be married in a few months. The weather was as perfect a day as could be imagined.

The old Ford had been used in the village to get around as needed. Today, it was to take them past the defense line to a small waterfall a few miles out; a picture-perfect picnic location. They felt confident that they would be okay. No one had even seen a tandoo in almost a year, and nothing else seemed to ever pose a threat.

The luggage rack on the running board and the space left in the back seat were piled high with the required provisions for a long, relaxing day. That included a chest full of beer bottles, which Astron proclaimed "Will be completely free of their contents before the day is through if I have anything to say about it." This was going to be a great day.

Celeste climbed in behind the steering wheel, Astron wedged himself onto the passenger side of the front seat, and they were off. When they got to the defensive barrier, the Marine on duty said, "The four of you need to stay alert. You should be fine, but you never know about those tandoo. Be back here at least one hour before it gets dark."

"We will be careful, Corporal, thank you," said Celeste and off they went. Since the Ford had been built before there many real roads on Earth, the old buggy had little trouble traveling over the rough ground dodging shrubs and boulders. The tall grass made a somewhat soothing sound from underneath as the car moved along. When they got to their spot, the practiced foursome took all of fifteen minutes to have everything out and beer poured into the chilled glasses that had been buried in the ice chest. An hour or so later, a campfire was built for cooking and Astron assumed the role of chef. The other three knew that was so he could continue to "sample," as he put it, while cooking. The only actual cooking was to roast some vegetables and one chicken sacrificed for the day. The usual solemn look on Astron's face was replaced with a cheerful smile that got bigger as the beers were consumed. The foursome had not a care in the world.

Mid-afternoon, Celeste excused herself to take care of a "personal matter" and wandered off to the tree line. Astron, Ben, and Carol were chatting when they heard a scream. Moving towards Celeste were the three largest tandoo they had ever seen. The tandoo didn't move quickly, but they were moving faster than Celeste, who was walking backwards. Astron jumped to his feet, told Ben and Carol to stay near the fire, and ran over to Celeste. He told her "stand still" and made some unintelligible sounds. The tandoo stopped. They started forward again, and once again Astron made some unintelligible sounds, but more of them and louder. The tandoo stopped once again, acting confused, and once again Astron made more sound—this time even louder. Finally the three tandoo turned around and sauntered off. Celeste looked at Astron with her mouth open and Astron looked down at her and said, "What?"

"You were talking to those things? What did you say?"

"I'm not sure talking would be the correct term, but I guess so. They're pretty dumb." Then somewhat alarmed he asked, "Are you okay?" as he saw Celeste swoon and start to fall. He caught her and carried her limp form back to the picnic as Ben and Carol watched.

Astron and Celeste had never touched each other before in any way, shape, or form. They hadn't held hands, hugged, or even brushed against each other by accident. When he caught her and had her comparatively light body so suddenly touching his, he became suddenly overwhelmed with an emotion he had never felt before and couldn't contain himself.

Celeste came out of her faint as she was being carried, and looked up to see Astron crying uncontrollably. She too realized she was feeling something different. When they reached their picnic area, Astron put Celeste down. Ben and Carol were staring and asked, "Are you all right?"

"Yes," said Celeste, as she looked up at Astron. "He saved my life, though I'm not sure how exactly." Then she reached up, pulled his face down and gave him a kiss.

Astron reached down, picked Celeste up once again, but this time vertically, and said, "Marry me."

Still a little dazed, Celeste mumbled, "Is that the beer talking?" Then she added, "By the way, the proper way to propose is to a lady is to ask politely if she will marry you, and in the old days only after asking the lady's father for permission!"

Astron thought for minute, while Ben and Carol looked on, waiting for what might come next, then finally he said, "I'll ask your dad later. Will you marry me?"

"Yes." Then to Ben and Carol, Celeste said. "You heard it. He can't deny it later when the beer wears off!"

"Right," Carol said, "And neither can you. This has been quite to day!"

The ride back to Mid Way seemed exceptionally smooth as the old Ford seemed to float over the ground. Ben broke the mood somewhat when he said, "Okay Astron, this is driving me crazy, and while this drive might be a short trip I gotta know, how did you get the tandoo to back off?"

"Oh, I just told them that Celeste was tough and stringy and they wouldn't find her tasty."

Celeste punched Astron on the shoulder and said, "You know you're not very funny, don't you? Don't give up your day job."

Ben added, "And you're not going to tell us, are you?"

"Oh, just call me the tandoo whisperer."

Chapter 39

Permission Granted

Celeste was beaming when she and Astron found Katherine and Dakota. Katherine was sitting outside the newly opened Proxima Pub at a little round table made of some yet-to-be-formally-named native wood. She had a very hoppy glass of beer. Dakota had some kind of dark beer that Katherine thought looked and tasted more like burnt motor oil. The beer glass was resting on his stomach as he balanced his chair on the back two legs and his feet were resting on the table. Dakota was feeling quite mellow when Celeste approached and sat down. Astron stood behind Celeste and seemed a bit nervous somehow. Behind Astron were Ben and Carol with odd smiles on their faces as they kept looking at each other.

"So," said Dakota in a mellow tone, "What's happening kiddo? How was the picnic? I didn't expect to see you guys until later."

"Oh daddy, it was a wonderful day. The waterfall was so nice. We had a wonderful time. Well, until the tandoo tried to get me."

Katherine spit out a mouthful of beer and Dakota fell over backwards spilling his beer all over himself.

"Daddy, are you okay?" Celeste said as she got up and ran around the table.

Looking up, Dakota asked, "What do you mean the tandoo almost got you? And yes, I'm okay."

"I said they tried to get me, Astron saved me by telling the tandoo to go away."

Katherine and Dakota knew Astron had the same ability to translate that Uri had, plus an uncanny way with domestic animals, so the communication part wasn't exactly a huge surprise. After all, he'd done it before. More relieved, Dakota could only say, "Oh," as he started to get back up. Halfway up, he turned his head to Astron and asked, "Do you have anything to add to this little story?"

"Well, yes sir, I do."

Still not yet on his feet, Dakota said suspiciously, "Sir? Since when do you address me as sir?"

"I have been informed by your daughter that I must use proper protocol when I ask your permission to take her hand in marriage." And as Dakota fell over once again, Astron asked, "Sir, with your blessings I'd like to ask Celeste to be my wife."

Katherine stared, still sitting with her glass in her hand halfway between the table and her wide-open mouth. Dakota just laid there on the grass looking up at Astron. Ben and Carol stopped smiling. The next few moments of no movement seemed like an eternity to Celeste and Astron until finally Katherine looked down at Dakota and said, "Get off your butt, shake hands with Astron and say 'of course!'" And that is exactly what Dakota, did to the relief of everyone. Ben and Carol hugged and laughed. It was quite the scene, after all.

Astron was smiling and looked around at all the smiling faces, except one. Celeste was looking at Astron with her hands on her hips, pursed lips, and half-closed eyes. "Well!" she nearly yelled.

Astron was puzzled, and said, "Well what? Oh!" Then he got down on one knee, took Celeste's right hand and said, "Will you marry me?"

Now smiling, Celeste held out her left hand, looked at it and said, "Maybe. Where's the ring?"

Carol said, "Knock it off you twit, you already said yes. We're witnesses. Let's celebrate."

More chairs were pulled to the table, stronger beverages were ordered, and the six of them celebrated into the night.

The next day, however, required a more serious discussion. Celeste was still flying high at breakfast when Katherine said, "Listen Celeste, I'm very happy for you and Astron, but there is something the two of you need to consider."

"Oh great, I'm sensing a downer moment."

"Maybe, maybe not. You have known Astron your whole life and of course you know his mom, but you probably don't know a lot about Astron's father, Raman. I did get to know him. He is not an evil person, but there is something you need to consider. Remember, he isn't a human and that makes Astron only half human. There was a considerably high level of surprise when Sharon got pregnant with Astron and that was followed by a very difficult childbirth. That is something you two really need to think about."

Celeste's happy mood was slightly deflated with Katherine's comments and said, "I know, Mom. In the not very far back of my mind, I am aware of Astron's history. I'm not sure what we will do in the kid department, but I do know I want to be with Astron. I have suddenly realized that I can't imagine what life would be without him. Maybe it is because we have always been together and don't know anything different. I think the same is true for him and it was only the tandoo scare that made us both understand what we should have realized all along."

Katherine then smiled and said, "You do know he will do whatever you tell him, right?"

"Huh?"

"Come on, you're not that thick. Astron has always followed you around like a puppy and done nearly everything for you."

"No he hasn't." Then thinking for moment Celeste added, "He hasn't, has he?"

"Yes dear, he has. In fact I'm a little surprised he asked you to marry him and not the other way around. My point is the kid thing will most certainly be your decision."

Celeste simply stared straight ahead and quietly said, "Oh."

On a perfectly beautiful day during the cooling season of Sanctum, people gathered at Mid Way for a double wedding. This was the big day for Ben and Carol as well as Astron and Celeste.

The weddings were important, but the underlying desire for most was to have a big party. Everyone wore their best—even though for most the best was their UNSC-issued uniforms. Celeste and Carol decided to adopt a variation of what the Gadans wore and they did it with it stunning results. Flowers were woven into their clothes and into their hair.

Some of the Gadans came, including Minda and her fellow Protector Soon. The Gadans were a little confused about the ceremony and what it stood for. In Gadan, people often paired up, but it was very informal and there were no hard feelings if the pairing wasn't always exclusive or if the pairings changed. The concept of pledging oneself to another for the rest of one's life was fascinating.

Sergeant Green managed to find a way to stand next to Minda without her seeing him right away. As the actual ceremony concluded, Minda turned to see Sergeant Green smiling at her and for the first time ever she smiled back. Green's warrior heart melted. This Minda person was the most fascinating and wonderful creature he had ever encountered. Her unintentional seductive Gadan clothing over an extremely beautiful, fit, body was almost more than he could comprehend.

The Pastor managed to keep the ceremony to forty-five minutes. It actually would have been longer except a few of the impatient witnesses keep interrupting with, "Hey Pastor, move it along already!"

The celebration kicked into high gear when the words, "I now pronounce you husband and wife." Within minutes the adult beverages were flowing freely. Celeste and Astron were as happy as they could be, when suddenly Astron stopped and started to cry.

"What's the matter?" asked Celeste.

"Oh, I wish my mother could have seen this. She would be so happy."

"Don't worry Astron. I am positive she is smiling down upon us right now."

"You think so?"

"Look, I may not be the world's greatest churchgoer, but I know what I know and I know she is in a wonderful place watching her son and is very proud of him."

Astron looked at Celeste with the warmest of looks and simply said, "I love you."

The Gadans had brought some of their beverages and in spite of warnings they flowed quickly. Fortunately, Sergeant Green was off duty so he was able to indulge, to the amusement of Minda.

Minda wasn't as stone cold as she sometimes appeared. She had been keenly aware of Sergeant Green. She had shown him no recognition, even though she had seen in him a ruggedness very few male Gadans exhibited. As the two of them drank and ate, they found themselves laughing more and more; partly because their translation of words was not always correct, and partly because some unseen force was growing between them.

"Hey Minda, are you an only child?"

"I am not a child. What is an 'only'?"

"No, I can tell you're not a child. I mean do you have brothers and sisters?"

"I am one. I have a bow and arrows. We are all one, I thought, but today that man in the funny clothes said two were one. That seems nice."

Green tried to explain siblings but it made no sense to Minda. Finally she stood up and said, "You talk too much." For a second Green imagined Minda taking him by the hand and leading him off to a quiet location where his fantasies might play out. She didn't. Instead she went off to talk to Soon.

Chapter 40

Schooling

Harlyn and Uri came to Katherine and Dakota with a proposal. It was something Dakota had suggested earlier and Katherine had been considering, so the proposal was easily accepted. "We like Dakota's suggestion of a school. Specifically we want to teach the Gadans English and to prepare them for a trip to Earth."

"I agree, but has this been discussed with the Gadans? A school with no students won't get us every far."

Harlyn answered, "We're way ahead of you. Two of the elders were very interested as were some of the Protectors. They understand the communication issue at least. Preparing them for going 'back' wasn't as clearly understood, but they trust that it is necessary. In all, there are at least twenty Gadans for the first class. These people have all exhibited a high level of intelligence, so I think they will suck up whatever we have to offer like a sponge. The Elders would like the school in Gadan, probably near the trailhead leading to Mid Way. We don't think a fancy schoolhouse is needed. Just a roof, some walls, a few windows, and maybe a wood-burning stove for heat when the weather starts to turn."

"And where will you be getting a wood-burning stove?" asked Katherine.

"Come now, dear," said Dakota, "Celeste said she'd make one!"

Shaking her head, Katherine said, "Of course she did. So you knew about this did you? No, don't say anything. Who is the headmaster?"

"Why me of course," said Harlyn smiling, "Am I not the Vice Admiral of Academics and Science?"

Katherine agreed saying, "There is a rumor that you have some fancy title involving academics. So what can I say? Go for it."

"That's good," said Uri.

With no expression on her face, Katherine looked at Harlyn and Uri and said, "You've already started haven't you?"

Harlyn said, Well, yeah, maybe." And without waiting for a response he added, "While Uri is working on language, I'm showing pictures of some of the natural features on Earth; some of the cities, towns, farms, weather events etc. Basically anything we can think of. The city stuff is not registering with them. It is too abstract.

"Teaching English will be interesting. The Gadans language is a weird combination of the different languages that were brought here by the first Gadans and new words that were either made up or had morphed from some other words. I'm guessing that maybe five to ten percent of the words are English or English based. Uri is putting together a basic Gadan/English book of translation for instructors to use. I keep thinking about the Tower of Babble and how it relates here."

"How long do you think it will take to get the basic training done?"

"By the time the Bird Island Gate is done, we should be able to bring a few Gadans back to Earth for a visit. Once that happens and these first visitors return, I'm thinking the other Gadans can get educated faster. We'll have to see how things go with this first group."

Katherine said, "I've been thinking about the Gadan business. We were all surprised to find people when we got here. Correction, all except Uri here, the grand keeper of secrets."

Uri made no indication that this was even aimed at him.

"Anyway," Katherine continued, "This has been a distraction from our original mission. Not that it has been wrong, but most of our attention has been focused on the Gadans and what we have come to believe is the need for them to be reunited with us back on Earth. I don't think the Gadans have it that bad here. Sure there are things that can be done to make their life easier, but I have come to find that the way they live is quite nice. They are healthy, they are happy, and with the tandoo threat under control, the Gadans are safe. Doesn't seem that bad to me.

"Now that I've shared that thought, I have also come to realize that except for Anna and her efforts, we have expended very little effort in understanding this planet and what it might offer. Anna's team discovered the curative properties of some of the water here and she wasn't even looking. What else might be out there that could be useful if we were actually looking? I say that with two things in mind. First I think that some—maybe many—people back home might want to settle here. Secondly, there might be other things here that the Trading Company might want to capitalize on.

"Bottom line, in my estimation, while we are schooling the Gadans maybe we need them to school us a little on how they manage to be so healthy. And at the same time, learn more about this planet we've named Sanctum. I'm asking Captain Loring to head up another exploration team under the general guidance of Anna. I want more detailed aerial surveillance and a few teams to explore areas of interest at ground level. And Harlyn, in your spare time, have some of the loafers in your groups get a better understanding of the climate here. So far we know that weather in these parts can change suddenly and be brutal. What about other places? Are there other places where a settlement might be feasible? Are there areas we need to leave alone? In short, get the brain trust busy and get into the details of this place. We need to be schooled as much as the Gadans, maybe more."

Chapter 41

Earth Orbit (2170)

Admiral Wu finally found some relief once his two ships, British Commonwealth and South America, were in orbit around Earth. Getting these two ships back was certainly an accomplishment, but it wasn't very satisfying, and he was exhausted. It had been twenty-one years on this trip with nothing new discovered. Worst of all, he had lost his flagship China. He wanted to blame his idiot VAAS Wang Fang but understood it had been his own fault for not paying attention to what she had been doing. There was always something that needed his immediate attention, while he had believed she was just playing around trying to look important. If he'd only investigated sooner, perhaps her microbes wouldn't have destroyed the ship. Wu felt certain he would be court-martialed and thrown in prison.

But here they were, his combined crews of about 20,000 worn out but mostly intact, ready to turn the ships over to new crews for the next phase of the mission. Still, a large part of him wanted to continue on. He was financially broke, meaning he would have to start over with nothing if he was tossed out of the fleet. Also, if he could stay with the fleet, maybe he could redeem himself by finishing the mission. He knew, however, that wasn't going to be an option. It was time to face the consequences and fade into obscurity. It was time for new blood.

Wu had been told that the UNSC directors had asked for funding for another ship to replace China with the understanding that with everything now needed to finish the Gate on Sanctum, it would be impossible to get all the supplies on British Commonwealth and South America. He felt confident there had been enough time to build the new ship before his two ships arrived. With this in mind, Wu had felt a little better knowing that the next Admiral would have enough ships. That, of course, was small consolation for the many disappointments he'd had to deal with. Not being Admiral and not having command of the new constellation class ship named Centaurus just added to the disappointment.

As British Commonwealth and South America were going into orbit, Wu could see what appeared to be the new ship. He hadn't received a lot of detail regarding the new ship's status even though communications with UNSC had improved as the fleet got closer to Earth. He supposed that the directors were focusing more on whoever the new Admiral might be, so why bother with him. On the other hand he was more than just a little curious. Enough so, that he decided that before he'd face the directors he'd exercise his rank and check out the new ship. It would likely be the last thing he'd be able to do as Admiral.

Wu and Captain Null boarded British Commonwealth shuttle #1 and they were ferried over for a close look. What they saw was extremely disheartening. Noelle spoke first, saying, "Admiral, am I missing something? That ship isn't going anywhere any time soon. The engine pod ring has only one pod on it."

Wu answered in a very soft voice, "No wonder they were staying quiet." There was, in fact, activity around the ship with shuttles, drones, and assemblers working on the ship, but the degree of activity didn't seem to match the apparent need to complete the ship in a timely manner. "This isn't good. I wonder what the UNSC has in mind. I'd be willing to bet they're going to delay the departure to Alpha Centauri."

Noelle, couldn't help herself when she said, "You're not allowed to gamble, remember?"

"Yeah, right, very funny."

The next day Wu boarded British Commonwealth Shuttle #1 once again and climbed into the co-pilot seat. "Take us down, Lieutenant," he said, and the shuttle left the shuttle bay and headed for Earth. When on the ground, Wu went into a waiting jet. Once on board, a cabin steward prepared him a drink and served him something he hadn't had in years—a hamburger with all the fixings. He savored every bite. The plane landed just outside Albany and from there a limousine took him to UNSC headquarters. Doors were opened for him, and everyone was cordial and seemed pleased to see him. Many applauded as he walked the corridor. *This must the preparation for the firing squad that will be waiting for me,* he thought. *Dead man walking.*

Inside the conference room were the newest Operation Director, Science Director, and most of the commissioners. Wu couldn't tell what the mood was in the room. There were a few smiles between commissioners after some words were exchanged. Some were reading some documents, while others looked bored as hell.

"Welcome back Admiral Wu," said the Operations Director, Augustus Tzounopoulos, who remained seated and waved to an empty seat at the other end of the table, "Please have a seat. We have a lot to discuss." Once Wu was seated, Augustus continued, "We have your official daily reports from your voyage that were sent. Unless you have something to add, we would like to focus on the unfortunate incident with the Star Ship China."

Admiral Wu took a deep breath and started, "Yes sir. As Admiral, I take full responsibility for what happened. I knew that Vice Admiral Wang Fang was selected with the understanding that she would be conducting experiments that supposedly needed to be conducted in a more controlled environment. Apparently something that could not be obtained on Earth. It was understood by me, however, that this would not take away from her main task to manage all the academic activities in the fleet and all the various branches of science, including the mathematical requirements for our safe acceleration/deceleration cycles. Perhaps within a year, the Vice Admiral had relinquished all responsibility for these functions to the three ships' CASOs as she focused more and more on her research. This did not seem to be detrimental to the mission as far as anyone could tell. Besides, she was so disruptive in meetings, claiming she needed to be in the lab and that we shouldn't be wasting her time, that it seemed prudent to leave her and her scientific pursuits alone.

"It was only when we were starting to receive warnings of a weakened hull that I began to investigate. At first I wanted to blame the Mobile Ones, but apparently they were smarter than we humans in this case. We then broadened the investigation, but it turned out this was too late, as we soon lost an engine room pod and the on-duty staff. Not knowing where to look next, there was some thought Fang might have an answer. I knew Fang was doing something with microbes, but that is a long way from my field of understanding. I soon learned that the microbes she was manipulating were intended to be an efficient means of pollution control, specifically, carbon neutralization. Vice Admiral Fang demonstrated complete surprise that the ships' hulls were carbon-based, and seemed to panic. It did not take long to understand the panic as it became apparent some of these experimental microbes had found their way to China's bulkheads and hull and were doing exactly what they had been designed to do. They were converting the hull to something else. As China's hull was being compromised, we gradually abandoned the ship, taking all precautions to avoid a similar fate to British Commonwealth and South America."

Director Tzounopoulos said, "Yes, your reports covered this rather thoroughly. So why do you think you were responsible?"

"I am, or at least was, Admiral, and am ultimately responsible."

The Chinese Commissioner said, "You are still the Admiral. The Chinese government selected the Vice Admiral and she was encouraged to continue with the research that she had started years previously, but that didn't mean she was to relinquish her duties as the VAAS. This is embarrassing, but it never occurred to anyone that the research might have a negative impact on the ships."

"You knew what her research was all about?"

"Well, yes. In broad terms."

Admiral Wu was quickly going from the stance of apology to controlled outrage. "You're telling me that you knew she was working with microbes with the goal of converting carbon?"

"Yeah, I guess we'd have to say yes."

"And this was done knowing the ships were built with an extensive use of carbon?"

"To be fair, not everyone knew that."

Admiral Wu could no longer contain himself. He stood up, his face beet red and his mouth was open in disbelief. When he regained some composure, he repeated, "Not everyone knew? Well, certainly the Vice Admiral should have known, don't you think? Didn't anyone evaluate her for the actual job she was supposed to be doing? You people are unbelievable. Being fired by the bunch of you will be a blessing." And with that he stormed out of the room and headed down the corridor.

Behind the Admiral was Operations Director Tzounopoulos. "Admiral. Wait up," he said.

When Wu stopped, Augustus said calmly, "Will you come to my office? We need to talk."

Wu was so furious, he almost said no, but he also knew Augustus was new to the job in the latest turn of the revolving door—the directors came and went far too frequently to keep track—so he agreed. Entering the office, Augustus told his assistant, "We don't want to be disturbed." Once in the office, he asked Wu to sit down and pulled a bottle of single malt scotch off the side bar. "I'm having one, would you like one?"

Somewhat tersely Wu said, "Yes."

"Admiral, do you prefer to go by Ying or by Wu?"

Few people ever asked him that, so maybe this guy wasn't all bad. A little more under control now, Wu said, "Wu is fine, thank you for asking."

"Wu, I've been in this position for almost a year now. Compared to you, that's nothing, but it has given me time to realize that the UNSC, especially most of the commissioners, are nearly useless. The Star Struck Trading Company has become the real power here. Their Board of Directors and each of their CEOs have shown vision, and now money; a lot of money. They took a chance building the newest Star Ships and I will tell you straight out, I think they have found something at Alpha Centauri that will change everything."

"Okay," said Wu, "I'm listening. What's this got to do with me? I figure I'm out of a job now."

"You were comparatively young when you were made Admiral. How old are you now?"

"You must know I'm forty-nine years old."

"That's right," said Augustus, "You're forty-nine. That's too young to retire. I want you to finish the job and take British

Commonwealth and South America to Alpha Centauri and join up with Admiral Hickey to finish the Gate."

"So I'm not fired?"

"No. Not at all."

This was not how Wu thought the day was going to go, not at all. He looked at his glass, which was now empty, and held it up indicating he wanted more. Augustus obliged, the two men clinked glasses and Wu said, "I'm honored. Yes, I'll do it, but only if I get to have final approval of any of the senior officers. And oh, I'm going to get paid this time, right?"

Augustus agreed saying, "Yes, you have the final say, but there are already recommendations from the Trading Company. "And" he added with a laugh, "you'll be paid this time, though the Trading Company seems to like making deals."

"Excuse me, but did I miss something? You haven't mentioned the new ship Centaurus. Don't we need the third ship? Based on what I've seen, it isn't going anywhere soon."

Awkwardly, Augustus said, "Well, ideally, the answer is yes, we need the ship. As you have apparently seen, the ship is being built, though for right now it is mostly for show."

"What do you mean, 'mostly for show'?"

"I'll get to that. Believe it or not, when the world learned what had happened to China there was a huge surge of caring for Admiral Hickey and her fleet. As a result the ship is being funded by private donations. Not the UNSC and not even the Trading Company. We have put everything we have into a schedule that would have had the ship ready by now."

"I feel a large 'but' coming on."

"Yes, the 'but' is we can't build the engines. Critical components don't exist and to replicate them will take years, or we may never be able to do it. We built one engine pod and it is on Centaurus now providing shipboard power, but that's it. The show part is to try and demonstrate that the UNSC is still an effective organization."

"It doesn't seem that effective to me. So what is going to happen now?"

"We are sending your two ships off to complete the mission to Alpha Centauri. Obviously, the original plan to outfit three ships to carry what was needed to finish the Gate is no longer an option. It now means each ship will have to carry at least fifty percent more. Besides what Dakota Bickmeier had requested to complete the Gate originally, we now have to cram in even more to make up for what was destroyed in storms. At least that part is ready as everything has been staged to go."

Wu said, "I'm beginning to see why I wasn't fired. You found another way to punish me."

Wu's head was spinning as he left the building in a mixed state of elation and confusion. He had expected to be fired—or worse—and instead was exonerated and asked to stay on. But the prospect of staying on for the next phase to set up a Gate on Sanctum was looking rather glum. The UNSC was becoming more and more confusing and inept, if that was even possible.

Wu spent the next two months on Earth working with the Trading Company selecting the new crews. It felt a little strange that the UNSC was now taking a back seat and was only nominally in charge, but with his first meeting with the CEO, Charles Woolrich, it was clear that at least the Trading Company knew what to do. Charles had been born on British Commonwealth when the ship was between Epsilon Eridani and Tau Ceti. He grew up and learned from the best on the ship. He completely understood the dynamics involved. Like many of the crew, he took a chance and bought into the Trading Company when it was getting started. He watched the company grow as it conscientiously worked with the indigenous populations of Epsilon Eridani b and Tau Ceti e to create fair and environmentally-friendly trade agreements.

With those agreements generating a significant cash flow into the coffers of the company, it took a chance and chartered the United States to explore YZ Ceti, yielding a major potential for wealth from the planet named Prosperity. Seeing that the UNSC was more and more inept, the Trading Company quietly partnered with the Union of African Nations and funded Orion and Perseus for the mission to

Alpha Centauri and for all intents and purposes took over the wormhole gate operations. Wu was impressed.

Augustus had warned Wu that the Trading Company liked to make deals, so it wasn't really a surprise to him when Charles said, "You have a choice. You can maintain your current pay grade, or it will be cut substantially in exchange for shares in the Trading Company. Our philosophy from the very beginning is to provide a potential for a large reward to those that serve on the ships and take a chance, but there must be a buy-in. All those that hold stock in Star Struck Trading Company have served on the starships. I can truthfully say they have reaped large benefits, but it is your choice. To be clear, however, I'm talking about stockholders. We do have financial partners as well that we can't ignore, but they don't own stock or run the company."

Wu laughed, causing Charles to ask, "What's so funny?"

"Did you know I haven't received any pay for the last couple of decades? I signed on in exchange for my gambling debts being paid off. To have my zero pay reduced further doesn't leave me with very much." Then, considering what Charles had said, he added, "Now then, part of the deal was that I wasn't to gamble during the trip. Not for money anyway. But that trip is over, so I guess I'm free to gamble again. What you are offering sounds like a gamble, so what the hell, I'm in!"

Just shy of twelve months later, British Commonwealth and South America separated and left Earth's orbit, headed for Alpha Centauri with Admiral Ying Wu in command. Consistent with his desire to keep the crews as small as possible because of space, he elected not to have Vice Admirals and instead would rely more heavily on his two captains and CASOs.

Captain Brian Null was the son of his former VAO Earl Null and former Captain of the British Commonwealth Noelle Null. Brian was five years old when they had left TCe. He was educated on the ship and received his engineering degree while on board. He knew nothing outside of the ships, and now at the age of twenty-six was Captain. Very much like his father, he was six feet tall, 195 pounds and sported a rugged full beard, something Wu envied. He was single and claimed he wanted to remain that way, though the women on board seemed eager to change that status.

That included the British Commonwealth CASO who replaced Kem. Bridget Pardon, age twenty-six, was five feet two inches with short, very styled blond hair. Bridget also doubled as the ship's doctor. She had entered college at the age of seventeen and by all accounts was brilliant, obtaining a medical degree by age twenty-two. She had never been in space before and seemed eager for the adventure. She also liked the idea of changing Captain Null's status of single to something else. This would be more than a hobby for her!

About half of the South America crew decided to stay on. This included Juan Martinez as Captain and Ere-Mi-El as CASO, though in Ere's case it seemed clear he wasn't given a choice in the matter.

Each crew size was 5500, far short of the design capacity of 18,000. The ships load of Gate and construction material cut into crew quarters, especially since as much redundant Gate material as possible was crammed in. Every available space was used for storage. Even the lounge and dining room tables were replaced with crates of parts. Some of the reasoning for the smaller-than-desired crews, in addition to everything they had crammed on board, was that with the time spent by the crews of Orion and Perseus on Sanctum, a smaller construction force could finish things up.

Wu felt confident he wasn't leading his two ships into something that was unknown. He had read all the reports and was getting daily dispatches; even though they were years old by the time they reached him. For the first time in a long time, Wu was feeling pretty good. This was a true mission, as opposed to simply ferrying the ships back to Earth, and it was certainly going to be a lot shorter trip than the one he completed the previous year. Plus there were no experimental labs to worry about this time. Wu was in control. And to top it all off, he would actually have something in the bank when the trip was over! He felt great!

Chapter 42

Welcome (2179)

Late in the year of 2179, Admiral Wu, with his two ships British Commonwealth and South America, went into orbit around the planet Sanctum. After some careful maneuvering, they went bow-to-bow with Orion and Perseus, connecting up and rotating. Admiral Hickey invited Admiral Wu and his senior officers to shuttle down to Mid Way for a welcoming banquet and to plan for the completion of the Bird Island Wormhole Gate. Over the next month everyone on board the ships would have a chance to go down to Mid Way and Bird Island for some well-deserved shore leave. The new additions to the construction crew would, of course, stay on the ground in quarters already built.

Katherine had sent detailed messages on a regular basis to Wu, so he was up-to-date on the overall status. So much early work had already been completed that it was just the logistics of getting the rest of what was needed on the ground and installed to complete the Gate. Everyone was anxious to get started with this final phase, but no one was more anxious than Dakota. Still, he was told by his wife, "Cool your jets for a day or so. Let the new people settle in for a bit."

Some of the Gadans, especially Minda and her Protectors, had become much more comfortable leaving their compound and traveling to Mid Way. A more regular path had been made between the two compounds that could almost be considered a road. Without Astron to convince the tandoo to leave them alone, however, occasionally Minda's group would have to wound or kill one.

When the second fleet arrived, Katherine made it a point to have the usual Gadans in attendance for the celebratory banquet. Minda asked Wu, "Are you here to take us back?"

Wu had been clued in so could only answer, "No, we are not the ones."

Disappointed, Minda had another question that Katherine was hoping would not come up. "We see a very wide path on the other end of your Mid Way and we see a machine sometimes on that path. Where does it go? Is it yet another commune?"

"Yes," said Katherine. "It does lead to another commune on an island in the sea."

"What is an island and what is a sea?"

This question was astonishing at first, but Katherine supposed that if you had never seen either one, why would you know what they were? She said, "The sea is a very big water. When you are in the middle, you can't see any land. An island is a piece of dry land that is surrounded by the water. That island is called Bird Island and can been seen once you get to the shore. This place, where we are now, is called Mid Way, because it is mid way between Bird Island and Gadan. Does that all make sense?"

"No. If this island thing is in the middle of the sea, how do you get there? How do you know where it is all the time when the wind makes it float away?"

At first Katherine was confused about the "floating away part" then laughed. She said, "It doesn't float, it's part of the sea bottom that rises above the sea. And we use the silver birds and boats to get there and a back."

"What are boats?"

"Boats are things that float like a leaf in the stream and we ride in them."

"So you make big leaves that float to islands, but islands don't float. That seems unnecessary."

Katherine could tell this wasn't going anywhere fast so she concluded with, "We will take you there so you can see, but not today. Would that be okay?"

"You people are confusing," said Minda. "It makes no sense to have so many things to worry about. I think you make up stories to confuse us."

Katherine and Wu both laughed. "Yes," said Katherine, "We do make things up, but not this. You'll see." Then she thought, *We do have a lot of things and do a lot of things. How did that all become so important?*

Chapter 43

An Open Gate (2181)

Two days later, after the second fleet was settled in, shuttles started bringing equipment and supplies down to Bird Island. Dakota and the construction superintendent checked each delivery and distributed as necessary. Within a couple of hours the construction crew that had essentially been idle for quite some time was attacking the project again. The additional construction workers that had just arrived took a little time to get up to speed, but before long Bird Island was an amazing beehive of activity. Excavators, bulldozers, and tunneling equipment took up where they had left off. Towers went up and cables were strung. The finishing touches to the gatehouse itself were completed and the last of the massive transformers were installed.

Orion had previously donated one of its spare engine room pods. It had been entombed in a deep bunker in case of a failure and was now gearing up from idle mode to produce the needed power for everything Gate related.

Dakota had brought all the very high-tech equipment with him and had completed as much as he could. It was now a matter of completing connections and testing each subsystem before the overall system test. It always sounded easy, but Katherine had learned much from her predecessors and the number one thing she was told, "Katherine, always remember the Pi factor; take a guess at how long anything is going to take and multiple by Pi, you know 3.14. That's usually about how long it will really take." That formula was usually more right than wrong.

The formula didn't fail so despite the four months estimated to finish the gate, it actually took a little more than a year. But it was completed in early 2181, and it was now time for the first tests. With Gates on Earth, New Hope on EEb, High Point on TCe, and now Bird Island on Sanctum, the dialing in of the desired destination was getting to be a little trickier. Dialing in wasn't all that complicated once the operators were thoroughly trained. But it was still always in everyone's best interest to not have people vanish during the planned transfer. That scenario would be considered rather rude! So making sure everything worked as designed was paramount. The goal was to have whatever was being transferred appear in one piece at the intended destination. Today, the destination was Earth.

Earth had been told well in advance that today would be the day. The Bird Island Gate was loaded up with inanimate objects. A hammer, some rocks, a letter commemorating the day, and a photo of their site. The plan was to send these items to Earth and the same items with some additional items, like a bottle of champagne, would be sent back. The Gate was fired up in transmitting mode and the items disappeared as planned. Once the Gate was placed in receiving mode, anxious people at Bird Island waited for things to return.

After an hour, Katherine turned to Dakota and said, "Umm, shouldn't we have seen something by now?"

An obviously nervous Dakota only said, "I thought so!"

Another hour went by and finally the Gate became active. The items sent were returned with a large sign saying, "We think there is a problem. We were not expecting anything from your site." And it was signed: Gate Keeper, New Hope Island.

"Damn!" said Dakota, with a mixture of relief and concern as he ran into the control room. Katherine decided to leave him alone and eighteen hours later Dakota emerged saying, "I think I found the problem. One of the relays was from the spare parts pile on Earth and it was calibrated for New Hope. I replaced the relay and we should be good to go…I hope."

Once again the Gate was fired up and the goodies were sent off. This was well past the predetermined schedule, so Dakota, and everyone else for that matter, hoped the Earth Wormhole Gate was still in receiving mode as the items disappeared.

"So Dakota, my sweet husband and Gate builder extraordinaire, where did they go this time." asked Katherine in a sticky sweet voice.

"Why Earth of course. I hope."

"I hope as well. And I don't mean New Hope either."

A few minutes later, back in receiving mode, the items that had been sent returned minus the letter and photograph, but replaced with the bottle of champagne. A cheer went up and the bottle was opened, as Katherine said, "We need to check this out for quality control purposes."

Over the next few days an increasing number of complex items were sent and received. A chicken and Labrador Retriever were "volunteered" as the last test before people might be transferred. However, when the Gate was placed in receiving mode, instead of the chicken and the retriever, they received a duck and a beagle. Dakota's heart jumped into his throat as he panicked. But then he read the accompanying note saying, "Ha ha, gotcha didn't we. Ostrich and cow made it safely."

Katherine and Wu laughed as Dakota said sarcastically, "Yeah, very funny. What a bunch of clowns."

It was always nerve-racking to have people test a Gate for the first time, especially for the ones that actually volunteered to go through the Gate. When asked for volunteers, a husband and wife team said they would do it. They were terribly homesick. When told that usually only one person would be the test subject, they looked warmly at each other and she said, "We have been married for forty-two years and do everything together. If this test fails, we want to go together." They entered the Gate holding hands, the Gate was activated, and they were gone.

Back in receiving mode an hour later, Gabe-Re-El appeared—much to everyone's surprise. Katherine looked at Wu and Dakota and said, "I'm willing to bet this is not just a social call."

"Agreed," said Wu. "Whenever Gabe shows up, there seems to be a shift in the cosmos."

Chapter 44

Gabe's Revelation

Gabe had come through the wormhole gate announcing he was there as an official representing the UNSC and the UAN. He had come to see firsthand what had been accomplished on Sanctum. At least that is what he had told people initially. There was a much more profound reason that he was getting ready to share, but only to those that should know and potentially understand. In any case, Katherine's and Wu's suspicion meters went off the scale.

Gabe spent a few days at Bird Island and Mid Way and then visited Gadan with Ere and Uri. They insisted on doing this without anyone else, which didn't sit that well with Katherine, but she didn't interfere. Ere and Uri had been to Gadan more than a few times, working with the Gadans in the school, so they accompanied Gabe without saying very much. They already had a good understanding of the workings within the valley. Outside of a few random questions to the Gadans and his companions, Gabe didn't have much to say either. He just looked around, which left the Gadans more than a little curious about this new person. Was he the one to take them back?

Gabe, Ere, and Uri did use their antigravity packs at times when out of sight of others, but they also enjoyed walking on this pristine planet. It was while they were leaving Gadan, walking slowly along what had now become a distinct trail, that Gabe broke his silence. "Uri and Ere," said Gabe quietly, "The time is fast approaching."

"Are you sure?" said Uri, "It seems to me we still have a lot of work to do."

Ere said to Gabe, "I already told him that. Maybe not so much here, but back on Earth, there are a bunch of issues."

Gabe said, "No, I am not sure, but the Boss has made it clear that it is time to move on. The Order was allowed to be more directly involved than in the past as a final push, or, in some cases, to make final gifts. The three of us will be going back to Earth in one week.

You need to clear up any loose ends you might have and say your goodbyes."

"Gabe, you've seen the Gadans and you've seen what Katherine and her crew have done so far to try and prepare them for what might come next. What's going to happen now?"

"So, from what I've seen, mankind has done a better job with the Gadans than our own people have done. It is clear that Katherine's people are looking for a way to preserve Sanctum, and I think the curative waters of Sanctum may have provided them with the means to do so. Mankind certainly has a ways to go, but at some point the level of competence has to be enough. I think mankind is as ready as they can be. Hopefully they will continue to learn and not make too many mistakes in the process. I mean the Order has made mistakes over the millennia, so we can't expect mankind to do otherwise. In any case, the Boss has made the decision so you and I have nothing more to say about it. This isn't going to happen instantaneously, but tomorrow I will start with a conversation and we'll have to see how it goes."

The next day Gabe asked Katherine if he could meet with her and her senior staff, with no explanation except to say he had an important announcement. Katherine and the rest of the officers naturally wondered what was to come next and weren't at all comfortable with the apparent cloak of secrecy. Once assembled in a quiet corner of the Proxima Pub, Gabe asked Ere and Uri to keep prying eyes and ears at a distance. Gabe said, "Please, everyone be seated and make yourselves comfortable. Today, I am not representing the UNSC or the UAN. As some of you may know, or at least suspect, I am a high-ranking member of a benevolent order assigned to assist, but not interfere, with the advancement of mankind. The Order has been in existence for thousands of years and has attempted whenever possible to maintain a low profile."

These words were making many in the room very uncomfortable, especially those that didn't know about the Order. But it was the next words that really got everyone's attention. "We are not of Earth. Where we are from is not important, but today, I'm announcing to you here before anyone else, that we will all be leaving, never to return. All of my people will return to Earth and from there we will depart as one. During these last few years we have led you to resources to be used as tools to improve the human condition. Consider these as gifts, but with these gifts there are subtle strings attached. It is our belief that mankind is now ready to take a leadership role throughout the universe. This will not be done quickly, nor will it be easy, or even guaranteed. But much of what our Order has done in the past didn't guarantee positive results either. The Gadan commune is an unfortunate example. Bluntly stated, the Order screwed up. You, on the other hand, have made major strides in addressing the errors we made and you have done so in a sensitive and methodical manner. You, representing mankind, have shown that you have the potential to use the gifts you have received to help others. We, that is to say the Order, hope you continue to use these gifts wisely.

"I have much work to do on Earth before our departure. Here on Sanctum, you have a number of initiatives underway and those should continue forward, especially as they relate to the Gadans. We will not be far away, but will no longer try to influence anything you do."

After too long of a pause, Dakota stepped out of his usual above-the-fray attitude and said in an almost-menacing voice, "My parents told me about you and your Order. I probably should have pieced things together, but I honestly didn't believe, or choose to believe, that what I was told could be the truth. You know you can't make someone believe, and I didn't. Now I am a believer and am torn between outrage and gratitude. Outraged that mankind has been manipulated; grateful that you probably saved mankind. And now with this revelation, my anxiety level is through the roof." Then looking around the room, he said, "It appears I'm not alone. Thanks a lot!"

It was Wu's turn, who only said, "When is this all happening?"

Gabe only said, "Not right away. For now Uri, Ere, and I will be going back to Earth to make preparations, but note that those preparations include whatever help I might be able to provide." And with that, Gabe left the room, leaving a less-than-satisfied small representation of mankind sitting in silence.

Chapter 45

Earth Visit (2181)

It had been months since Gabe, Uri, and Ere left Sanctum. Remembering what Gabe had said, Katherine felt it was time to do something. She thought, *We'll do something. It might be wrong, but we're going to do it.* When she laid out the plan, it was obvious no one in Katherine's group felt comfortable about this trip, but it was time. For the past twelve years, Gadans had been gradually introduced back to the human race with formal and informal teachings. Some Gadans had been allowed to interact more directly at Mid Way with the starship crews, especially those assigned to construction activities. This inclusionary tactic was thought to let these Gadans learn at their own pace, but just as importantly it allowed Katherine's people to observe the Gadans.

A good portion of the formal teaching had initially been aimed towards language. Uri had done an excellent job developing tools to translate the mixed babble language the Gadans had developed to English and back again, so it was English that was being taught, with mixed results. Some of the Gadans like Minda really got into it. Some didn't see a need, saying, "Well if Minda knows what they are talking about, I don't need to learn anything." Minda wasn't any happier about this than she was about all the other things she ended up doing. Somehow, she had been trapped into a leadership role that kept expanding. Everything she did seemed to place her in a position where she was being asked to do more.

And so, on this historic day, Minda was the first one pushed to the front of the line of volunteers to go through the Gate back to Earth. With her were another Protector, Soon, and two elders called Taback and Weha. They weren't sure what this Gate thing was; in fact they had no idea and as a group were quite unnerved. They had observed people and things entering this Gate and disappearing while other people and things seemed to simply appear. If they had any concept of magic, this would certainly be it.

Dakota had tried to explain, but as any explanation needed to be based on simple concepts, it was impossible. "We call this a Gate. It like opening a door to another room."

"What is a door?"

So Dakota had to show them a door in one of the shops. Any technical explanations were simply meaningless to the Gadans. The concern for Katherine was that once the "door" was opened to Earth, it might just be too overwhelming for the Gadans to handle. Fingers were crossed.

The escorts for the Gadans were Dakota, Astron, Celeste, Harlyn, and Sergeant Green, the one Marine that somehow managed to be in Minda's vicinity whenever she was away from Gadan. Arrangements had been made for Gabe to meet the group at the Earth Wormhole Gate in his role as a UNSC Commissioner. It took a little coaxing to have the Gadans wear something that would be less revealing than their typical warm weather attire, but eventually they were convinced to put on one-piece jumpsuits over their own clothes and to wear sandals.

The nine entered the Bird Island Wormhole Gate on October 10, 2181. After a few psychedelic minutes as they were transported to the Earth Wormhole Gate in South Dakota, they emerged. The Gadans were obviously shaken. Minda expressed her discomfort as best as she could, saying, "Not like that. Thought you friends. Friends not do that to friends. Where are we?"

Dakota answered, "We are back from where your people first came. This land is called South Dakota. I am named for this place."

"Look like Bird Island. Tall poles with long vines. Not lot people."

There were, in fact, some people. The people that maintained the Gate knew about the Gadans story and were curious to see these people being reunited on Earth. What they were expecting wasn't clear, but what they saw was certainly interesting. The Gadans were simply beautiful people. There was some expectation that the Gadans would be joyful as they emerged from the Gate room. Instead they had looks of confusion and dread. They certainly weren't joyful and weren't receptive to welcoming gestures. As promised, Gabe was there to greet the group.

Dakota said, "This is not our final destination. We are going to fly in a silver bird to a big village where our elders live. This will be another new experience for you, but you will be safe. There are important people that want to meet you, but we will try not to move things along too quickly."

The four Gadans just stared at Dakota, making him feel rather uncomfortable. Things were already moving too quickly. Gabe was remaining uncharacteristically quiet, observing the Gadans and noting every little nuance in their behavior.

A van took the group out through the Gate compound to a small airstrip. Two planes were on the strip. A military Lear jet was waiting to take everyone except Astron and Celeste to Albany. The other private jet was to carry Astron and Celeste to Star Struck Trading Company Headquarters for a meeting called by the Board of Directors.

The Gadans had to be shown how to get into the plane and be strapped in for the flight. They didn't like being restrained. Even the brave Minda showed some fear as the engines were started and the plane started to move. Sergeant Green sat across from Minda and smiled to try and reassure her that it was going to be okay. The cabin was small, but large enough that the cabin steward, dressed in an Air Force uniform, was able to offer lemonade and some vegetable snacks. That helped calm things down a little.

Looking out of the windows, the Gadans saw fields and towns of a size they couldn't believe. The fear that they might have experienced from looking down from a high altitude seemed to be overridden by the wonder of what they were seeing. Not much was said during the flight to Albany.

Harlyn said quietly to Dakota, "I wish there was some way to slow this whole show down so the Gadans could catch a break. I'm starting to think the videos we showed them beforehand didn't register."

"Yes, I agree. This kind of thing is nothing close to anything within the realm of my training. It is far outside my comfort zone." Then, looking at Gabe, he added, and you, who I thought was supposed to be helpful, haven't said much of anything. What do you think?"

Gabe said, "Since the eventual goal for the Gadans hasn't been clearly defined, I think you're doing fine. I think things will work out in the Gadans best interest."

"Great. When we ask for help, we get nothing. When we don't ask for help, you offer more than your two cents' worth."

Gabe just shrugged.

As the plane started to descend, the Gadans showed more and more concern as the ground got closer and closer. When the plane came to a complete stop and the engines were shut down, the tensed muscles of the Gadans finally relaxed. The plan was to spend a quiet night in a small hotel and then meet with the UNSC Directors and Commission members in the morning. The concern was that the hotel experience alone was going to be stressful. And it was.

The ride from the airport to the city was dreadfully quiet. The Gadans were so obviously overwhelmed that it was unsetting to both Dakota and Harlyn. Gabe was stoic in appearance. Sergeant Green smiled at Minda, but that didn't seem to help.

At the hotel, the Trading Company had reserved four suites for them. Each had two bedrooms. Each Gadan was paired with an escort to guide them through the use of the water faucets, showers, and toilet. Everything was so totally alien to the Gadans, they just wanted it all to stop. One thing they didn't need was instructions for the bed. That was something they took to immediately.

The eight of them met for dinner out on the patio, away from prying eyes. Partly because it was out of doors and would be more comfortable for the Gadans, but also because the Gadans ate with their hands and that information didn't need to be shared. Sensitive to the Gadans usual diet, the food served was all vegetables. Only Sergeant Green grimaced, as he really wanted meat! The Gadans didn't eat very much. They were too keyed up. Gabe, as usual, made up for it so no food was wasted.

Before going to their rooms, Dakota told everyone to sleep well. "Tomorrow is going to be busy. We will meet for breakfast." Seeing the blank expression on the Gadans face, he explained, "I mean a morning meal, and then go over to headquarters."

Taback asked, "What are headquarters?"

Patiently, Harlyn said, "Where elders meet."

In their separate rooms, the Gadans laid on their beds with their heads swimming. Minda and all Gadans had lived their lives believing that "going back" would be a wonderful experience. *Maybe it will be*, Minda thought, *but so far I don't like this. Everything seems complicated.* Supposedly settled in for the night, Minda was alone in her room and she didn't like it. Time meant little to her, but it was two hours later when, unable to sleep, she got up.

Across the living room from Minda's room, Sergeant Green was asleep, dreaming of Minda. He woke as a warm, naked Minda crawled into bed with him. He thought he was still dreaming. *Can this be true?* he thought. It was true, and it was a wonderful night fulfilling a fantasy he thought could never happen. At breakfast the next day, Sergeant Green was smiling. Minda, however, was expressionless.

Before 9:00AM the van pulled up to the UNSC headquarters and the party entered the building. This was the largest building the Gadans had entered and they simply couldn't believe what they were seeing. There were dazzling, colorful pictures of spacecraft on the very tall walls of the vestibule and a model of one of the starships hanging from the ceiling. And although it was very dazzling, to the Gadans these things meant nothing. These were just shapes of, well, something. Even the name of this place meant nothing, even though the schooling they had received was supposed to prep them. United Nations Stellar Commission? What are nations? Stellar they had discovered meant stars, but what's a commission? The Gadans were totally and completely overwhelmed.

When they entered the conference room, Operations Director Augustus Tzounopoulos was surprised to see Gabe. "You're with them?"

"Yes," Gabe said, "I thought it might be helpful."

After a moment of silence, Augustus said, "You just pop in and out of places. Are you the UAN Commissioner today, an ambassador to Gadan, or a Trading Company lobbyist?"

Smiling Gabe said, "What would you like me to be?"

"Humph," was the only muffled reply.

The Gadans had no idea what was going on. As a group they sat down on the soft conference room chairs. Protector Soon admirably rubbed her hands over the smooth walnut conference room table.

To the Gadans, Augustus said with a smile, "So, how has your visit to Earth been so far? Are you ready to come back?"

Dakota winced. The directors and commissioners had been told they should take their time with the Gadans. He supposed that compared to the speed of light, this very direct question was slow, but it wasn't what he had in mind. So he said, "The Gadans are taking in the sights and so far haven't seen very much."

"Yeah, okay, but we need to make plans to reunite them with their own people."

Minda, as usual, was the first Gadan to speak. "We Gadans are a people. Gadans are own people. You confused."

Sergeant Green nearly burst out laughing, but held it in. His feelings for Minda were getting stronger and stronger.

Augustus was flummoxed and looked at Minda with his mouth slightly opened, considering what to say next. Looking to an amused Gabe, he said, "Ah, so what's next on the agenda for our guests."

"Well, we wanted you to meet so that faces could be attached to names." Trying not to laugh he added, "You have now met Minda," and then introduced Soon, Taback and Weha. "With the limited time up to this point we've not had a chance to show the Gadans much beyond Albany. We'll be heading to the countryside next. I think that will be more to their liking."

"Yes, well, ah," stammered Augustus as he looked around to the few still quiet commissioners. "If there is anything we can do to help, please let us know."

With no sign of any emotion as she stood up, Minda said, "You need help. You confused," which produced more than a couple of smiles.

And with that, the visitors all got up and left. The meeting was a lot shorter than expected. After the visitors left, Augustus said to those remaining. "I'm not sure what just happened."

The British Commissioner laughed and said, "I think that Minda was right, you're confused. Probably more than usual." And he laughed some more.

Arrangements had been made for a small bus to transport the Gadans and their escorts. Dakota really wanted to slow things down, so using ground transportation seemed the best. They traveled into the New York farm country and spent some time on a few farms. The Gadans seemed most favorably inclined towards those operated by the Amish, who were even more inclined to avoid technology than they had been a century earlier. Dakota tried to avoid any place where animals were raised as food, but that proved impossible and when the Gadans realized what the animals were for, they were horrified. "You just like tandoo," said Taback.

Days later they traveled to Massachusetts and into the hills that reminded the Gadans of their valley. They were curious about the different animals, and the houses, barns, and other structures they saw. Bridges really got their attention. Everyone ate meals together, but at night each was provided with his or her own room. The Gadans, being more communal, didn't appreciate what Dakota was trying to do for sleeping arrangements and it became apparent that among the Gadans, only Weha slept alone. Soon and Taback shared a bed. To the delight of Sergeant Green, Minda found her way to his room every night.

Because the tour was during autumn, the Gadans got to see harvests and sample some of the bounty the farmers brought in. The use of machinery was mesmerizing, but to Dakota, Harlyn, Sergeant Green, and even Gabe, it wasn't clear what the Gadans were thinking. After more than a week of touring Harlyn asked, "Is this what you were expecting? Have you seen anything that would meet your needs when you all come back?"

Taback said, "Not ready."

"Not ready for what?"

Taback looked at his three companions and repeated, "Not ready."

Finally after two full weeks on Earth, the party, minus Gabe, went back to the Earth Wormhole Gate and returned to Sanctum.

Gabe seemed to be the only one that understood what had transpired, but wasn't ready to say anything.

Chapter 46

Board Room

After they arrived on Earth with the Gadans and their escorts, Astron and Celeste headed off to Iowa and the Star Struck Trading Company. The Board of Directors had called a meeting and wanted Astron in attendance. Charles Woolrich was retiring as soon as the Board elected a new President and CEO.

Charles had been the third President following the company founder Admiral Dodson and then Astron's mother, Sharon Hooding. The Trading Company stockholders were still limited to those that had at one time or another served in the starship fleet. These people had proved their willingness to take chances and because of the corporate mentality, took investment chances—chances that had paid off handsomely. The other big investor, the Union of African Nations, had also reaped huge financial rewards investing the funds and become a world leader in many fields, but most especially in ecosystem preservation and restoration.

The Trading Company and the UAN didn't need more financial wealth. They collectively believed they were to do what the rest of world was either unwilling or incapable of doing. Their mission statement was clear. They were to continue to manage the wormhole gates. They were to continue to fund explorations with the starships under the general guidance of the UNSC. They were to protect what needed protection and take only what was needed.

The Board knew Astron; how could they not? They knew the secret of his parents. They also knew he had the power to persuade when needed and that he was more capable than anyone of seeing many problems simultaneously, organizing the real issues, and often devising a simple, single plan, to resolve everything. And he did it all quietly with no fanfare.

The Chairman of the Board said, "There is no need to beat around the proverbial bush. Astron, we want you take over as President and CEO of the Star Struck Trading Company. We already know your position on most subjects. If you accept the job, you will, of course, have our complete support."

"I need to ask Celeste."

"You can do it now," and with a nod to the door, a board member opened the door and Celeste entered. Celeste said, "They already asked me. Of course you'll accept, you big goof."

"Yes dear," said Astron and the entire room burst into laughter. Everyone knew that as intelligent as Astron was and with all his abilities, he would still do whatever Celeste wanted. That had never changed from when they were children rebuilding the old Ford.

More seriously, Astron said, "I am honored that you have asked me to take the helm. Honestly, I expected you to choose from among yourselves. After all, you've been right here in the thick of things guiding the company."

The Chairman said, "Of course we considered many possible leaders, but we wanted some fresh blood that hasn't been tainted with too much time in the Board Room. Besides, we will be watching and hopefully keep you from straying too far from our core values. Though we collectively believe that if you were to stray, it wouldn't be done purposely. In other words, we think Celeste will be great!"

Astron looked puzzled and repeated, "Celeste?" bringing a hardy round of laughter.

Realizing the joke, Astron also smiled and said, "Thank you! I, or should I say Celeste, am very comfortable with the Trading Company mission statement, but I want to detail my thoughts of taking only what is needed and protecting what needs to be protected. Celeste and I have spent more time on Sanctum than just about anyone. We shouldn't destroy the place by taking anything more than what we need. Specifically, the waters we have come to call the Elixir. We are close to determining what is a sustainable harvesting of these waters. We may have to judicially distribute these healing waters, but that is what we should do. We could exploit this and make huge profits, but I propose the money we charge should cover costs, nothing more.

"It seems reasonable that we can create small outposts on Sanctum for the purpose of harvesting the Elixir. These outposts could also provide accommodations for tourists. But they must be kept small and basic. In this case, however, we should charge large sums of money to visit Sanctum in order to keep demand low.

"It isn't clear to me that the Gadans will actually return to Earth either as a group or as individuals. Whatever they decide, we need to provide for their needs. And I mean needs. There are big differences between a want and a need. They are basically very happy people, but some real tools would make a huge difference for them.

"I have no problem exploiting Prosperity. That is especially true for Lehtolarite. That stuff has already proved it can be beneficial in many ways and there are indications we can do even more with it. That is something we can charge large sums of money for and in this case, the benefit far outweighs anything we might charge. Now, we should not allow chain of custody out of our hands. We should mine it, process it, make products, and whether we sell it, rent it, or franchise the end product, we need to make sure it comes back to us when the product use has come to an end so we can reuse it."

"Well now Astron," said the smiling chair, "I'm pleased you have taken some time to think about this during your thus far lengthy tenure as President and CEO. It will be interesting to see what else you might come with after you've had the seat for more than five minutes. What are your thoughts on further exploration?"

Astron said, "Sorry, I was actually expecting someone else would be asked to take over so it was all there waiting to come out. As far as further exploration is concerned, oh, that must continue. We need a larger pool of thoughts on that subject, however. We essentially have two fleets right now. Of those, mining is the only real activity at the moment. What I'd like to see happen is the UNSC redefine itself with stronger leadership and then we would collectively develop a plan. Supporting exploration is good for us, but it isn't our business. We need to focus on what we know, fair trading.

"That said, some of you have learned what Gabe-Re-El revealed to us on Sanctum. I was perhaps as surprised as many of you about what he had to say, but much of what he said made sense; even if it damaged the pride of those that thought mankind was in charge of its own destiny. Anyway, he made it clear that his people, not of Earth, have been prodding mankind onto the right course when we strayed too far. This has been going on for thousands of years, quietly making people think proper action was their idea and not that of the Order.

"In more recent times, this Order has been more upfront and active. Now, the Order will be leaving Earth and mankind. The recent increased activity was to provide us with parting gifts, with the more obvious ones being the Elixir and Lehtolarite. But these gifts come with strings attached. It is clear we never had a say in accepting the gifts. We might not have taken them if we knew there were strings attached, but as it turns out the so-called strings were something we had already accepted unknowingly. In this, it is safe to say our Trading Company has been the leader. We have helped species not of Earth, protected and corrected ecosystems, and we are guiding the Gadans to a better life of their own choosing. To continue this mindset as we travel to other worlds is what we are destined to do. We are to take up where the Order leaves off, and it will be the Trading Company leading the way. This seems to be a significant shift in the cosmos and a definite alteration of what we have come to expect on the horizon."

"Excuse me, Astron," said a board member, "But we know your father was a member of this Order. Where are you in this? Are you going to be leaving also?"

"That's a fair question." Then smiling and glancing towards Celeste before answering, he said, "You know, you should have asked that before offering me the positions of President and CEO." For some in the room Astron took too long to answer the question, but there was relief when he did. "The human half of me means I cannot be part of the Order and leave. Even if I could, I wouldn't, because it would mean leaving Celeste and that is something I could never bear. I was oblivious to my feelings towards her until she was nearly taken from me by the tandoo. It is clear to me that we are one and shall always remain as one. I shall never leave her, and by extension, hope to be President and CEO of the Trading Company for many, many years."

The Board could see Astron was serious, and at the same time Celeste was smiling and tearing up simultaneously.

"Okay," said the same board member, "You convinced me. And oh, that little speech seems to have scored a few points with

Celesta as well," the member added, to which everyone chuckled at Celeste's embarrassment.

Chapter 47

First Governor (2182)

The control of Earth's interstellar space program was continually being given up by the UNSC. Since the Commission was weak and lacked a willingness to commit the resources necessary for any kind of a viable program, it was leaving a vacuum; and Mother Nature abhors a vacuum. Only a few commissioners exhibited anything that resembled competence. This translated into Science Director and Operation Director selections getting worse with each turn of the revolving door. As the entire UNSC became more inept, the Star Struck Trading Company continued to fill the vacuum with leadership to the point where nothing was being done by the UNSC without first checking with the Trading Company. So while the UNSC maintained the authority on paper, it was the Star Struck Trading Company, with its accumulating resources, wielding the real power. This power could have easily been abused, but where the UNSC made poor choices, the Trading Company looked beyond financial gain. It combined a corporate philosophy of taking only what was needed, while maintaining good stewardship of everything they touched. Some tried to find fault with this, but most chalked that attitude up to jealously.

Astron Hooding and his wife Celeste Bickmeier held the corporate philosophy high, and it was this philosophy that would determine the fate of Sanctum. They decided that the entire planet should be considered a place of limited access and of limited resources. It wasn't to be kept completely isolated, but resources, of any kind, weren't to be taken beyond sustainable levels.

The Bird Island Wormhole Gate would be maintained for travel and the movement of goods. Gadan and its people were free to come and go as they pleased, but as Gadans were content in their ways for the most part, no outside pressure was placed on them. Gradually over time, if they chose to assimilate into the Earth culture, that would be left to them.

Mid Way was designated the center of the Sanctum's political power and resource management, but someone needed to be put in charge to provide needed oversight and rule enforcement. Astron and Celeste made it clear to UNSC what kind of person they thought should be "selected" by the UNSC, and went out to find this person. Following their usual modus operandi, the UNSC relinquished the responsibility but maintained the token authority.

Charles Canton, or Chuck to everyone that knew him, had been the Pastor on the Star Ship Africa before returning to Earth. His beliefs were considered liberal when it came to religion. He preached about and believed in a Supreme Being, but also that there was no one religion that was "the correct religion." Any religion that offered sincere peace and goodwill was fine with him. During his time in space and interacting with the members of the Order, he at first started to question his beliefs, but in the end he had an even stronger understanding of his own beliefs. He was practical, worked hard, played hard, and certainly knew how to have a good time. He never argued with anyone, but could easily bring someone around to his way of thinking using calm logic. By the same token, he was more than willing to change his mind on any subject if the facts that were presented made it clear he had been wrong. The respect for Chuck was unquestionable.

From a physical standpoint, Chuck wasn't impressive in size, standing at five feet six inches and 140 pounds. He was wiry and regularly would run ten miles or more just for fun. At the tender age of forty-eight, his hairline was receding much faster than he would have liked, but he shrugged it off until he had a chance to drink some of the Elixir from Sanctum. Within weeks, the hairline stopped retreating and started making a mild advance. Chuck was impressed and became nearly obsessed, thinking about Sanctum and how it might help his family.

Chuck's wife, Abigail, was a petite and very frail individual, but—with Chuck's help—Abigail produced two boys, now five and seven years old. Both were well-mannered and intelligent, but prone to every illness that came along. The idea of resettling someplace where his family could thrive was exciting, so when he had a chance to interview for the Governorship position he didn't hesitate.

Astron and Celeste had known of Chuck and hoped he would meet their expectations. He did. "Tell me Chuck," asked Astron, "what would be your vision of governing Sanctum?"

"Well, of course things will change over time and while I might have ideas now, those too will likely have to change once the reality of the place sets in. That said, I see the same vision as you of a planet that, for the most part, should be left alone. Bird Island, Mid Way, and Gadan should be encouraged to be models of good stewardship. I'm not sure what the ideal human population should be, but it should stay small and once obtained it shouldn't change. That is, the numbers shouldn't change. People changing places with those on Earth, High Point, and New Hope shouldn't be discouraged, but should be carefully managed.

"Exploration of the planet should continue with Mid Way acting as a supply depot for these efforts. But while exploration should be encouraged, leaders need to make certain little, if any, trace of any explorations are left behind. Discoveries, and I'm certain there will be some, need to carefully studied with the goal of helping mankind, and we shouldn't forget, the indigenous wildlife."

"What about the tandoo?"

"What about them? From what I understand, there is a kind of unofficial truce between the humans and the tandoo. The human compounds are small relative to the size of the planet. While I don't think hunting tandoo, or anything else should be condoned, any tandoo threat should be dealt with as required. I like the Gadans' approach to the tandoo threat.

"By the way, I like a lot of what the Gadans do and I would encourage no meat eating on Sanctum; especially any native species and certainly never in the presence of the Gadans."

Celeste asked, "What about alcohol consumption?"

"My answer is simple and truthful even if it eliminates me from consideration. No drugs allowed. With the Elixir, there would be no health reasons for them. I see no reason to eliminate responsible alcohol consumption. No one could reasonably expect abstinence, by the way. I understand even the Gadans figured that one out. I think it was Benjamin Franklin that said 'beer is proof God loves us.' I agree. I like my beer and wine."

Astron and Celeste both laughed, but Celeste said, "I would think you would be incapable of managing Sanctum if you were that rigid. But I'll warn you not to consume whatever the Gadans brew up. That stuff can knock you on your butt, big time!"

Astron asked, "What about tourists? There are a lot of people that would like to visit Sanctum."

"Yes, I'm thinking it would be good, but a tourist bureau should monitor it closely. Something like eco-tourism might be good, but it needs to be limited. Maybe have some of the tourists involved with exploration. Tourists would need to be vetted, and I think a sizable fee might be good to offset the Gate costs," and then, he added chuckling, "and my exorbitant salary."

"You think this is a paying position?"

This threw Chuck off. He said, "well, yes, I thought so."

Astron smiled, "Yes you'll get a salary with an annual review that could also result in termination if we, oh, I suppose officially if the UNSC doesn't like what is seen. I doubt you'll ever hear from them."

There were many more questions and interviews of references, but in the end Chuck Canton became the logical candidate. So on April 1, 2182, the Canton family entered the Earth's Wormhole Gate located in Zeibach, South Dakota and reemerged from Sanctum's Bird Island Wormhole Gate. From there, they were taken by launch to the mainland and then driven to Mid Way. There were some that greeted the first Governor with tempered enthusiasm. Many had a wait-and-see attitude before getting too excited. After all, they seemed to be doing just fine without a Governor.

The Governor's Palace, as it was being dubbed, was still under construction, but it was plain to see that the grandest aspect of the building was the designation of "palace." It was being built of brick just like all the other permanent structures. Thick reinforced walls, windows with storm shutters, and a roof connected with cables to the foundation. All built to withstand the sudden intense storms that could last for days. Living quarters were on the second floor with limited bedroom space for visitors. The offices and communications center were on the first floor. All administrative and security offices were to be in the Governor's Palace. While Anna Giblin was building a lab for environmental studies nearby, her work was considered so important she had an office next to Chuck's. Plans called for a wing that would be used for receptions and entertainment. The building was designed to be efficient and in this case, it was design that took a distant second place over function. Abigail could see right from the beginning that it would take her many years of decorating before it could feel like something other than a bomb shelter. "Well Governor," she said to her husband, "Start governing!" And they laughed.

Chapter 48

Choices

The settlement of Polyarnaya on TCf hadn't exactly been forgotten, but because the people there were mostly mutineers and wanted to be there, everyone else seemed satisfied to leave them alone. The biggest TCf issue for the UNSC and the Trading Company was the still-contaminated Star Ship Russia that remained in orbit around the planet. For lack of any other explanation, the working theory remained that some sort of addictive pollen allowed the TCf inhabitants to live on the planet, but once off, they became ill. The problem was that whatever the source, the same stuff had been brought on board and contaminated the ship. The one major effort to decontaminate the ship failed, so the ship was still in orbit, useless to everyone.

That decontamination effort was now years ago and since then only maintenance trips to the ship were made by citizens of Polyarnaya; quick trips to make sure the engines, still in idle, were behaving themselves. But those temperamental engines needed more love than could be given in these short visits, and as a result another engine room pod was ejected and exploded at a safe distance. The ship was now down to three engine room pods, so even if it were decontaminated, moving it would be a little more challenging.

Captain Gigory Kazakov had been the individual that had first learned that life on the planet was possible, and actually quite pleasant. He had befriended what he first believed to be an indigenous species of animal that seemed to have a kind of telepathic ability. These sheep-sized animals—with coats that were more feather-like than hair or fur—seemed to be content, but hinted strongly that they were also not of the planet. A ship of some kind had been discovered and it appeared to have crash-landed. It had never been said, but Gigory had speculated that some time in the past these sheep-type animals had been the occupants of that ship.

There was news from off planet, but it was also old news by the time the citizens of Polyarnaya received it. One piece of news that generated interest was that the Star Struck Trading Company, with permission from the UNSC, was showing interest in a new initiative to rescue Star Ship Russia. Captain Kazakov had died since the first attempt and the current leader of Polyarnaya was the son of the mutineer spokesperson, Sara Brown. Sara wasn't sure who the father was, so the child was named Elias Brown. Elias wasn't exactly brilliant, but he wasn't stupid either. He had a fierce look that said, "Don't mess with me," even though he never had, or wanted, a fight. Combined with the fact that no one else was interested in being in charge, he assumed the role and continued enforcing the rules Gigory had set in place.

Astron Hooding exited the High Point Wormhole Gate on TCe and found the communications building. He was on a mission. He sent a message to Polyarnaya saying that he believed he now had a means to decontaminate the Star Ship Russia and perhaps even allow people to leave TCf. But he would like help from Polyarnaya, if they were willing.

Elias received the message and responded with, "What do you have in mind? I have taken the same position as Captain Kazakov and therefore pledge all reasonable support. We are curious, however, that it is the Trading Company asking and not the UNSC."

"For some time now the UNSC has been giving up responsibility and is now just a shadow of its former self. They have turned the majority of the operations of the starships and wormhole gates over to the Trading Company, and as a result we have been able to capitalize on our discoveries. One discovery is a source of water that has amazing curative qualities. The source is limited, but continuous, so that we can collect these waters and build up a reasonable supply.

"Scientists at our lab have been testing these waters, which we just simply call Elixir, and have come to believe that if enough is placed in the ventilation systems of Russia, it will neutralize the contamination—but only because of the previous efforts to clean the ship. In other words, the heavy lifting has been done, so we think the Elixir can finish the job. But we will need your help if you so choose. It would mean some of your more technical savvy people would need to go the ship and introduce the Elixir into the ventilation systems. If you agree, we'll transfer the Elixir shuttle-to-shuttle and your shuttle would bring it into Russia. We're thinking 12,000 gallons would do the trick, if it works at all."

"So if it does work, then what?"

"Then your people would have another choice. We don't know if the Elixir would be effective on the planet because what is on the planet would likely overwhelm the Elixir qualities. However, once an individual is off the planet, it should work and counter the effects of the pollen. But we're not 100% certain of that either."

"Let's say it does work, then what?"

"Anyone choosing to leave Polyarnaya would have to agree not to go back. I have to stay firm on that, but leaving would be an option if it works."

Elias asked for few days to discuss the proposals with his people. The staff that periodically went up to Russia to check on it always returned sick, needing days to fully recover. Every one of them, eighteen in all, agreed to give it a try. They also agreed they would try and stay on the ship to see if they could be "cured" as well. Exactly half, however, were firm in their desire to return to Polyarnaya because of family. The rest were single and wanted off. Astron agreed.

It took months to collect enough Elixir on Sanctum and send it through the Bird Island Wormhole Gate to the High Point Wormhole Gate. From there it was shuttled up to Africa and when loaded, Africa headed for TCf and Russia. Elias, true to his word, had his shuttle meet the Africa shuttles and from there the Elixir was brought over to Russia. It all sounded easy, but there were many trips with each trip transferring many containers. Adding to the time required for the transfer was the need for the Polyarnaya shuttle crew to recover from the pollen withdrawal. Finally the Polyarnaya volunteers were brought up to Russia.

The eighteen from Polyarnaya moved as quickly as they could to keep from getting the deadly withdrawal symptoms. It was close, but they did get everything in place in time for the Elixir to be pumped into the ventilation systems just as the headaches and nausea were taking over. A few weren't taking any chances and went to the shuttle. The rest crossed their fingers, said a little prayer, or just stood waiting to see what would happen. Two managed to find an overlooked bottle of vodka and decided they would empty the bottle while waiting for the results.

Kem-U-El had been sent from Earth to assist with the mission and was assigned as the Africa CASO. As usual, this assignment was made without any input from the Captain, Frederica Armanda. And as usual, the arrival of a strange, large man with an equally strange name created a number of questions that would remain unanswered. About the only thing known was that he had recently completed the trip to Earth as CASO on the British Commonwealth, so he had experience. On this relatively short trip from TCe to TCf, Kem performed his duties as CASO without a lot of interaction with the Captain. Frederica was, therefore, a little surprised when Kem said, "If this works I'd like to go aboard Russia. I think I can be useful there." Frederica agreed and placed Kem in charge of the Africa crew contingent.

On the prearranged schedule, the Elixir was discharged and the fine droplets infiltrated everywhere in the zero-gravity ship. Within minutes the crew from Polyarnaya started to feel better. Within an hour they felt better than they had in years. The exception was the two vodka drinkers who were feeling exceptionally well until the Elixir aerosol was inhaled and the drunken stupor disappeared. "What good is that stuff? It ruined a perfectly good buzz!"

Except for the vodka drinkers, there were smiles everywhere. The next phase of the operation was to have people from Africa go on board Russia to confirm that the ship was now contagion free. Two volunteers went aboard with Kem and met up with the Polyarnaya team. The plan was to spend a week on the ship to be certain of the results. Cautious optimism was the rule of the day. Since the ship had been pretty well stripped of everything in the first salvage attempt, those on board Russia were supplied with plenty of food and drink as they roamed the ship and waited. There were some imaginary symptoms but those also vanished, and the mission was declared a success.

Now was the time for the crew from Polyarnaya to make a choice. Do they stay on Russia or go back down to the planet's surface? Eventually, five of the eighteen decided to stay on Russia and join the fleet. Of those on the planet's surface, 251 more decided to leave Polyarnaya. These were shuttled up in groups over a period of two weeks.

The sheep-like creatures on TCf had somehow understood what was going on and the leader of the critters, Downy, sent a thought message to Elias. *We would like to sample this Elixir you have.* When told, Captain Armanda gave this some thought and finally decided, "Why not?" And Downy was brought up to Russia where the creature was given some of the Elixir. When the creature took a drink there was a gradual transformation over a couple of days of the front legs to something more like arms with odd-looking hands. Downy remained on all fours, but the neck seemed to elongate and the head was more erect. Downy looked around and caused Kem to hear thoughts of, *Thank you, my mind is much clearer now. I am the leader of my people here. When our ship was having problems we were forced to land here. It was a difficult landing and some did not survive including our Captain. I am, or was, the chief flight engineer. We have been here a very long time. In observing your kind, we have determined that our life span is generally much longer than yours, but also this planet extended our lives even longer. This Elixir you have brought will make us whole once again if you will share, but we need help in repairing our ship so we can return home. If you can help us, we would be very grateful.*

Kem suspected something like might happen, but it wasn't even close to anything Frederica was expecting. She asked Kem," Is this Downy creature reading minds?"

"Partially. When we speak, it forms the thoughts that he can understand."

Frederica was having some trouble wrapping her head around this, but had enough composure to tell Kem, "Find out as much as you can and then we'll see what we can do."

And with that Kem started making inquiries and relayed the responses back to Frederica. "How many of you are here?"

We are 353.

"I'm not sure we can help you with your ship, but I will ask for permission to try. It isn't my choice to make. If agreed, we will also need to collect more Elixir for your people and to eventually decontaminate your ship. Do you know how to repair your ship?"

There will need to be modifications to use your technology, but I am confident that with your engineers working with me we can make our ship fly once again.

"Why are you here in the first place and where are you from?"

We are explorers like you. We are from what I believe you call the Betelgeuse solar system. That is over 630 light years from here. Our star will explode at some point so we have sent ships off in many directions to find an alternate home.

"Have you visited our planet Earth?"

Others from my world have explored Earth, but not my crew or me.

Frederica was quite stunned when she heard this, but decided to stop this line of inquiry for now and told Kem, "Give me some time and I'll get back to you. Downy can stay on Russia for now if it so desires."

Frederica sat back in her chair, ran her fingers through her hair a couple of times before resting her hands on top of her head. After perhaps twenty minutes of this while thinking about the conversation, she sent a message off to TCe to be relayed to Earth asking for instructions.

"Proceed with caution and make certain Kem is involved," was the response.

Chapter 49

Resurrection (2184)

Downy continued to morph ever so slowly even after going back down to the planet's surface. Apparently, the Elixir had a positive overriding effect on what everyone had come to call "pollen," at least on Downy's species. With that discovery, five more of Downy's "people" were given Elixir to drink. Within days the humans were more than simply fascinated, as they could easily observe a transformation. With the transformation, Downy's team of six moved to their disabled ship with the hopes of getting it to fly once again. Elias had a couple of his most technically-trained people in the mix and Kem took charge leaving Russia, against Frederica's wishes, and going down to TCf. At her insistence he did wear a spacesuit. After so many years of not much new happening in the Polyarnaya settlement, this sudden change was exhilarating.

The technology on Downy's ship was nothing any of the humans had ever seen, but somehow, to Frederica's astonishment, Kem seemed to understand enough that this crazy mix of species was able to redesign the broken systems to enable the use of human-made components. This was not done overnight, however, because determining what a problem might be was often the hardest part. And you can't fix a problem until you know what the problem might be, and there were multiple problems. Not just from the crash, but also from the amount of time the ship had been subjected to the local environment.

First there was the evaluation phase to determine what was broken; then the need to find out what parts were available from Downy's stash of spares. When they didn't have spares, they had to determine what those parts were intended to do. Once that was done, human technology was studied to see what might work. Next was a redesign and modification of the ship components to accept the alien technology. Once installed, each system had to be checked one by one. This was not a ten-minute job. In fact it took closer to two years.

During this time there was a lot of questions and answers between species. Answers from Downy, of course, were in the form of projected thoughts, so it did take a little time simply to get comfortable with that aspect. But they all had plenty of time. The distance that Downy and his crew had traveled was incredibly long; certainly many times further than the humans had thus far. So an obvious question was "How can you do that?"

In ancient times, our scientists learned how to project what you call a wormhole in front of our ships, like a stream. Travel time isn't as instantaneous as you enjoy going between what you call Gates, but it does cut down travel time by a significant amount. There are drawbacks, however. We cannot be near anything when it is activated as it pulls whatever is behind us along and when we reach our destination, whatever might have been behind us retains some momentum. In our case there had been some kind of rocky debris behind us and to one side. When we opened our wormhole stream, we pulled the debris in directly behind us into our wake and when we stopped, the rock kept going right into our ship causing us to lose most of our control. We were only able to manage a controlled crash landing on this very handy planet.

The other drawback is our navigation systems get thrown off when we enter the projected wormhole stream, especially if we have something unintended in the stream, like the rocky debris. The result is we don't have pinpoint accuracy, even on a good trip, so we aim for open space and hope to get reasonably close. We weren't supposed to end up in this solar system, but in one way it was fortunate, because our ship was damaged and we needed a place to go. And here we are! But because we didn't end up as planned, our people couldn't trace our route and we couldn't send out a message.

"And over time the planet changed you?"

Yes, though we didn't notice at first. Our people are what you might call grain eaters. The grasslike vegetation here is similar enough to what we usually eat that we started consuming it when our supplies ran out. We did plant some of what we usually eat, but the local plants were dominant. Over time, our bodies started to change. We could communicate easily enough, but our ability to solve problems, or build, or make anything with our appendages left us.

"Have you now reverted to your original form?"

No, not yet. Actually I'm not sure we will ever completely return to our original form. The change seems to have stopped. I think that Elixir you discovered has limitations.

Kem had heard of Downy's planet, but none of his people had ever been there. This tidbit of information he kept to himself. There was no need to have awkward questions directed towards him.

Naturally, not all the work at TCf was directed towards Downy's problem. When Russia was finally decontaminated, it still had to be brought back into operating condition. It had only three engine room pods remaining; so one spare was donated from Africa, providing the needed engine balance. But the ship was also devoid of much that would make it fully functional. So while the ground team was still determining what was needed for Downy's ship, Africa returned to TCe leaving Russia with a skeleton crew. Relayed information allowed much of what would be needed for Downy's ship and Russia to be either waiting for Africa to pick up, or soon be available after design work was completed on Earth. There seemed to be a number of loose ends, with information flying around between all sectors, but fortunately, Captain Armanda was able to take a step back to calmly bring everything together with incredible efficiency.

Finally with the required components for Downy's ship and Russia on board, Africa set off to TCf once again. This time back in orbit, Russia and Africa were able to connect and rotate, providing the appreciated artificial gravity for the crews. Elias's pilots were kept busy getting what was needed down to the planet's surface to complete the repairs on Downy's ship and transferring people back and forth as needed.

Captain Armanda and her staff paid close attention to what was being done on Downy's ship and had learned a few things that would eventually help the UNSC and the Trading Company, but the one thing Frederica had really wanted to learn was how the wormhole stream worked. That technology, incorporated into Earth's starships, would really be something. Frederica thought it was suspicious when Kem said, "That technology isn't transferrable. There are specific attributes of their ships that would be impossible to replicate." Kem certainly wasn't about to tell Frederica that he and Gabe had discussed that very issue and they had decided mankind needed to develop some things on their own. And they felt it might not take that long!

There were a few other revelations that were disturbing. Downy had "said" in a rather offhanded way, *there are forces out there in the universe that we cannot possibly understand. Some are good, some are evil, and some are both with a point of view being the determining factor. When our people visited Earth, it was decided that it could be a very suitable home for us, but obviously mankind was already there. Some of our more radical people decided that if the human population was eradicated, we could move in. From this radical groups perspective, that would be good, but not good for you. You had a pandemic in what you call year 2071. That was watched closely and there was a hope your species would be eradicated and we could move in. There are still those among my kind that want to finish the job.*

You have gone out of your way to help us and have never asked for much in return. I can assure you, that this act of kindness shall not be forgotten. When we return home, this will be instilled into our collective conscience and Earth will not have any interference from us.

Many heard this declaration. It was sobering. Even Kem, who seemed to know more than he would let on, was disturbed. While his Order had been trying to provide a positive guide for mankind's development, he had never considered that there were other life forms that might have the opposite intention. He had a hard time coming to the realization he had been that naïve.

It was fully two years and one month before Downy's ship was ready for a full operational test. During that time, the rest of Downy's people had been treated to the Elixir and reached the same level of transformation as Downy. With Downy's people ready to go and the ship hopefully all set, the moment of truth had arrived. The ship launched and went into orbit close to African and Russia. Once in orbit, Elixir was pumped into the ventilation system to neutralize the pollen effect. When satisfied with the level of decontamination, some additional calibrations were made, and the ship left orbit. Over the next few months it moved out and away until it could activate the wormhole stream. The resurrection of the crashed and abandoned ship was complete.

The last question that was on all minds was, "Do you think your species and our species will ever meet again?"

"*Perhaps.*"

Chapter 50

Farewell (2186)

It was time. Gabe had wondered, over the thousands of years he had been on Earth, if this day would come. *Thousands of years?* he thought, and then with a little smile he said out loud, to no one, "My, how time does fly!"

It seemed clear that the course of mankind would have been much different if the Boss hadn't sent members of the Order to Earth those many millennia ago. Gabe had been on Earth from the beginning and witnessed firsthand how the course of mankind had been corrected over and over again. Gabe estimated that 99% of what the Order had done was positive. There were mistakes to be sure. And there were those in the Order that thought they knew better than their leaders and made a mess of things. These few—plus a few that had developed evil intentions—were captured and exiled, but not before the damage was done.

The exact direction of mankind really didn't matter that much. After all, every civilization should be able to chart its own course. But when that course isn't clear and a species is headed for a complete collapse, a course correction, through some guidance at the right time, can be essential.

Gabe had stepped in on a few notable corrections, but the one where he acted alone and where he thought he had made a significant difference was in 1944 when the Allies were preparing to retake Europe from Nazi Germany. General Eisenhower was having second thoughts about invading on June 6th because of the weather forecast. Gabe's ability to see the bigger picture helped the General make the right choice for the greater longer-term benefit of mankind. Even though the outcome was positive, Gabe still bore the burden of being unable to stop the carnage that resulted. But even he had limits as to what he was allowed, or even capable of doing.

Fast forward to when mankind entered into interstellar space travel, a whole new chapter was written. Actually it was more like a whole new book, not just a chapter, in mankind's progression. Technology and spiritual enlightenment seemed destined to merge rather than be considered mutually exclusive. With that merger, it was now time for the Order to step aside and for mankind to help guide other civilizations.

In fact, they already had done so, proving they were ready. Not in the way the Order had been doing it, but still helpful. Mankind had provided enlightenment to the Second People on EEb, rescued the indigenous populations on TCe, and recently helped stranded aliens on TCf to return home. In addition, and to the embarrassment of the Order, the descendants of those abducted by the Order over 200 years ago were being treated with compassion. Subconsciously, mankind was adapting and learning how to guide themselves though difficult times. They didn't need the Order any more. Perhaps now was the proper time for a shift in the workings of the universe.

When the Boss informed Gabe that the Order's mission on Earth was to end, it had been assumed that all Order members were to leave. It wasn't that simple of course. In these final days on Earth, Gabe listened to Charm-E-Ine's passionate plea. "Gabe, you once convinced me to give up my plan to live out my natural life and rejoin the Order. I did so, partly to accompany Raman into stasis with the hopes he would be rejuvenated. When we returned to the land of the living, Raman was better, but it didn't last. He started to fail once again, and today his cognitive abilities are again severely impaired. He realized this was happening once again and in one of his more lucid moments he begged to be allowed to die a natural death. I think that wish should be honored.

"I once vowed to unite Africa and did so. When I returned after being in stasis, I had to nearly start all over to cleanse Africa of those who wanted to take power forcibly. You allowed me to use means I would never have been able to utilize previously with the notion this was to be a last effort. I don't want what was accomplished to regress again. I also have had enough of the skipping from time frame to time frame through history, going in and out of stasis. I want to stay as Princess Charmy of the Union of African Nations until it is time for my natural ending. I beg you to allow Raman and me to do this. We will give up all of us that has been the Order and be part of mankind's world."

Gabe had expected something like this so was prepared and said, "Charmy, you are truly something else. You will be missed by

Africa if you leave, but if you stay you will be missed by us. Your wishes will be honored, however. You may stay."

"Thank you Gabe. I will take care of Raman as long as I am able. Quite frankly, I think he has but a few years."

Gabe understood that others in the Order would be confused, as each team being activated would expect an assignment. For these teams he decided that the currently activated team members would be present as the other teams came out of stasis and help prepare them for what would be coming next. As part of the preparation, they were to meet with the human leaders in each area, except Africa of course, and provide a little clarification for the history books. They were to be told there was no need to be subtle. The veil of secrecy was removed. That didn't mean they were allowed to be obnoxious, and when he told his team this part, he looked squarely at Ara and said, "Ara, you got that? None of your so-called jokes. Act with some dignity for a change."

"Geeze, Gabe. Lighten up."

"Ara, I mean it or you won't like your next assignment. Guaranteed!"

And so it was. Over the next year, all Order members that had been off planet made it back to Earth. Order teams that that had been in stasis were activated and they went out into the world. By this time, everyone that had a close relationship with Order members had been told what was coming. As receptive government leaders were provided with a history lesson regarding the Order and then told what was coming, there was initially a general feeling of indignation. Stripping away human self-esteem was not received well. History was now seen as having a significant introduction of an alien intervention, though "interference" was the word most commonly used. "How dare these aliens interfere with us? Who do they think they are?" After many thought about it, however, they realized that a little help once in while was probably a good thing. Then after a little more thought, these same people panicked. "We're going to be left on our own?"

The general population was not generally enlightened, leaving it up the various governments to decide what they wanted to say, or not. This left some government officials in a quandary, as the sight of Order members gliding through the air with their antigravity panels unfurled became more and more common. Initially there was one of two reactions, especially as the sightings were obviously becoming more frequent worldwide. About half of the people were convinced there was religious significance. Of this group, the interpretation was certainly not consistent. Some saw this as a sign the world was coming to an end. Some saw this as sign that mankind was about to enter a new age of salvation. And of these, there were as many variations in the interpretation as there were people. Overall, however, attendance at religious services skyrocketed.

The other half of the people thought it was some new military tool or perhaps some new personal transportation device that had just been introduced to the marketplace and wanted to know, "How can I get one these things?" Confusion was added in when the Order members got up close and personal with people and their size was apparent. Many government leaders made up stupid stories. As difficult as it was for some leaders, they told the truth, but were often not believed.

Gabe's sincere wish was that the Order's efforts to pass the torch to humans would take hold beyond what he felt the Trading Company would embrace. Time would tell. While all the Order teams had told Earth's leaders that they were leaving Earth and that mankind would now truly be on its own, there were a few facts being left out.

For one, it seemed very few had put two and two together and realized that Princess Charmy and her Internal Ambassador, Raman were of the Order. It should have been obvious with Raman flying around with his anti-gravity pack, but there seemed to be a mental block in this regard. And those that did realize that Charmy was from the Order simply chose to believe that the Princess was here to stay. And as it turned out, they were right.

In addition to Charmy and Raman, a few others petitioned Gabe to stay on Earth and live out their natural lives. Most of these were individuals, but there was one entire team of six that wanted to stay. All of these Order members had been on Earth a very long time and simply wanted to live as normal a life as possible. The cycle of renewal each time they went into stasis was unnatural and they were tired of it. They wanted to live like humans as much as possible. They offered to spend their time preparing mankind for their new role. Gabe let them know, it was their choice, but none of the Order's technology or their habitats would be available to them. They would each be allowed to have some gold and silver coins to help with the transition, but they would have to take care of themselves. "And it won't be easy with the metabolism you have."

The one that wanted to stay that really surprised Gabe was Uri-I-El. Seemingly out of the blue, Uri said he wanted to go back to Sanctum and continue teaching at the school he set up for the Gadans. As he told Gabe, "I don't think I will ever get over what was done by the tandoo to our sister Evan and her group. I also feel a huge sense of regret for what was done by our Order creating the Gadans. I think the Order has a debt that needs to be repaid and I want to do what I can. I understand what this means for me, but I am willing to accept it. Actually, I look forward to it, as it will finally put my mind to rest."

Astron Hooding was in a conundrum. His father had been an Order member and therefore not human, but his mother was human and he was raised as such, eventually following the human tradition of marriage. Gabe wanted very much to do the right thing for Astron, but for one of the very few times that he could recall, he didn't know what "right" was in this case. He decided to go directly to Astron.

In Earth years Astron was now fifty-one years old. When Gabe realized that, he thought, *how can that be? How could Astron possibly be that old?* He was, of course, but only in terms of Earth years. Astron looked much younger, and Gabe suspected he would likely live a very long life. Celeste was aging gracefully. In many respects, especially when it came to displays of energy, she put Astron to shame. Celeste still bounced around, never sitting still. Astron, by contrast, displayed physical energy only when required, while his brain was moving a million miles and hour.

"Astron," said Gabe, "The Order is leaving Earth. A few of our people will be staying but as members of the human society. I want to do something for you before I leave, but don't know what that might be."

"You need do nothing. I know who I am. I consider myself human. I was raised that way and have been blessed with the most wonderful person in this world, or any other world for that matter, to have Celeste as my wife. If I died tomorrow, I would have no regrets. Celeste and I will continue managing the Trading Company as long as we can. We have taken from the Order the credo of doing good with our company's fortune. You and the Order need give us nothing more. Know, however, that I will profoundly miss you."

Gabe was surprising choked up as he shook hands with Astron and then hugged him.

Not everyone on Earth, or for that matter humans anywhere, were aware of the legacy being passed on from the Order to mankind. Most never even knew about the Order at all. For them, it was spooky enough seeing human-like beings all aglow and floating around on wings. But the next series of events really got them spooked, to the delight of Ara, who had been assigned the task of organizing the Order evacuation. Ara had asked Gabe for this assignment and though reluctant at first, Gabe gave into Ara's begging. Gabe figured Ara would arrange things for his own amusement, so told him not to get too carried away with whatever he had up his sleeve.

The year was 2186; not coincidentally exactly 5000 years from the time Gabe and his team, the very first team, had reached Earth. The evacuation started on June 1, with citizens of Earth witnessing a sight no one ever expected. Over one hundred shallow bowl-shaped flying machines entered Earth's atmosphere. Long-range sensors saw them appear as they closed in towards Earth. Military units around the globe were activated in case what they had been told was false and this was a hostile attack, but fortunately no one fired a shot. The saucers made no attempt to hide. They boldly flew over the landscape, clearly in view of anyone daring to watch. Instead of targeting populated areas, the saucers flew to the most unusual locations, mostly in remote areas. Volcanoes, thermal vents, and hot springs were especially targeted.

Nervous pilots assigned to aerial surveillance watched the saucers land, but nothing seemed to happen. All saucers remained on the ground for one week, making some people extremely nervous, while others that had embraced the notion of an alien invasion of some kind were simultaneously scared and thrilled waiting for "whatever might be next." Citizen militia groups made a big show of force—but it was all show with no concept of what they might do. Simultaneously, as it was later determined, groups, mostly of six, appeared from seemingly nowhere and entered the waiting saucers. After boarding, the saucers remained unmoving for precisely four hours until they all lifted off at the same time and went into low orbit. It was far more dramatic on the night side of Earth, but no matter where they lifted off, it was impressive. Surveillance from aircraft and satellite captured the event so anyone with access to a screen could watch.

Then, on June 7, every form of electronic communication was interrupted. Large and small viewing screens of every description came alive. On screen was a very large man with shoulder-length hair, wearing all white and surrounded with a glow. Behind him were what appeared to be wings. At first, everyone was petrified. Everyone, that is, except those few that recognized Gabe-Re-El. To them, Gabe was a familiar and friendly face.

To many, Gabe's message was confusing because so few even knew about the Order. He began, "People of Earth. My people have been with you for thousands of years. At times we have tried to guide mankind towards prosperity and to move you toward ever more enlightenment. We have done this by suggesting course corrections when your apparent clear horizons were altered. In recent times, we have been more direct in our actions, as we knew our time here was coming to a close. The course of mankind that has been followed must now be altered as you take your place as a guide for other societies on other worlds. There will always be more that can be done here, but as a society, it is time for my people to leave you to your new destiny. A destiny that requires altering what you may come to believe to be the only course of action. Do not be afraid to alter your beliefs as you continue to reach out towards new horizons, finding new challenges and other societies. The United Nations Stellar Commission and the Star Struck Trading Company have been led to understand this as a long-range goal, so it is only incumbent upon you to support these organizations.

"As a people you have made discoveries that are truly gifts to all of Earth and elsewhere. Continue to use these gifts to make Earth a better place. And as your home planet of Earth improves, share your bounty with others in need. As you do so, remember that others may want more, but quietly fill only true needs with guidance. Simply giving into wants of any society not willing to put in effort is not helpful in the long term.

"As you look to the future and the horizons before you, recognize that your horizons have been altered in the past and each horizon you will reach for in the future will also be altered. Likewise, guide other societies as their horizons become altered. Provide guidance where possible as they decide whether to steer towards what has appeared before them on their horizon or to steer away."

The speech wasn't long. Fewer words often have larger impact. When done, all screens went blank for the next thirty-seven minutes leaving many questions to be answered. How dare these people interfere with mankind. How will we survive without them? What did he mean they had recently been more direct and provided gifts? Gifts to whom? What did his people do wrong? How many are there? Why have we not seen them before? Or did we?

More sensible questions focused on details. It made sense that the UNSC should be strong and lead mankind to other worlds. After all, wasn't it a world-supported organization reaching for the stars? But the Trading Company? That seemed more than odd until much more serious consideration made it clear that it was the Trading Company that had made all of the major discovery breakthroughs that benefited Earth.

But there wasn't time to consider the answers right now, as the focus was on the sky as the orbiting saucers formed into groups of three. Over the next hour, the saucers slowly flew low over populated areas before they rose up again into space and disappeared. Ara made sure it was an awesome sight to be remembered and recorded for posterity.

Chapter 51

Contemplation

It was a quiet dinner. Just the two of them, sitting on the back patio under an awning in Iowa, as the Earth's sun was getting ready to say good night. The weather was absolutely perfect. A bottle of good Merlot had been opened and aired. A healthy glassful was nearly consumed while Dakota was grilling some very expensive steaks over charcoal, which was an indulgence Katherine allowed Dakota to make once in a while. Katherine had to admit, nothing beat the taste of a steak cooked over charcoal, even if it wasn't exactly the green thing to do. While he seared the meat, he sat in an old-fashioned wooden Adirondack chair and watched the antics of the many birds and squirrels in the yard. He was as relaxed as he could be. Katherine had busied herself cooking up some onions and peppers to go over the steak, some potatoes, and some green beans. This was something she never was allowed to do on the starships as the Admiral, so she took great pleasure in this simple task while humming away.

Katherine and Dakota were working hard to learn how to retire. Not really having any hobbies, the transition was proving to be difficult. The closest thing Dakota had to a hobby had been the ancient Ford, but Celeste and Astron weren't about to give it back. Dakota had visions of maybe finding another that he could work on and enhance with Lehtolarite power. *Katherine wouldn't mind,* he thought.

The feast was ready just as the Lehtolarite-powered solar lights came on, giving the patio a very romantic feel very much enhanced by the wine. They ate slowly and talked quietly.

Katherine said, "You know we were manipulated by Gabe-Re-El and his Order."

"Yes," said Dakota, "But really only near the end of their stay on Earth. Up until then they only gave advice to be taken or not."

"I suppose, but you know I wasn't exactly complaining. I mean look at what happened. We discovered the Elixir water that cures so many ailments. We have Lehtolarite, which is a miracle by itself, essentially providing all the power we need with no negative by-products. Well, all the power we need, not counting the obvious 'want' of your charcoal that is."

"Hey, that's just once in a while and even that is made from wood scrap. Besides a little burnt meat is good for you. I think."

"Oh don't go getting defensive on me."

Dakota considering the Order efforts said, "Do you think we could have done what we did without any of that whole Order thing? I mean they didn't design the wormhole gates or get them established. They didn't develop the starships." Then pausing for moment added, "Or did they?"

"I don't know, but they certainly helped when it was needed. Think about that language thing they do. Without that we would still be struggling with the Second People, the Tall Ones, the Mobile ones, and even our own people, the Gadans."

"Do you think they had a grand plan or where they winging it?"

"'Winging it?' Very cute. You mean when they fly into places? But, no, I don't know. I do wonder what our world would be like if they weren't there when things got dicey."

Dakota took a sip of wine and, looking up into the sky, said, "So what do you think is next? I don't see the starships being mothballed."

"No, there will be more missions. They might be defined differently, but there will be missions of some kind. But it won't be for you or me. Like it or not, we are done. It is the next generations that will make things happen. They will be charting the course of mankind, and as Gabe said, changing course from time to time as mankind's horizons alter. We can only hope they don't screw it up when the unexpected appears on the horizon."

"Yes, the next generation must be as perfect as we were."

"Very funny, dear husband, very funny. Have some more wine."

As Katherine and Dakota savored their meal, they silently agreed, without saying a word, that the anticipated view of any horizon could never be guaranteed. With that in mind, it was now clear that mankind had a new role in the universe. What that might be exactly could only be answered over time. But the one thing that they did know was that as this chapter of the progression of man was closing, they had each other—and that would never be altered.

Epilogue

Once the Gadans got past the initial shock of Earth, they took a serious look at what was around them. They didn't care for much of it. The Gadans had liked what they had seen of the Earthbound Amish and asked many questions of their culture. Eventually the Gadans, as a whole, determined that what they had on Sanctum wasn't all that bad. "Going back" no longer seemed like a great idea. With the addition of some horses and simple tools, their way of life felt good. Oh, and the tandoo not bothering them was certainly a plus. They did like the idea of letting younger members decide what they wanted in life. So when a Gadan reached the age of fifteen Earth years, they were allowed to go to Earth if they wanted, or anywhere else where there was access. Then, on their twentieth birthday, they needed to decide whether to stay as a member of the Gadan community or leave. But even that wasn't very rigid. Travel between Gadan and Mid Way had become so common, it became quite acceptable for people to go back and forth and mix in.

In fact "mixing in" became a major event for Sergeant Green and Minda. Minda had been educated on the concept of marriage and so when the sergeant proposed, she readily accepted. They couldn't decide whether to live in Gadan or Mid Way and since neither of them feared the tandoo, they built a home halfway between the two settlements. They built a tavern into a hill fortified against the weather and served the alcoholic beverage the Gadans had come up with, plus the usual Earthly fare. They had a few rooms for tourists, acted as local guides, and had two children. They called the tavern "No Tandoo Inn."

Astron and Celeste brought even greater success to the Star Struck Trading Company. Celeste finally did decide to have a child, to Astron's delight. After a difficult pregnancy, they were blessed with a boy they named Kenning. Their old Ford returned to Earth, much to the disappointment of Sanctum's governor, who had thought it was there for his use.

The United African Nations continued to prosper in every endeavor. Africa's environment was restored to a level not seen in hundreds of years. Even the Sahara Desert was retreating. Wildlife flourished and the people of Africa self-implemented population control measures to maintain a sustainable healthy population. Raman did pass away in a couple of years as Princess Charmy had predicted. Charmy went on to enjoy a very, very, long life adored by the entire continent.

Besides the starships Orion and Perseus, the Trading Company took over ownership of the starships United States and Russia. These two ships continued to bring back valuable ore from Prosperity. Most of the remaining starships would eventually go off to explore further reaches of space, and more wormhole gates would be built.

Star Ship Africa had a different mission. In helping Downy and his people return to their home planet, the humans did acquire knowledge that would eventually lead to the development of their own wormhole stream. The first experimental use was on Star Ship Africa. When the system was activated, the volunteer crew and ship disappeared as expected, but did not return as planned. Many years later, another class of starships successfully utilized the technology. These would eventually be called "Horizon Class'" ships in recognition of the direction given to mankind when the Order left Earth. Because of this new technology, they would actually overtake the aging starships sent out on earlier missions.

Katherine and Dakota did finally learn how to retire. Katherine took up gardening and cooking. Dakota found that owning one ancient automobile was very much like eating potato chips. He didn't stop with just one.

Admiral Wu returned to Earth. But rather than giving up gambling, he built a casino in China, which naturally generated a very healthy income. He named the casino "Safe Bet Casino."

Governor Chuck Canton and his family flourished beyond any of his expectations. The Elixir gave his family health. Both boys joined the starship fleet managed by the Star Struck Trading Company. Chuck managed every detail mankind was involved with on Sanctum, with 100% resolve to keep the planet as unspoiled as possible. He was extremely successful.

Dr. Anna Giblin maintained her office in the Governor's Palace, but spent most of her time at the Elixir extraction sites, to make sure collection remained sustainable, and doing additional research. She had little worry with sustainability, as the field teams were a very conscientious bunch. Her spare time was spent exploring the rest of Sanctum with research assistants from the best schools on Earth and setting up field research sites. From these sites discoveries were made continually. Added to this, the many volunteers that worked at the research sites on Sanctum returned to Earth after their stint with contagious enthusiasm that helped shape policies affecting both Sanctum and Earth. Anna had become as famous as Suzanne Lehtola.

The Mobile Ones that had been in the fleet joined their companions on Coat Island in Hudson Bay. The tales they told of the humans would have been considered ridiculous, except no species from TCe could ever fabricate a false impression. As a collective species, they also had difficulty trying to understand the beings from the Order. Why had these beings spent so much effort helping mankind and no effort to help them when it was truly needed? Was the intent to teach mankind how to help others? If so, maybe it worked, but it would remain a great mystery.

Some Significant Dates

1971: President Nixon listens to a proposal from Tam-I-El

Book 1: *Course Correction* story line

2067: First Star Ship fleet leaves for Epsilon Eridani (EE)

2071: Death Flu pandemic

2096: Star Ship fleet establishes wormhole gate on EEb

Book 2: *Carbon Neutral* story line

2144: Wormhole gate established on Tau Ceti e

Altered Horizon story line starts

2147: United Nations Stellar Commission (UNSC) lays out new missions

2148: Order members receive assignments

2153: Lehtolarite discovered on YZ Ceti planet c (named Prosperity)

2157: New Constellation Class Star Ships Perseus & Orion launched

2160: Star Ship China lost

2165: Star Ships Perseus and Orion reach Alpha Centauri star Proxima, planet b   (named Sanctum)

2168: Elixir discovered

2170: Star Ships British Commonwealth & South America reach Earth

2179: Star Ships British Commonwealth & South America reach Sanctum

2181: Wormhole Gate on Sanctum opens

2186: An altered horizon for mankind revealed

www.ingramcontent.com/pod-product-compliance
Lightning Source LLC
Chambersburg PA
CBHW071743190726
48292CB00003B/852